M

Rave Reviews for
Emily Toll's Travel Murder Mysteries

MURDER PANS OUT

"A truly delightful cozy with a great deal of Gold Rush lore thrown in."
—*I Love a Mystery*

MURDER WILL TRAVEL

"A clever, charming novel that readers will relish on many levels. Its wine country setting is both exciti⋯ its complex plot will satis⋯ buff. An admirable and ⋯ world."
—Ea⋯

"A splendid new series ⋯ mosphere. Rich and full ⋯ oughly original mystery."
—Tamar Myers

"Flawless. The plotting is tight and realistic; it's a pleasure to read a mystery that doesn't require a conscious suspension of disbelief. . . . Toll perfectly captures the Sonoma Valley—its scenery, its history, its atmosphere. All of Toll's characters are fully rendered, which is a particularly notable accomplishment in a novel with a cast of about twenty . . . An auspicious award-worthy kick-off for a new series."
—*BookBrowser*

"Delightful . . . *Murder Will Travel* is a classic who-done-it and Lynne is a character I'm looking forward to meeting again. Toll's story is rich in plot, character development and history and I'd recommend this to all who love classic mysteries."
—*I Love A Mystery*

"A second exciting outing in California Gold Rush country sends travel director Lynne Montgomery on the track of a culprit bent on destruction in *Murder Pans Out*. Wonderful setting, excitement, and dead-on tour group characters come together in a great mystery by Emily Toll."
—Mystery Lovers Bookshop

Berkley Prime Crime Titles by Emily Toll

MURDER WILL TRAVEL
MURDER PANS OUT
FALL INTO DEATH

FALL INTO
Death

Emily Toll

BERKLEY PRIME CRIME, NEW YORK

FALL INTO DEATH

A Berkley Prime Crime Book/published by arrangement with the author

PRINTING HISTORY
Berkley Prime Crime mass-market edition/May 2004

Copyright © 2004 by Taffy Cannon.
Cover art by Dave Schweitzer.
Cover design by George Long.

*For the Teabuds
and the
Second South Sobriety Society*

Acknowledgments

It all started with Sally Lynch and scrimshaw earrings on a road trip in the summer of 1969. While any errors that remain are my sole responsibility, I'm grateful to the many people who shared their knowledge and expertise for this book:

- Aileen Schumacher for concrete and D. P. Lyle, M.D. for skeletonization

- Bruce and Helen Blake for New Hampshire and for New England plumbing and heating

- Debby Conrad, Cheryl Exner and Craig Williams for Massachusetts

- Anne and Jose Goico for Hartford

- The late Jack Koehler and Mary Catherine Hurlbut for Vermont

- Rev. Harper Welch and Dr. Robin Waldron for Maine

- Massad Ayoob for New Hampshire law enforcement

- Evelyn Williams for Roller Derby

- Keith McClain for mortgage banking

- Lynne Borow for taxidermy

- Kitty McMahon and Dana Whitson for UC Santa Cruz

- Joseph Lisiecki for the U.S. Marine Corps

- A whole raft of people for the U.S. Navy: James Lincoln Warren, Hap and Marilyn Meredith, Bill Rosenthal, Anne Gallagher, John Prophet, Marlene Satter and Connie Spencer, with particular appreciation to my erstwhile student, Stephen Fetters

- Martha Bushko for fine editing and Jane Chelius for fine agenting

- and finally, Bill and Melissa Kamenjarin, for everything.

Chapter 1

RAT-*a-tat-tat! Rat-a-tat-tat!*

The insistent woodpecker's staccato message filled the misty forest air. Coming slowly awake, Lynne pulled the sleeping bag tighter around her body—a body, she realized suddenly, that was naked in the zipped-together bags. She smiled a bit as she remembered the night before, the way the moonlight had filtered through the screened top of the tent. She'd been plenty warm enough then, but this forest morning was downright chilly. The tall canopy of redwoods shut out most of the sunlight that would fight its way through the dense vegetation to penetrate and warm the forest floor as the day moved on.

Rat-a-tat-tat! Rat-a-tat-tat!

She breathed in deeply, noticing the welcoming aromas of coffee and bacon added to the rich forest smells. The tent door was partially unzipped and she scooched the sleeping bag toward it, pulling the nylon aside and peeking out into the clearing. Monty had the cookstove fired up with the cof-feepot on one burner. On the other, he deftly moved the skillet of bacon from side to side, stopping to turn the strips carefully. He sat crosslegged in the fern-bordered clearing with his back to the tent, his shock of sun-lightened blonde hair spilling over the collar of his blue-and-green plaid flannel shirt.

Rat-a-tat-tat! Rat-a-tat-tat!

He pulled the strips of bacon from the skillet, shut off the propane flame and laid the bacon on a plate. Now he stood deliberately and headed into the forest, his muscles flexing beneath the plaid shirt and snug faded jeans. He didn't look back.

Lynne tried to call to him to wait, but no sound came from her mouth. He kept on marching purposefully into the woods, brushing aside shrubs and low branches, sidestepping to avoid a soft green fern. She tried again to call, then pulled her own flannel shirt from the floor of the tent and hurriedly slipped into it, stepping out barefoot into the clearing. She tried a third time to call, unsuccessfully, then realized she would have to run to catch him.

Rat-a-tat-tat! Rat-a-tat-tat!

She stood now in the clearing utterly paralyzed, her feet rooted in the earth, her voice mute. The more she tried to run after him, the more firmly her feet stuck to the ground beside the cookstove. She glanced down at the cookstove and saw frost on the coffeepot, green mold on the bacon.

When she looked up again, Monty was gone.

Rat-a-tat-tat! Rat-a-tat-tat!

LYNNE Montgomery's eyes flew open and she felt cold sweat cover her body. The forest was gone. The tent had disappeared. And Monty—Monty was gone, too, forever gone, dead far too soon, leaving Lynne to face each morning alone, to waken from tantalizing dreams and discover they were cruel hoaxes.

This time she was really awake.

Rat-a-tat-tat! Rat-a-tat-tat!

Too loud for a woodpecker, the noise seemed to shake the four-poster bed in which she lay. This, at least, was real. As was the bedside table with its blue ceramic washbasin, the simple rocking chair with its blue gingham cushions, the lace curtains gathered at the window. Beyond the curtains a large tree shaded the window, its bright green leaves tinged with a tantalizing red.

She inhaled. The scent of maple-cured bacon was real, at least, as was the coffee.

And so was this would-be hostelry, the grandly named Maple Leaf Inn, the latest project of Lynne's ceaselessly energetic mother Priscilla, who at 82 ought to be leaning back and enjoying her sunset years, not starting up some cockamamie business.

Now it all came flooding back: the flight from San Diego to Manchester, New Hampshire, the midnight arrival and rental car pickup, the half-hour journey down dark, deserted roads to South Hadford, her mother's sleepy greeting, the immediate impression of utter chaos.

Certain parts of the place were at least superficially ready for paying customers, and almost everything smelled freshly painted. Other areas, however—the dining room, a self-contained manager's apartment in the rear where Priscilla planned to live, and at least one guest bedroom and bath upstairs—remained a jumble of mismatched furniture, uncurtained windows, unmade beds, and large brown moving company boxes.

It had been a relief to find her own assigned bedroom nicely finished, wallpaper dry above the wainscoting, coordinated bedding and curtains, fresh carpeting and a functional bathroom that she shared with her traveling companion. Her twenty-six-year-old daughter Jenna slumbered on the other side in her own charmingly appointed guest room.

Rat-a-tat-tat!

Maybe Jenna wasn't sleeping, after all. Lynne's dream of Monty in the woods might be gone, mercifully receding into nothingness, but the woodpeckers were still at it. Except that this didn't sound like any woodpecker Lynne had ever heard, not even the cartoon Woody at his most relentless. It sounded very much like a jackhammer, somewhere in the nether regions of the Maple Leaf Inn.

Her mother had spoken, in recent months, of carpenters and handymen, plumbers and carpet layers, the tile setters and seamstresses. But she was fairly certain that her mother hadn't mentioned any jackhammers during those conversations, and she knew with absolute certainty that the subject had not arisen when they arrived last night. Not that it was surprising that her mother might omit such a detail. Throughout her three marriages, two of them to ambitious and adventuresome Navy officers, Priscilla Chenonceau Westbrook Doolittle Jones had plenty of experience embroidering reality to suit her own self-image.

Lynne sat up, straightening the quilt, a charming log cabin pattern in shades of blue and white. Her mother's calico cat Hester lay curled on the foot of the bed, nestled into the quilt. It might be autumn, but the morning was surprisingly warm and Lynne had shucked off most of her covers during the night. Hester opened a sleepy eye, then slowly pulled herself to her feet and began a sinuous set of feline stretches, purring all the while.

Smart cat. Lynne mimicked the movements in her own clunky human fashion. First she stretched her arms and shoulders, fluttering her hands gracefully like those Belarusian figure skaters, moving every joint. Then she swung her legs out of bed and extended them deliberately one at a time, pointing her toes, flexing her ankles, lifting each leg skyward, then bending it at the knee. She was not about to think of herself as old—AARP membership be damned—but she had discovered that these few stretches made it much easier to get out of bed and proceed with the business of her day. If she kept it up, maybe she'd never have to think of herself as old.

She glanced at the old-fashioned clock on her bedside table and discovered it was after nine A.M. For all she knew, Jenna and Priscilla had both been up for hours. Jenna might be back from a five-mile run around town, full of observations about the hometown of her maternal forebears. Lynne chuckled at the notion. Jenna was a notorious night owl and was doubtless still asleep. After all, on California time it was barely six A.M.

Jenna's presence on the trip was a last-minute substitution. Initially Lynne had planned to bring along her friends and sometime traveling companions from Floritas, the Harpers and the Martells. Then Mark Martell flunked a blood test and found himself undergoing radiation for an early prostate cancer, with his wife Pat providing chauffeur service and pep squad duties. Alice and Don Harper had still been slated, however, until Alice slipped on a dropped sample of four-cheese ravioli at Costco and shattered her kneecap.

All four swore that if the trip worked out as Lynne hoped, they'd be part of her first official group the following autumn. But it was just as well that they weren't along now, on a trip that might offer more challenge than she'd bargained for.

Autumn in New England.

It had a wonderful air to it, like April in Paris, Christmas in Aspen, Cherry Blossom time in Washington, D.C., summer on the Outer Banks.

With a little bit of luck, it would live up to its billing.

October in New Hampshire was when billions of leaves turned crimson and russet and gold in a dazzling display of fall foliage. It had been too dark to tell anything about the color of vegetation when they arrived last night. Now Lynne crossed to her window and looked outside. The Maple Leaf Inn, named for two stately trees on its front lawn, sat at the end of a cul-de-sac on a quiet residential street shaded by mature trees that were still mostly green. The two trees in front of the Inn seemed on the verge of turning, their crimson-edged leaves promising an even grander display later.

Jackhammer notwithstanding, this ought to be a fabulous trip.

Chapter 2

AFTER showering in a bathroom so freshly painted that the switch plates hadn't yet been replaced, Lynne dressed in a ribbed cotton sweater and jeans, then peeked into Jenna's room down the hall.

This room too was an oasis of calm. Her daughter's soft blonde curls poked out from under an intricately patterned quilt in shades of burgundy and white, with a smattering of forest green. Lynne was pretty sure she was supposed to know the name of the pattern, but this was the kind of information she usually kept in her scratch-pad memory only as long as it was absolutely essential. Two more cats were curled up on Jenna's bed, one on the pillow beside her head. Neither stirred as Lynne quietly closed the door and headed downstairs. The felines at least had enough sense to stay out of the construction zones.

There seemed no likelihood of breakfast being served in the dining room, which was stacked floor-to-ceiling with brown cardboard boxes. Nearly all were labeled DISHES or CRYSTAL, with further subdivisions into WATERFORD, WEDG-

WOOD, WINEGLASSES, and LIMOGES. Where on earth had they all come from? Back when the Westbrook family was circling the globe at the behest of the US Navy, there had been only the most basic in formal tableware. Now Priscilla had somehow accumulated entire boxfuls of brandy snifters and butter dishes.

If the B&B didn't work out, she could open an antique store.

The large, sunny kitchen seemed finished, for the most part, with a big Sub-Zero refrigerator and gleaming new stovetop, dishwasher, and set of matched microwaves. Here the green and beige curtains were hung, the linoleum shiny, the kitchen chairs dressed in green ruffled seat cushions that matched the curtains.

Her mother sat at the kitchen table reading the morning newspaper. Two places across from her were set with cheerful stoneware plates, glasses of frothy orange juice, empty coffee mugs, and color-coordinated cloth napkins folded atop the plates to look like flowers. The tablecloth featured bright sprays of fall leaves.

When Lynne walked in, Priscilla looked up and beamed. "Well, good morning, sleepyhead! Did you sleep well?"

Best not to mention the jackhammering yet. "Absolutely. Do I smell breakfast?"

Priscilla stood and moved to the stove, her step sprightly. Her body remained trim and she was dressed to match the kitchen in hunter green slacks, a beige blouse, and a full-length pink ruffled apron. Her mother had been in denial about her age for as long as Lynne could remember. When Lynne was in grade school at various naval bases, her mother always claimed to be twenty-nine, a fiction she maintained until Lynne got a driver's license, when her mother quietly turned "thirty-five." By then Lynne had sneaked a peek at her mother's own driver's license and learned the truth.

"You most certainly do. Can't have a bed-and-breakfast without breakfast, now can we? Even if in your case it's more like brunch. I made crepes. I thought we'd just breakfast in the kitchen, since the dining room's not quite finished yet."

A masterpiece of understatement. Not to mention that breakfast was not a word Lynne was accustomed to using as a verb, or a meal she was accustomed to eating at all. But she just smiled.

Lynne poured herself a cup of coffee from the carafe on the counter while Priscilla fiddled with the microwave, then reached into an oven and pulled out a serving plate holding some thin, dispirited pancakes and several slices of limp, undercooked bacon. Her mother had never been a particularly enthusiastic cook, which made her new career as innkeeper even more problematic. Folks at bed-and-breakfasts expected fancy morning meals: Belgian waffles, eggs Benedict, huevos rancheros. And they expected variety, as well. There'd better be a good bakery in town or this venture would be doomed from the get-go.

The microwave beeped and Priscilla pulled a charming little pitcher from it. "Here's some warmed maple syrup, from New Hampshire's finest maple trees," she announced, "and there's whipped butter in that little crock on the table." She might be in her ninth decade, but her expression—her entire face, for that matter—remained perky. Lynne had a sudden flash of recognition: her mother was living out a private version of that TV show *Newhart*. Any minute now, Darryl and Darryl would pop in through the kitchen door.

"Sounds g—" Lynne began. A sudden burst of jackhammering cut her off.

But of course. The Darryls were already at work.

The noise went on long enough for Lynne to help herself to the alleged crepes, their French authenticity called into question by the Bisquick box on the counter. Priscilla herself was a quarter French, her paternal grandfather having emigrated from Lyons. It was, however, a very aggressive quarter, and, like the Coneheads, Priscilla always claimed to be from France.

The jackhammering stopped.

"How long has this been going on?" Lynne asked, pointing

toward the floor. "And *what* is going on? I notice that there's a bit more to be taken care of before you put your sign out on the lawn."

"Oh, the sign's already done," Priscilla said, missing the point—deliberately was Lynne's guess. "It's in the garage."

Lynne could only imagine what all else would be in the garage. No vehicles, at any rate. Her mother's Lincoln was parked in the driveway.

"And I'm sure it's a lovely sign. But what's going on down there?" Lynne pointed again at the floor.

"Oh, I told you all about it," Priscilla fibbed.

"Refresh my memory. And you better hurry before it starts up again."

"Well, you may have noticed that a couple of the bathrooms upstairs aren't quite finished yet." More understatement. A boxed toilet sat in the hall just past Jenna's room, along with several cartons of ceramic tile. "But my plumber's discovered some sort of problem with the pipes down in the basement. And, unfortunately, those particular pipes are embedded in the floor. So we have to chop up part of the floor to get at them. That's all. I tried to put it off until after your visit, but you know how plumbers are. I had to take the time slot he offered me."

Lynne nodded sympathetically, all too willing to commiserate about capricious plumbers. "Is this going to affect our water supply while we're here?"

Priscilla shook her head. "Absolutely not. We're just chopping up the floor now so he can get started right away after you girls leave. I'll go stay with Abby while the water's off. In any case, you shouldn't have any trouble with the plumbing in your bathroom."

Lynne wondered how this could possibly be the case and decided to let well enough alone. She'd already showered, after all, and nothing blew up or flooded when she did.

"I've put most of the renovation work on hold during your visit anyway. So probably the only workmen you'll run into are Jason and Ralph. Ralph's had the flu this last week and Jason's here today by himself." Priscilla nodded at the floor.

Jason? It was better than Darryl, but not much.

Now the noise started up again. Lynne noticed her juice glass bouncing lightly on the table, performing a regular little tap dance. What this experience actually resembled was a mild earthquake.

Breakfast finished, Lynne waited for a break in the noise, then asked, "Could I get the grand tour?"

"But of course," her mother replied. Grandly. She was playing the role of Newhart's wife—what had her name been?—the one with all the great sweaters.

Lynne would have been concerned about the purchase of the Maple Leaf Inn under any circumstances. The extent of the renovation was certainly alarming, but matters were also further complicated by the fact that Lynne herself had been cast in a supporting role in its future. Her mother expected her to refer clients from her Booked for Travel agency to stay here. Year-round, not only during the autumn, Priscilla having brightly noted on more than one occasion that New Hampshire was a "Four-Season Vacation Wonderland."

Lynne was also assigned to develop a Fantastic Foliage tour that she had tentatively committed to leading next fall. The idea was to bring the joys of crisp autumn days and dazzling foliage displays to Southern Californians who usually only marked the arrival of fall by exchanging their white shorts for khaki ones.

It wasn't a bad idea, actually. She'd booked many a client on other agencies' "leaf peeper" autumn tours. And whether or not the tour materialized, Lynne had long wanted to revisit New England in the fall.

As a child she had sometimes come to visit New Hampshire relatives with her mother, often when the Westbrooks were on their way to a new naval base and a new duty assignment. One of those trips had coincided perfectly with New England fall color. All these years later, Lynne could still recall the amazing display of color and the leaf collection she had carefully pressed between sheets of waxed paper. The leaf collection had bit the dust in the next year's move, or maybe the one after that, but the memories lingered.

It had been too dark to tell much last night, but from photographs that Priscilla had sent, Lynne knew that the Maple Leaf Inn was a two-story white frame building with a wide porch across its entire front, set at the end of a cul-de-sac. The front of the ground floor featured two large common areas, a good-sized living room on one side and a formal dining room that was only slightly smaller on the other. The dining room opened into a large, sunny kitchen in the rear. A small apartment, two rooms with private bath, occupied the other back corner of the ground floor. One of those rooms was set up as a library and the other was full of boxes. Priscilla planned to move down here, she had said, before she opened.

Her mother started the tour upstairs, where there were six bedrooms that would be open to the public. Priscilla tiptoed past Jenna's still-occupied room and ignored the toilet in the hall. Two other bedrooms and the bath between them were finished, down to the dried floral arrangements on the dressers. One had a brass bedstead, the other twin beds with mahogany headboards, and each featured a different quilt pattern and color scheme.

"You've been having fun, haven't you?" Lynne asked fondly.

"The time of my life," Priscilla responded.

When her mother expressed appreciation that Lynne had made up her bed, Lynne made a mental note to bring up the issue of just who would be doing what at the Maple Leaf Inn. There was a lot more to running a successful bed-and-breakfast than decorating talent and personal charm. Somebody needed to clean the guest rooms, scrub the toilets, fix and serve as many as a dozen breakfasts daily, handle credit cards, and book reservations.

Lynne was not, however, foolhardy enough to raise these questions now, just as she was keeping her mouth shut about the much more disturbing question of how her mother was paying for all this. Best to wait and buttonhole Aunt Abigail about that, since she was the one who'd brought the subject up in the first place.

Still, the completed rooms in the Maple Leaf Inn were undeniably charming. The furniture looked old, whether or not it qualified as bona fide antiques, and the accessories and little touches added coziness without crossing that fuzzy border to terminal cuteness, a common affliction of B&Bs.

"Everything was just a terrible mess when I started," Priscilla explained, "and it still has a long way to go. It probably would have been absolutely impossible except that there were already extra baths from back when the place was a boardinghouse, though I must say they were rather primitive. And there was such a limited water supply that I can't imagine how everybody stayed clean. But all that will be fixed."

At great cost, Lynne imagined. "Where did you find all these contractors?" she asked carefully. "Did Aunt Abby recommend them?"

Priscilla laughed girlishly. "Abby doesn't particularly approve of this little project of mine. My financier recommended Ralph and he found the plumber and the others. Ralph's been doing this sort of thing forever in South Hadford. He's a little . . . well, confused, I guess is the best way to say it. He had a stroke a while back, maybe two. So he's got some memory problems, but fortunately he remembers everything there is to know about home repair."

A mixed blessing, a forgetful handyman. Though they never seemed to forget the bill.

Priscilla continued. "Ralph and his dear little wife used to live across the street till they moved out to a place where she can get nursing care. He drives in every day to work here." She frowned. "Except, of course, for when he forgets."

It seemed to Lynne that renovating a home was difficult enough without having a contractor who sometimes forgot to show up. But she kept her mouth shut. For all she knew, Ralph was the cleverest fix-it guy in all of New Hampshire.

"But Ralph doesn't do all the work himself. You said that's somebody named Jason downstairs now."

Priscilla giggled. "My goodness, Ralph's not steady enough on his feet to use a jackhammer, and besides, he's been laid up with the flu. I thought I already mentioned that. Anyway, Jason is kind of like Ralph-in-training, to be an all-around handyman. Or handyperson." She frowned. "Am I supposed to call him a handyperson?"

"Call him whatever you want, Mom. Do I get to meet this miracle worker?" If he was as good as Priscilla claimed, Lynne would have to figure out a way to clone him and stick him in her suitcase. Competent, reliable handymen were an endangered species in California.

"But of course. I'll take you down to meet Jason just as soon as we finish up here."

Now Priscilla opened the last door on the upstairs hall. "Welcome to my boudoir, my own little retreat. I'll be moving all this downstairs before I open, of course, into the private apartment."

Her little retreat looked like a preteen girl's fantasy bedroom, in shades of pink and white, awash with ruffles and bows. This surprised Lynne not one bit.

"It's wonderful, Mom." She gave her mother a hug. "And it's great to see you."

The jackhammering stopped.

"Come on," Priscilla said, disengaging herself from the hug. "Let's go down to the basement before Jason starts up again."

JASON turned out to be a ponytailed fellow with buck teeth and a bit of a paunch. He was probably in his late thirties, wearing a faded black Patriots t-shirt and jeans with a rip at the knee that did not seem to be a fashion statement.

"Nice to meet you," he told Lynne as he reached for a

water bottle and took a long pull. "Your mother's fixing this place up real nice."

"She gives you and Ralph much of the credit," Lynne told him, her tone carefully neutral. "It seems like quite an ambitious undertaking."

She looked around. The basement was large, unfinished, and for the most part filled with large, ominous pieces of equipment. Any empty space was cluttered with junk: broken chairs, out-of-season fans, and lots more boxes with labels like CHRISTMAS ORNAMENTS and NAVY STUFF and PENSACOLA KNICKKNACKS. Several windows high on the walls were too grimy to let in much light.

Shelves under the stairs held Mason jars that looked like they'd been there since the Revolutionary War. It was a certainty, Lynne thought, that her mother hadn't been involved in filling them. In front of the canned goods stood a couple of litter boxes that could do with some attention.

A portable workbench that probably belonged to Ralph and Jason was set up in a corner near the stairway, and plastic sheeting covered laundry equipment behind the workbench. Near the washer and dryer stood what had to be the mangle Priscilla had recently mentioned finding on eBay, also shrouded. It would, she'd assured Lynne, make short work of ironing guest linens. Lynne now added laundry to her mental list of innkeeping chores.

Everything down here was covered with a layer of dust and grit. And the floor itself, the part that wasn't already in pieces, was rough and uneven.

There were several large pieces of equipment that she'd never seen before, including some big rusty tanks. A massive furnace had large pipes that seemed to be tentacles extending in different directions up through the ceiling. Various exposed pipes crisscrossed the ceiling and a six-foot-tall tank resembling a large rusty bullet stood on an equally rusty wrought-iron stand. In the opposite corner, the floor rose at a forty-five-degree angle toward the top edges of a three-foot-diameter circle with a flat concrete top that looked rather like a concrete footstool. Underneath one of the dirty windows, a fuel oil tank of gargantuan proportions sat quietly rusting.

"So what exactly are you doing down here?" Lynne asked, looking down at the chunks of concrete Jason had already broken and set aside. The area affected seemed to bisect the basement from corner to corner, starting around the rusty bullet and moving toward the concrete footstool.

"That over there is the well," Jason said, pointing at the concrete footstool. "That's the water supply for the whole house. There's a pump that takes the water out of the well and sends it to that tank." He indicated the rusty bullet. "Problem is, the pipe between the two is galvanized iron and it's starting to rust out. It'll be re-piped with copper, and then there'll be two of those water tanks, on account of folks at a place like this use a lot of water."

He spoke with a tone of resentment. Lynne wondered if the antagonism was directed at her mother, or at tourists in general. Of course there could be a simpler reason. Jason might have done a little research on bed-and-breakfast rates and compared them to his own earnings.

"The floor's really thick over here, isn't it?" Lynne moved toward the footstool. The concrete there was more than a foot deep and seemed honeycombed with open spaces. She squatted to examine an opening. It looked more like a small tunnel than a hole, perhaps three inches in diameter, circling the well.

But wait.

There was something in that tunnel. Loose, just lying there. Lynne cautiously touched what looked like a bleached piece of driftwood. What on earth would driftwood be doing in this landlocked basement?

She pulled it out to examine it and realized, in a moment of pure horror, that this was no driftwood. It was bone. A long straight length of bone, like what you might find in somebody's leg.

Resisting the urge to scream, forcing herself to stay calm, Lynne stood and looked around for a clean surface on which to set the bone. The *whatever,* she mentally corrected. She didn't know it was a bone, though she felt an odd sense of certainty. In any case, it definitely seemed wrong to just stick it back into the concrete floor in the path of the jackhammer.

Jason and Priscilla were both watching intently.

"I don't guess this is a nine-one-one emergency," Lynne said, "but we definitely need to call the police."

Chapter 3

THE relative calm of a small-town New England morning rapidly deteriorated into the Marx Brothers scene in the ocean liner stateroom.

First on the scene was a South Hadford patrol officer, responding to Lynne's matter-of-fact call to the local police. This impossibly young man came down to the basement, regarded the chopped-up concrete suspiciously, then looked sternly at Lynne when she showed him the apparent length of leg bone that she'd pulled from the honeycombed concrete. She had, before he arrived, gotten down on her hands and knees with a flashlight to see what might be farther in the hole. She wasn't sure if she was relieved or disappointed when she realized that without actually poking around in there, a fairly horrifying concept, she really couldn't see much.

"Ma'am, you shouldn't disturb a crime scene," Officer Chapman chided. He had a baby face and probably hadn't been shaving much more than a year. But he seemed to take his work seriously. His uniform was crisply pressed, his shoes and holster polished to an ebony sheen.

Lynne looked at him and smiled sweetly. As the mother of a young police officer—though not as young as this pup— she had plenty of experience interacting with the law. "I didn't know it was a crime scene when I picked that bone up. If it even *is* a bone. For all we know it's a chunk of something that got dropped into the cement by mistake."

They both stopped to look at the object in question, now resting on a clean shop rag on Jason's workbench. Jason himself was doing his best to fade into the unfinished basement walls. Indeed, he seemed to be sidling toward the outside cellar door, which opened into the back porch via steps leading up to ground level.

"If anything disturbed it, I'd say it was probably the jackhammer, don't you think?" Lynne went on. She was starting to realize that while this situation was bad now, it might well become considerably worse in the near future.

Upstairs the teakettle started to whistle and the doorbell rang.

A few moments later, an older man in blue denim overalls lumbered down the basement stairs. He wasn't particularly large, but he seemed uncertain on his feet.

"Jason?" the man called as he came. "You down here, boy?"

Jason moved away from the backyard exit and came to the foot of the stairs. "Right here, Ralph."

"I was feeling better so I thought I'd check on things. But what are you all doing down in the basement?"

Ralph got to the bottom of the stairs and looked around in genuine confusion at Lynne, Jason, and young Officer Chapman, who was moving rapidly to intercept the older man. As he took in the details of the jackhammer and the chunks of broken concrete, his face grew very pale.

"Who in the dickens—"

Then he fainted.

Jason lunged forward to break the older man's fall, then

settled Ralph onto the bottom stairs. There was nothing in the basement resembling a chair.

"I'll call for an ambulance," Officer Chapman said, reaching for his radio.

But Ralph was coming out of the faint. "I'm okay," he said weakly. He turned his head from side to side, still pale, then put his hands on his knees and dropped his head between them.

A few very long moments passed. Then Ralph slowly raised his head. "Jason? Help me get across the street to Cindy's place."

"Are you sure we don't need the paramedics?" Officer Chapman asked again.

Ralph shook his head. "Been sick, that's all. I'm okay. Jason?" He pointed to the back door. "Less stairs."

Officer Chapman opened the back door and then helped Jason assist the older man up the stairway. A few moments later he was back.

"Tough old bird," he said. "You weren't messing with anything while I was gone now?"

Lynne almost laughed. Did he think she'd been rearranging the chunks of concrete? Alphabetizing the Mason jars? "Didn't move a muscle," she assured him.

Upstairs the doorbell rang again.

"LYNNE?" Her mother's voice from the top of the stairs had an edge that hadn't been there half an hour ago, when her cellar was just her cellar and not a possible burial ground. "Can you help me, please?"

"Excuse me," Lynne told the young cop, heading gratefully upstairs.

The bone and the concrete rubble were both starting to give her the willies. There was probably some totally innocuous explanation, of course. Maybe this had been somebody's pet—a Great Dane, say, or an Irish Wolfhound—that died in winter when the ground was frozen. You weren't supposed to keep dead animals, but Lynne knew from personal experience that a sympathetic vet would allow you to take a euthanized pet home. If that pet died at home it was even easier. In a bushy back corner of Lynne's own backyard, several beloved cats were buried with their favorite toys beneath the buddleias and hibiscus.

So maybe instead of waiting till summer, they buried old Bowser under the basement floor.

Yeah, right.

As Lynne stepped into the hallway, she was greeted by the sight of her mother, looking decidedly harried, and her mother's sister Abigail.

"Lynne! You look wonderful," Aunt Abby said. She was Priscilla's younger, more responsible sister, a long-retired supervisor at a South Hadford knitting mill that produced fine sweaters, mostly for the tourist trade. Few locals could afford them.

"And so do you, Aunt Abby." The woman's steel gray hair was cut in a precise and utilitarian cap that hugged her scalp. Abigail wore a brown gabardine skirt, a blue button-down Oxford style shirt, and sturdy brown clogs. Had the weather been cooler, she'd undoubtedly have added a Golden Mills cardigan.

Abigail's sharp dark eyes flickered behind rimless glasses as she made a reciprocal inventory of her niece, her gaze moving steadily from head to toe. When Aunt Abby was done and had nodded a brief approval, Lynne moved forward to offer a hug. It was the standard welcoming hug that Southern Californians offer anyone they've ever met before, even for a minute, but it seemed to make her aunt uncomfortable. Abigail allowed herself to be only briefly hugged before extricating herself and stepping back out of reach, all but brushing off cooties.

It wasn't considered polite to call an unmarried woman an old maid anymore, or even a spinster. In the case of Abigail Chenonceau, however, both terms fit tidily.

"What's the matter with Ralph?" Abigail now asked. "I saw that young fellow going across the street with him. Didn't look too steady on his feet. And what's that police car doing out there?"

Priscilla waved her hands helplessly.

Lynne took over. "Ralph's been sick and he felt faint. And the police car is here because Jason exposed something that looks like a bone when he was breaking up the basement floor."

"Come now, that's ridiculous."

"Probably," Lynne agreed. She explained what had happened.

"What rubbish," Abigail said. "And where's my grand-niece?" She was one of those people who understood all the nuances of third cousins twice removed. Jenna actually did refer to Aunt Abby as Great-Aunt Abigail behind her back, but only because she said it sounded like the name of the woman who brought the Siamese cats to stay in *Lady and the Tramp*.

"Still sleeping, I think," Lynne said.

Abigail set off toward the kitchen, casting a disparaging look at the dining room and its vast collection of boxed dishes. "I certainly didn't anticipate that you'd be entertaining the police, Priscilla." Abigail's tone was sufficiently accusatory to make Lynne glad she'd never labored under this woman at Golden Mills. She would have been a fearsome and unforgiving taskmistress. Lynne remembered her father saying, on more than one occasion, that Abigail should have been a man, and an officer. While hideously sexist, it was his highest form of praise.

"All I did was agree to rip up the basement floor to fix the plumbing." Priscilla slunk toward the kitchen, trying to look pitiful and succeeding all too well. She poured boiling water into a teapot shaped like an English country cottage, complete with a thatched roof and flowering vines climbing the walls. From all that Lynne could tell, accessorizing the Maple Leaf Inn was her mother's favorite aspect of the entire innkeeping experience.

Jason came in the back door without knocking. "Took Ralph over to Cindy's," he said. "Says he's fine, just going to lie down a bit." He lingered for a moment in the kitchen, checking out the counters, probably trolling for doughnuts. Away from his workbench and jackhammer, he looked dusty and uncomfortable. "I'll be outside," he told them. "Can't do any more down there till they figure out what's what."

"There's the gazebo," Priscilla reminded him, suddenly in authority again. "You could start sanding that down to paint it."

"My tools are all in the basement," he said, "and that cop said I couldn't bring any of them up here. Think I'll just go have a smoke and wait."

Abigail shook her head, muttering, "Filthy." It wasn't clear if she meant Jason or the habit. Probably both.

Oblivious, Jason went back through the kitchen door, ambling toward a gazebo that was peeling paint as if shedding a bad sunburn. He pulled a pack of Marlboros out of his shirt pocket and stopped on the path to strike a match and light up.

Priscilla looked helplessly at Lynne, just as Jenna, dressed in running shorts and an old UCLA t-shirt, bounded down the stairs and turned toward the kitchen, pulling up short. Her hair was pulled back in a scrunchy, her face scrubbed and free of makeup.

"Why, hello there, Aunt Abby," Jenna said politely. "I didn't know we'd see you so soon."

"I came to see my relatives, Jenny. But it seems there's been a bit of a rather distasteful discovery here this morning."

Jenna frowned, and Lynne was grateful that her daughter didn't immediately correct her great-aunt on the currently used variant of her name.

"Does this have anything to do with that police car parked out front?"

Score one for the UCLA grad.

"It does indeed," Abigail answered.

Jenna looked around, noticed Priscilla hovering in the kitchen, and appeared to relax. "So what's going on?"

"You might have heard some jackhammering this morning?" Lynne said.

Jenna laughed. "Yeah, I might have."

"Well, that jackhammering seems to have unearthed . . . a problem."

"A problem requiring the police?" Jenna asked.

Lynne nodded, then explained what had happened. "We're waiting for a detective now."

"Should I stick around?" Jenna asked. "I was going to go for a run."

"Go ahead, dear," Priscilla told her. "We'll just stay here and hold down the fort until— Oh my Lord, the party!"

"Party?" Jenna asked.

"Party?" Lynne echoed.

Priscilla sounded stricken. "I set up a little gathering for this afternoon, an afternoon tea to introduce you two to my friends and neighbors here."

Moving into major league histrionics, she buried her face in both perfectly manicured hands—hands, Lynne assumed, that would not be performing any of those menial chores she'd been wondering about earlier. "What on earth can I do?"

Aunt Abby looked at the basement door. "Postpone it, I'd say. It'll give you more time to get ready, which would probably be a good idea. You might even be able to get some of those boxes emptied in the dining room. But heaven only knows when you'll be able to reschedule. There's likely to be all manner of riff-raff through here if that thing actually turns out to be what Lynne thinks it is."

Lynne detected the slightest hint of blame in Aunt Abby's tone, as if Lynne had somehow created this potential problem by discovering it.

"I'd better start making calls," Priscilla said, with just enough petulance to make it clear she was already feeling abandoned.

"I'll stay and help," Abigail announced. "And I'd suggest that you girls run along and take in some of the local sights before you get stuck here with the old folks."

Lynne might have felt insulted at Aunt Abby's implication that she would be in the way, but she chose instead to focus on the "girls" part of the pronouncement. "Maybe I'll walk into town and check out some antique shops while Jenna takes her run. Then we can go over to Portsmouth to Strawbery Banke, which was actually what I'd planned to do today anyway."

The doorbell rang again and Lynne moved swiftly to answer it. A serious looking man in his forties stood on the porch, wearing a navy blazer and khakis. His tie was so badly knotted that Lynne, who normally didn't pay much attention to male neckwear, found herself staring in fascination as he held up his badge, right next to the tie.

"I'm Detective O'Keefe," he said. "Mrs. Jones?"

"That's my mother," Lynne told him, opening the door. For the first time she noticed artistic displays of pumpkins, gourds, and chrysanthemums on the wide front porch, flanking the front door on both sides. On the door itself hung a spectacular fall wreath with intertwined leaves and berries. "She's in the kitchen."

Detective O'Keefe followed Lynne back to the kitchen, where he nodded at Aunt Abby in slightly surprised recognition.

"Good morning, Miss Chenonceau," he said carefully.

"Good morning, William." Abigail turned to the rest of them and announced, "William worked summers at the mill while he was a student." Her tone suggested that he might have been a slightly less-than-perfect employee. "Have you met my sister, Priscilla Jones, William? She grew up here and recently moved back."

"Pleased to meet you, ma'am." Detective O'Keefe listened and nodded as Abigail took over matters, identifying Lynne and Jenna. Realizing that the Californians had been in New Hampshire less than twelve hours, he offered them a hint of a smile. "Sorry to inconvenience you, ladies. You're here for peak?"

Lynne had done enough homework to know that "peak" referred to the entire autumn phenomenon, a fleeting season that the natives did everything they possibly could to prolong. Each day that the leaves performed meant dollars in the till all over New England. The *Yankee Magazine* website featured interactive foliage maps where you could track the changing leaf colors from regional generality to town or county specificity. Whole battalions of hometown leaf-watchers reported back to *Yankee* as the season shifted.

Lynne nodded. There was no reason to explain the tour she was planning, or her own reservations about her mother's somewhat impetuous dive into inn keeping. A woman half her age might find the prospect daunting, but Priscilla was a rebel who thrived on challenge, a propensity that had sent her on the road with the Roller Derby as a teenager, then served her well during the decades when she traversed the globe with her first two husbands and the United States Navy. Priscilla had always been a strong-willed woman, despite her nominal acceptance of the social restrictions and obligations of an officer's wife. In her third widowhood she had become even more stubborn and determined to have her own way.

Lynne, who had known all three husbands, figured it was time for her mother to make her own decisions. She just wished she believed that opening the Maple Leaf Inn was a good one.

Detective O'Keefe excused himself to go down into the cellar, returning a few minutes later. "I'm not sure exactly what you have down there, ladies, but I'm going to ask some folks from the State Police up in Concord to come down here and take a look. Officer Chapman will stay downstairs until they get here."

Roger, the long-haired black cat who'd been sleeping on Jenna's bed earlier, cautiously rounded the corner from the hall and slunk toward the basement stairs and the litter boxes. Roger looked a bit anxious, as if this were an emergency.

"Whoops!" Detective O'Keefe said, reaching a quick arm down to scoop up Roger. The action was so unexpected that Roger didn't have time to object, and by the time the cat realized he should be protesting, the detective was rubbing his neck and speaking softly. Roger took the easy way out and began to purr.

Priscilla explained about the litter box. "I can't let him outside. These are strictly indoor cats."

Yet another concern. Lynne filed "animal dander" and "allergies" on her mental list of problems requiring resolution at the Maple Leaf Inn.

"Then I'll have Officer Chapman bring the litter box up for you. Perhaps you could keep it on the back porch for the time being?" It was more expectation than request. "And I'll need to close off the entire cellar till we determine what's going on. We can just shut the door here for the time being. And now I'll go see what the fellow who was working down there has to say."

"He's out in the back," Abigail said. "Smoking."

As Detective O'Keefe headed out into the yard in search of Jason, Lynne stole a glance at Aunt Abby. She wondered when her aunt would explain just what was worrying her about Priscilla's purchase of the Maple Leaf Inn.

Though Lynne's mother didn't know this, part of the reason Lynne was here was to check up on Priscilla's finances. Abigail's handwritten, lavender-scented note to Lynne last summer had hinted, in perfect, Palmer-method penmanship, that something might be amiss with the arrangements her mother had made to buy the Maple Leaf Inn.

Lynne, whose handwritten-note days were long behind her, had immediately picked up the phone and called Aunt Abby. "Come and see for yourself," Abigail instructed, in a maddening and uncharacteristic fit of coyness. "I may be entirely mistaken, after all." Her tone, as always, left little doubt that this might possibly be true. But she refused to elaborate.

"I think we should both get out of everybody's hair," Lynne told Jenna. "I'm going for a walk and I know you want a run. Maybe there's someplace we can meet up in an hour or so for lunch, and then head out to Strawbery Banke." At Jenna's blank expression, she explained. "Strawbery Banke is a collection of restored historic buildings in the town of Portsmouth down on the New Hampshire coast."

"Sounds nice," Jenna said, her tone carefully neutral.

"Why, that's a lovely plan," said Priscilla. "There's a darling little restaurant called Angelina's downtown, right next to The Curiosity Shop, which is a pretty nice antique shop that you'll want to check out. It opens at eleven. And if you go a bit farther down Main Street, there's an antique mall on the outskirts of town."

"Is all this within walking distance?" Lynne asked.

"That depends," Abigail answered, "on what you consider walking distance."

Lynne smiled. "Jenna's been running for years, and I walk three miles just about every morning along the seawall in Floritas with some friends. Five when we're feeling truly virtuous."

"You should manage, then," Abigail conceded.

Detective O'Keefe returned through the back door, offering a pro forma knock. He stepped inside and asked Priscilla to take a seat at the kitchen table. The aroma of the breakfast "crepes" still lingered in the kitchen air. It seemed a long time since breakfast, even though it was barely ten-thirty.

"If the rest of you could excuse us please?" Detective O'Keefe said.

As the three women moved toward the front of the house, Lynne could hear the detective's voice quite clearly.

"Mrs. Jones," the detective began, "how long have you lived here?"

"About a year and a half. I came here in the spring, so this is my second autumn in South Hadford."

"Did you move here to buy this place?"

"Heavens no!" Priscilla offered a little titter. "I came here to live with my sister after my husband, rest his soul, passed away. Then I learned this property was available and I decided to open it as a bed-and-breakfast."

Lynne followed Abigail and Jenna out onto the front porch. Abigail offered directions to Jenna, who then jogged off toward the heart of town.

"You know that detective?" Lynne asked her aunt as they watched Jenna's receding figure.

"I told you so. He worked for me summers. Three or four years."

"Satisfactorily?"

"Satisfactorily enough. I knew he wouldn't be staying on after he graduated from the university, but he was bright and reasonably reliable."

Bright and reasonably reliable. Talk about damning with faint praise.

"Has he been on the force here for long?"

"He was working with the State Police up in Concord before he came here," Abigail said. "He's been here four or five years. His wife grew up in South Hadford."

All told, this sounded like somebody who might put forth some real effort to determine what was in that basement and why. And with a hometown connection, he might be able to come up with leads that no out-of-towner would ever unearth in this typically taciturn New Hampshire town.

A young woman in overall shorts with a skimpy tee was crossing the street toward them. A little boy holding her hand strained to get away from her as they crossed. Once they were on the Maple Leaf Inn's side of the street, the woman let the boy break away. He ran toward an apple tree at the side of the porch and started to climb.

"Be careful, Bradley," the woman called out. Bradley ignored her as he shinnied up the trunk and came to rest about eight feet off the ground in a crook of her mother's Macintosh apple tree. Rosy windfalls lay on the ground beneath the thick canopy of leaves that hadn't yet begun to change color.

"I understand Daddy got a little dizzy over here this morning," the young woman told Abigail. "He's lying down at my house right now." She gestured to the police cruiser, the unmarked Ford that belonged to Detective O'Keefe, Abigail's stodgy Buick, and the two pickup trucks that the handymen had arrived in. "What's going on?" She smiled at Lynne. "I'm Cindy, by the way. Ralph's my dad."

Lynne introduced herself and explained briefly what had

happened. "Is your dad okay? He was very insistent that we not call the paramedics."

"Oh, he's fine," Cindy assured them. "He's had the flu, that's all. But golly, that's weird about the basement. You really think it's a bone?"

"I don't know," Lynne said, though in fact she was all but certain that it was.

Chapter 4

JENNA Montgomery looked around the antique mall, stunned silent by the staggering quantity of material that looked to her like pure and absolute junk. The term "mall" was certainly a misnomer, too. The building was a cavernous place, much longer than it was wide, its interior aisles twisting and turning among the various consignment spaces that exhibited the Crap of the Ages.

"Hey, Jenna, check this out." Lynne, who seemed utterly unfazed by any of this, stood next to a pile of board games that looked old enough to be trash but not quite old enough to be collectible artifacts: Clue, Game of the States, Yahtzee, a knock-off Monopoly for Atlanta and a very pink box offering a female version of Careers. She pointed at Careers. "Remember that game?"

Jenna laughed. "I sure do, but mostly just because you got so mad about it. Didn't it have maybe four choices? Like teacher, nurse, stewardess, and marry a millionaire? Grandma sent it to me for Christmas one year, didn't she?"

"She did indeed."

"And after we played one game you threw it in the fire-place. Does Grandma know that?"

"Not from me," Lynne said, "and I assume you're smart enough not to bring it up. I guess I was a little less flexible back then. Women were still really struggling with a lot of equal rights issues. Maybe I overreacted. But it sure was sat-isfying watching that sucker burn. I'm half tempted to buy this one and do it again. There's a fireplace at the Inn." She examined the box. "Scratch that idea. The moment of satis-faction I'd get isn't worth seven bucks."

"Remember Boggle?" Jenna asked, picking up another box. It had a dusty look, though when she stroked a finger along the top of the box, it came back clean.

Lynne grinned. "Not only do I remember it, I still have it."

"Cool." Jenna looked around. "You know, it looks like no-body in this town has ever thrown *anything* away. For hun-dreds of years."

"I'm inclined to agree," Lynne said. "I'm sure there are some interesting things here, but you'd have to go through mountains of junk to find them." She gestured at the nearby consignment areas. Broken picture frames, tattered books, crockery of all descriptions, including some faux Mason jars that had recently held spaghetti sauce. Ads from *Life* were tucked into clear poly bags and marked ten dollars each. Uninspired postcards from long-defunct motels were offered at a dollar and up.

"I wonder," Jenna said, picking up a hairbrush that just looked like a hairbrush, neither old nor interesting, "whether tourists buy a lot of this stuff and take it back home to wher-ever they came from, or if the locals here just keep churning it back and forth to each other. I bet a lot of the furnishings at the Maple Leaf Inn came from here or places like this."

Lynne nodded and continued down the serpentine aisle. Every time Jenna thought they'd reached the far end and could finally start twisting their way back, it turned out to be a fake wall that turned toward another half-acre of thrift-shop rejects.

"Look at all this depression glass," Lynne said, stopping at another display. "It almost makes me wish I collected it, just to be able to get some of these pieces."

"Don't get any ideas, Mom. You've already got more junk than you need." Though after just a cursory appraisal of her grandmother's house, Jenna had a much clearer sense of how her mother had become a minor-league hoarder. Grandma herself was championship material.

Of the Montgomery family, Lynne had always been the one with the most serious packrat tendencies. Jenna's dad had claimed it was because Lynne had moved all the time when she was younger. That once she was settled in a single place, she wanted to have more possessions simply because she could.

Jenna had a feeling that this trip might involve far more time in this sort of place than she'd anticipated. She also realized that this was exactly the kind of thing that the older folks who took the Booked for Travel tours seemed to like, which was, after all, why they were in New England in the first place.

Jenna passed a display of elderly Book-of-the-Month Club selections and joined her mother in front of a decrepit shelving unit marked NOT FOR SALE. Not to worry. Nobody in their right mind would want this broken-down excuse for furniture, though she imagined that it would fit nicely in that nasty cellar at the Maple Leaf Inn.

Of course she hadn't actually *seen* the basement yet. By the time she got up, it was already off-limits with the cops standing guard. She didn't have much experience with basements, actually, since hardly anybody in Southern California had them. Still, Jenna had seen enough scary movies to know that when you were in Stephen King country and somebody said there might be a body in the basement, you Did Not Go Down There.

She picked up a faux ivory folding fan with fluffy black feathers on the end of each segment and opened it. It appeared to be intact. She swished it dramatically. "I thought you said it was going to be chilly here, Mom."

"Well, maybe it will be." Her mother didn't seem the least

bit perturbed by the weather, or the change in the day's plans, or even by an apparent body in Grandma's basement. Her father had been the same way, Jenna realized. When she'd been growing up, she'd taken for granted that the two of them were pretty much unflappable.

"Are we going to be able to leave town?" Jenna asked. "Because the whole idea that there might be a body down there really creeps me out."

"It creeps me out too," Lynne admitted. "But of course we'll be able to leave. We don't live here and don't know anything. By the time they get the folks from the state crime lab down here and figure out who or what is in that concrete, it could be Christmas. The only thing that concerns me is that Grandma's kind of freaked out. I really don't want to just run off and leave her right away."

"You could have her come with us."

"Yeah, I could. And I probably will, a little bit later. But your grandmother tends to be a full-time job, and I need to concentrate on finding interesting things for this tour I'm trying to put together."

"Then I could distract her while you run around doing whatever you need to run around and do."

Lynne said nothing.

"Or how about this? She can stay here and we can go. She won't be alone. She's got her sister right across town. She could go stay with her."

Lynne shrugged. "Also a reasonable plan. Jenna, I just don't know."

"Is this going to mess up the plans to develop a tour?"

"Oh, no, not at all. It doesn't matter if I can't see everything I wanted to check out. I deliberately planned more than any tour can possibly do because it's hard to know what will actually be interesting until you see it in person. So if we don't get everything done that I hoped to, I'll just make the tour next year fit what we *do* get to see. That's the beauty of being the boss. You get to make the rules."

Jenna glimpsed a little plaque standing on a dusty shelf, surrounded by kitschy salt and pepper shakers. She reached behind a set of lobster claws and a ceramic mermaid with salt holes in her breasts to pick the plaque up, then solemnly presented it to her mother. "I guess you'll be needing this, then."

REMEMBER THE GOLDEN RULE, the plaque counseled in glittering letters on a black enamel background. HE WHO HAS THE GOLD MAKES THE RULES.

"Well, I can certainly go along with the theory," Lynne answered, grinning. "But I think the only gold we'll encounter on this trip will be the foliage."

THERE was a bit of a nip in the air as the two of them hiked back to the Maple Leaf Inn, though it was still rather warm and the natives they passed all seemed to be dressed in shorts, tank tops, and flip-flops. As a native of body-conscious Southern California, Jenna couldn't help but notice that these garments were not particularly flattering on many of them.

The body in the basement—if indeed it *was* a body in the basement and not a dead dog or some other, less sinister something—was getting things off to an odd beginning, but even with that, the trip seemed like it would be fun.

As Jenna slowed her normal pace to accommodate her mother's shorter legs, she decided that the opportunity to come along on this trip had been too well-timed to be mere chance. Some kind of guardian angel was hanging around on her shoulder, and about time, too.

It was, of course, only a matter of time before Grandma started in with the questions. *Are you seeing anyone special, Jenny? Still playing the field? How's that little job at the bookstore? Isn't David's baby girl adorable?*

The blatant transparency of these questions and their relatives—which Jenna had been fielding ever since she turned sixteen—seemed to escape her grandmother altogether. Jenna had even thought about having a t-shirt made up for the occasion: NO BOYFRIEND, CRUMMY JOB, LOUSY PROSPECTS. But it would have cost twenty bucks that she didn't have.

She was pretty much resigned to having her grandmother ignore her preferred name. Christened Jennifer Lee, she had been known as Jenny until college, when she decided that name was too cute and cheerleadery, never mind that she herself used to be inside the stuffed mascot at Floritas High football games. At Floritas she'd been an honor student, a sometime surfer, a big-time beach partyer. At UCLA she'd majored in English with a minor in Women's Studies.

Currently she was sharing a crowded and overpriced apartment in Santa Monica with two other girls, working as a clerk at an independent bookstore that was clinging to solvency by the narrowest of threads. She had no interest in teaching and didn't write very well, though in LA that didn't preclude calling oneself a writer. She knew several fellow grads who'd majored in film and were currently clawing their way into the film industry. Business seemed pretty boring, for the most part, and she hadn't taken any college courses that could remotely be construed as vocational. Grad school didn't appeal much either, because (a) she didn't know what she wanted to study and (b) it was expensive and (c) when it was over she'd probably still be unemployable.

Kind of a lost cause, she was, but her mother didn't seem to mind and indeed had quietly left the door open for her to come back and live in Floritas, maybe even go to work at Booked for Travel. Of course her mother's job security wasn't too hot either, even though she owned the business outright. Travel agents were running scared these days. People were afraid to travel and money was tight and those who *did* want to go somewhere could make all their own arrangements on the Internet at lower prices than Booked for Travel could ever hope to offer.

Still, it was good to see her mother so happy, adjusted finally to the isolation of her widowhood. Mom and Dad had always seemed so very close. Jenna found it cruel and horrifying that her robustly healthy father could drop dead. No cancer, no warning signs, no special low cholesterol diet, no nothing.

Just here one day and gone the next.

And now, to her dismay, she realized that her mother was turning into a cemetery adjacent to the First Congregational Church.

"COME and meet your ancestors," Lynne said now, turning into the well-maintained churchyard.

Jenna instinctively disliked cemeteries, and had long before her father died. Near the UCLA campus a military cemetery covered acres of prime real estate, with thousands of white markers parading in every direction. The thought of the lost lives they represented had always seemed too staggering for contemplation.

Without speaking, Lynne led the way to a back corner of the cemetery.

Jenna followed, reading names and dates, seeing that despite the age of the graveyard, it was still up to date in sad and disturbing ways. Beyond some softly faded white marble stones with dates in the 1700s, she passed a shiny new green marble marker for a soldier killed in Operation Iraqi Freedom, a pink granite tablet for a nineteen-year-old girl GONE HOME TO JESUS just last year, a collection of identical small stones each labeled BABY LUCINDA TRACY.

Along the way back to the family plots, Jenna noticed a few as-yet-unoccupied graves with stones that listed birthdates, hyphens, and "19—." How would their heirs deal with this exercise in creative stonecraft? These penny pinching Yankees, the folks trying to sell their old spaghetti jars, would almost certainly be too frugal to buy new stones.

The rear of the churchyard was ablaze with scarlet sumacs, while a bed of soft blue asters bloomed alongside the stone wall.

Lynne stopped in front of a stately white marble obelisk engraved BRADDOCK. "These are your earliest American ancestors, Jenny," she announced, with a small sweep of her hand.

The childhood nickname seemed somehow all right here,

and Jenna realized her mother wasn't even aware she had used it. Lynne seemed off on a journey of her own, one that was taking her far from these well-tended white marble markers.

Jenna read more names and dates, the information flooding over her. She had known that this cemetery was here, of course, without ever thinking about it. If her mother's family had lived in a particular town for two hundred fifty years, a lot of people had to have died and been buried somewhere. She tried to step back psychologically, to view this as an exercise in genealogy rather than an immersion of the lives and deaths of her ancestors.

There were more women than men, it seemed, partly because so many of the men had gone through several wives. Take JOSIAH BRADDOCK, BORN MAY 4, 1764, DIED DECEMBER 16, 1847. Josiah was buried front and center at the large rectangular BRADDOCK tombstone, surrounded by smaller white marble tablets labeled with the names of his wives: PRUDENCE, MARY, ELIZABETH, MARY CATHERINE.

Jenna did some fast math. Prudence had lived to be thirty, while Mary had barely made it to twenty-three and was buried with the infant whose birth had apparently killed them both. Elizabeth and three of her children had died in 1824— influenza? Diphtheria? Polio? Only Mary Catherine had come close to equaling her husband's longevity, surviving him long enough to see the start of the Civil War. All told, Josiah had sired a dozen children, though barely a handful made it to adulthood. Their family tales spread out in other directions around the plot.

This area of Braddock and Chenonceau forebears was immaculately maintained, the grass clipped precisely away from the stones. Jenna pictured Aunt Abby on her knees with a jar of marble polish and a well-worn toothbrush. The Chenonceau branch of the family appeared in the late 1800s, the numbers of family members dwindling from one generation to the next. Stones were already in place for Grandma and Aunt Abby beside two brothers already deceased: Wendell James, who had died in a childhood accident, and John Jacob, killed in Okinawa in World War II.

"Do you miss not having a cemetery to visit for Dad?" Jenna asked suddenly. In keeping with his oft-expressed wishes, Monty Montgomery's ashes had been scattered from an old friend's boat off the shore of Floritas, out beyond the rolling surf he so adored, within sight of the beach where he had died.

Lynne turned and regarded her thoughtfully. "A little. But you know, when I walk on the seawall in the morning, I kind of feel as if he's there with me sometimes. And I look out at those big old waves rolling in and I remember how much he loved those beaches and that ocean." Her eyes misted and Jenna saw a tear begin to fall.

Jenna moved to hug her mother so quickly she wasn't aware she'd even done it. And as the two of them stood there among the ghosts of all those Braddocks and Chenonceaus, they both cried for the man they had loved, taken from them far too soon.

IT was her mother who ended the embrace, finally, moving to the side of the lot to deadhead some soft blue asters blooming against the stone churchyard wall.

"There was a song we sang when I was in first grade," Lynne told Jenna. "We were living in San Diego then, actually, down at North Beach on Coronado." She began humming, then sang in a soft clear voice:

Goldenrod and asters, all your hands can hold,
September wears a party dress of lavender and gold.

"I was so excited because we had asters in the garden where we lived," she said when she ended the verse, "and my mother found some kind of yellow flower that may or may not have been goldenrod. I took the bouquet in to school, all proud of myself. And it turned out my teacher had hay fever."

Jenna laughed. She loved to hear her mother talk about her childhood, which seemed so idyllic and romantic, moving around all the time, living in interesting places around the globe. The hay fever story was one she'd never heard before, at least not when she was actively listening.

"So what do you say?" Lynne asked. "You up for a trip to Strawbery Banke?"

This was one of the things that Jenna found most appealing about this trip, the sense that they were just winging it, not on any schedule, open to whatever might happen to fall in their path. Though for somebody who wasn't on a schedule, her mother sure had a lot of lists and guidebooks.

"Sure," Jenna said. "I wasn't really clear. Are we going to go to a lot of these restored town thingies?"

Lynne laughed. "Thingies indeed. Actually, this may be the only one, because it's so close to the Inn. There's a lot of them in New England—Mystic Seaport, Sturbridge Village, Strawbery Banke, a couple of Shaker places, Plimoth Plantation. Generally the quality of those places is reliable enough that I could take a group there without visiting first."

"Whatever," Jenna said. "Just so long as I get to visit Orchard House in Concord and Mark Twain's place in Hartford." Jenna had immersed herself in a crash review of the literature of New England once she was invited on the trip. The experience had reminded her, not unpleasantly, of studying for exams in college.

"Absolutely," Lynne told her, just as Jenna felt a splotch of water hit her arm.

"Is that a raindrop?" She looked up at some clouds that seemed to have arrived since the last time she'd checked, which was not all that long ago.

"I think so," Lynne said, stepping up the pace. "It hadn't occurred to me that rain might be a bit of a potential problem on this trip. Maybe even more so than uncooperative foliage."

They turned a corner and the Maple Leaf Inn came into

view, wearing a fresh coat of white paint, its wide porch inviting behind the shade of the two large red maples. It looked like an inn, Jenna decided, and she'd lived long enough in LA to know that looking the part was often nine-tenths of the game. Just then she felt another raindrop. Two more vehicles were parked out front, and as they watched, a van labeled NEW HAMPSHIRE STATE POLICE squealed around the corner.

"Let the merrymaking begin," Lynne announced, as the skies opened.

Chapter 5

LYNNE was enthralled by the array of gardens at Strawbery Banke.

Even before they'd entered the park, Lynne had seen massive coleus plants across by the harbor, reaching shrub-like sizes that she'd never been able to match in her own yard. Now that she was in the park, she appreciated the period authenticity of its various gardens. Like the buildings they were allied with, they were true to the different time frames represented, from Colonial to a World War II Victory Garden.

The Sherburne Garden, which they visited first, was early eighteenth century, with an emphasis on its raised-bed kitchen garden. Half an hour later, they were roaming the Victorian-era Goodwin Garden, largely ornamental, with a summerhouse and a hemlock archway and a border of climbing roses.

Lynne kept one eye on the clock and the other on Jenna as they proceeded on this self-guided tour. She watched the clock because they were due back at Abigail's house in South Hadford for dinner at six, a meal that would most definitely be served on time. And she watched Jenna because she wasn't entirely sure how her daughter was going to be as a travel companion. The Montgomerys hadn't traveled much as a family because Monty had believed he was already living in the finest place on earth. She and Jenna had spent a couple of weekends in San Francisco together and had gone to Hawaii, where they mostly lay on the beach, but that was about it.

This planning trip presented particular challenges because it would be necessary to see far more sites and attractions than she'd end up including in the final tour. Not every place would be appropriate, so some sites she would eliminate. And the weather and foliage might not cooperate, this or any other year, so she needed indoor alternatives to leaf peeping. She hoped that Jenna would be energized, not put off, by the spontaneity.

Strawbery Banke was a bit more urban than most historical parks, named by the first English settlers in 1630 because of the wild strawberries that grew by the ocean's shore. Today it featured buildings here when the area was rescued from proposed urban renewal in the 1960s, along with other buildings moved to the location. It wasn't Colonial Williamsburg, to be sure, the restored community which served as the gold standard for all others, but it was interesting and convenient to the Maple Leaf Inn, so for tour purposes the place was a definite keeper.

Outside the gift shop at the afternoon's end, they came upon a hybrid rocking horse/tire swing. Pieces sliced from an inside-out tire had been fashioned into body, head and tail, hanging from a sturdy rope.

"So is this that Yankee ingenuity we're always hearing about?" Jenna asked with a grin.

"You betcha," Lynne answered. They might not be back on the dot of six for dinner, but the afternoon had clearly answered her other concern. Traveling with Jenna was going to be great fun.

"AUNT Abby, you're not playing fair."

As Lynne spoke the words, it occurred to her that she had never seen any evidence that Abigail Chenonceau was interested in justice or equity or even openmindedness.

"Your mother would be furious if she thought I was speaking behind her back."

"Well, you already *have* spoken behind her back. That's why we're having this conversation. If you're worried, I need to know why."

"She's a grown woman," Abigail said, as if this might be news to Priscilla's only child, "but she's always had an irresponsible side."

Again, no surprise. Lynne's very existence was a product of her mother's reckless youth.

Priscilla Chenonceau had accompanied an invalid to Chicago during the Depression, then joined the Roller Derby when she ran out of money. The act scandalized her family and prompted her father to disown her publicly, though she'd later rehabilitated herself in South Hadford's eyes by marrying Gregory Westbrook, a dashing young Navy lieutenant, shortly after Pearl Harbor. On a two-week leave in Boston, Lt. Westbrook met the young, beautiful, irrepressible Priscilla Chenonceau at a USO dance. They were married before his leave ended.

Against all odds, the marriage lasted, and while it could hardly have been described as idyllic—at least not by anybody who observed it at as close range as their daughter had—it had worked pretty well. According to Priscilla, however, her sister Abigail had never forgiven her for being prettier and for finding a handsome husband.

Lynne thought about all this as she and Aunt Abby washed the dinner dishes, by hand, in Abigail's kitchen, a room curiously untouched by time. No microwave, no dishwasher, no icemaker, no disposal. The appliances were white with rounded corners, not retro models but simply well-maintained originals.

The bland but wholesome pot roast had been simmered with an assortment of mushy vegetables in an ancient cast-iron Dutch oven, then served promptly at six. This meal originally had been slated for later in the week, but once the Maple Leaf Inn was taken over by state police officials, Abigail had rearranged her schedule without complaint. Aunt Abby had also assisted with the cancellation calls for Priscilla's previously scheduled tea. Lynne presumed that the announcement wasn't much of a surprise, since the neighbors could hardly fail to notice the steady parade of law enforcement vehicles throughout the day. Word would have spread swiftly, like that telephone tree in *Bye Bye Birdie*.

There had still been several investigators at the Maple Leaf Inn when the group left for Abigail's austere two-story frame house on the other side of town. They'd shut the cats up in various second-story bedrooms before leaving, but none of the investigators had answered specific questions about what was downstairs or what might have become of it. How would you remove a body encased in concrete, anyway? By wheelbarrow?

Now Priscilla sat out on the screened front porch of Abigail's drafty frame house with her granddaughter, no doubt interrogating Jenna about her professional and matrimonial prospects. Separating mother and daughter after dinner had been no accident. Priscilla wanted a clean shot at Jenna and Abigail wanted more than Lynne's assistance with the dishes. Lynne had been given a threadbare dish towel and very specific instructions on where to put things as she finished drying them.

"About those financial matters . . ." Abigail began. Then she fell silent.

"Mom hasn't shared much about her finances with me," Lynne said, once it became clear that the next move was hers. "Ever. Some of this I know only because it's a matter of public record. When Dad died, she got the standard Navy survivor's benefit package and a modest chunk of life insurance."

Calling it modest was an exercise in hyperbole. Even allowing for thirty-some years difference in time, what Greg Westbrook had left Priscilla was paltry compared to the coverage Monty, an insurance agent, had carried on himself. Once, about two-thirds of the way through a bottle of nouveau Beaujolais, Priscilla had told Lynne that Dad had felt more insurance would invite disaster. As if a military pilot didn't invite disaster just by going to work.

"My concern," Abigail said after a few moments, "is that she has invested more than she can afford to lose in the Maple Leaf Inn. When she was a little tipsy, she mentioned an enormous balloon payment due in four years."

Thank God for red wine. If Priscilla didn't regularly get snockered, nobody would be able to keep track of her life. The balloon payment, however, was not good news. Lynne could easily see her mother making that kind of commitment, confident that she'd turn this old boardinghouse into a five-star Michelin hostelry lickety-split, simply by the purchase of some nice quilts and a few rocking chairs.

Lynne, however, knew enough about the travel industry to realize that the odds against this happening were astronomical. "Do you know how she was able to get a mortgage in the first place? Even if she had a huge lump sum to invest, which I'm inclined to doubt, any bank is going to want to see regular income to write a mortgage on a commercial property. Above and beyond any social security. And I know she lost all the Navy benefits for good when she married Harvey." Priscilla's third husband, plagued throughout his life by flat feet, had never served in the military at all.

"She called it creative financing," Abigail said, "and the sound of that makes my blood run cold."

Lynne's blood felt a little chilly too. "So the problem is her investment advisor?"

Abigail gave a most unladylike snort. "Investment advisor my left foot. Snake oil salesman is more like it."

"So how did this happen?"

"Priscilla was living with me when she first encountered the reprobate. All of a sudden she decided to take her holdings out of Merrill Lynch and invest them with Will Colwhistle. His financial package offered a much greater return, she told me. But I think it's one of those scams—what is it called? Ponti?"

"Ponzi," Lynne told her, heart sinking. "You mean the kind of thing where the early investors are paid out of what comes from the later ones?"

"I do indeed. Except I'm not aware of any other investors. For all we know, he's just paying her back out of what she gave him herself."

"But somebody has to be holding the mortgage."

"I believe that somebody is Mr. Colwhistle. So far as I can tell, he's a cosigner on one note with Priscilla and then he supposedly arranged more private notes that liquidated some of her assets. He also had her take out a larger mortgage than she needed to provide sufficient funds for renovation."

"Which would be a serious chunk of change," Lynne said. "I haven't noticed that she's skimped on much of anything."

"Hmph. Never in this lifetime." Abigail added another "hmph" for emphasis.

Lynne liked this less and less. "I guess I should have pushed a little harder to be sure she was okay financially. But she always brushed me off when I'd ask anything specific, and you wouldn't believe how uppity she got when I tried to sound her out on her financial situation after Tony Doolittle died. I always had the impression that Tony's family had money, and they certainly lived nicely enough, so I didn't much worry."

But she should have. A truly responsible daughter would have worried like crazy. Obviously Lynne was not a truly responsible daughter. Though it didn't really seem reasonable to expect responsibility, given her bloodlines.

"Well, she should have been able to get by quite nicely, collecting on two dead Navy husbands," Abigail said.

Lynne shook her head. "It doesn't work that way. This I do know. She lost Dad's survivor benefits when she remarried. Then she was eligible again after Tony died. I always assumed the amount was about the same as what she got when Dad was killed."

Tony Doolittle had been Priscilla's second Navy husband,

a charming alcoholic and sometime philanderer who bought half-gallons of bourbon by the case. When loaded, which was to say most of the time, he groped any female in range, including his stepdaughter, Lynne.

The Doolittles had lived in Pensacola for most of Priscilla's second marriage, in a ranch house they'd built before Tony retired. For a while the couple had visited Southern California regularly, usually during the Del Mar racing season. After a few years, however, Lynne got tired of avoiding her stepfather's roaming hands. She stopped inviting them altogether when Jenna—then Jenny—emerged from puberty as a tall blonde knockout.

There were a lot of things in life you couldn't protect your children from, but this was one potential problem Lynne knew how to solve. When she came upon Tony Doolittle leering at Jenna in the Montgomery kitchen one hot July night, Lynne had made a scene and asked them to go back to their hotel immediately. Priscilla got on her high horse and the Doolittles returned to Pensacola the following day. For a number of years thereafter, Lynne had hardly seen her mother. Sadly, Priscilla hadn't seemed to much notice.

"Well, at least Harvey was a levelheaded businessman," Abigail said. Levelheadedness carried a lot of weight in her universe.

Harvey Jones had been husband number three, a heating contractor in Buffalo. Hard to go wrong providing heat to Buffalo, where the natives shrugged off seven-foot snowfalls and negotiated travel around town via underground tunnels, like humanoid prairie dogs.

"I assumed that Harvey left her well provided for," Abigail went on. "But from things she's let slip, I don't think he was quite as wealthy as she believed. Which makes me even more nervous about that Colwhistle fellow. I simply do not trust him. Taking his advice on investments was bad enough, but to put all her financial eggs in that one rickety basket is absolute folly."

"Have you met him?"

Abigail looked pained. "Once. I dropped her off at his of-

fice in Manchester when I had other business up there. I went
inside when I returned to pick her up. She was just coming
out of his office and she introduced me."

"And?"

"And he was very smooth," Abigail said disdainfully, "and
middle-aged, probably around fifty or sixty. The sort of good
looking man who is accustomed to having women go along
with whatever he wants."

Lynne wondered fleetingly if Abigail was making oblique
reference to some kind of sexual liaison, then dismissed the
idea. If Abigail thought her sister was sleeping with a financial advisor two-thirds her age, she wouldn't have waited this
long to involve Lynne. And she probably would have tried to
find some way to have Priscilla committed for psychiatric
observation.

"Did you talk with him?"

Abigail shook her head vehemently. "Ours was the briefest
and most superficial of conversations."

"You didn't try to stop her from buying the Inn?"

Abigail sighed. "At first I thought it might be good for her,
something to keep her occupied after Harvey passed away.
She wanted her own space again."

Harvey was dead three years now. Lynne was frankly surprised that her mother and Aunt Abby had lasted more than a
week under the same roof.

"So let's get back to Will Colwhistle. Is he local?"

Abigail shook her head. "He's not from around here. And
not only that, I've been unable to determine where he *is*
from. He's got a fancy-schmancy letterhead that lists offices
all over New England, but where he himself might be is anyone's guess. It isn't even clear to me where he lives, and your
mother says she never asked."

"How did she meet this guy?"

"He gave a lecture on financial planning somewhere up in
Manchester, I believe."

"Did she talk to some of his other clients?"

"I don't know. I asked that very question and you might
have thought. . . . Well, never mind. No, I don't think she

did. But I'll tell you one thing, I happened to be up in Manchester not long ago, and I stopped by his office."

Lynne realized that she'd been wiping the same glass, now dry as the Sahara, for several minutes. She set it on the counter and picked up another. Here was where the story got a little awkward, as Abigail stuck her nose further in where it clearly did not belong. "What did he say?"

"Nothing. He wasn't there. I spoke with a young woman at the reception desk in the lobby, and she explained that Mr. Colwhistle stopped in regularly to pick up his mail, and occasionally to meet with clients, which of course I already knew. But she also said that he was absent from the office far more than he was there. I tried to get her to show me his office, but unfortunately she refused."

"Did you tell the receptionist why you were there?"

Abigail shook her head, then frowned as she held a glass Lynne had wiped earlier up to the light and found her performance lacking. She handed it over for a more thorough drying. "I didn't want to make a fuss. I didn't even tell her my name, and I doubt very much that she remembered me from before."

"If he wasn't there and didn't come in often, why would he have a receptionist?"

"Oh, he wasn't the only tenant in the office suite," Abigail explained, "though I didn't actually see anybody else while I was there, either. But there were other professional services there, a number of them. Some lawyers, I believe."

"Do you have the address in Manchester?" Lynne asked.

"Of course. I also have one of his business cards and a copy of the letterhead, with all those addresses. He has offices in Hartford, Portland, Manchester, and Montpelier. I thought that since you were going to be traveling around New England anyway, you might be able to look him up somewhere." Abigail shook her head again, frowning. It seemed to be her default expression. "I considered telephoning, but even Manchester is a toll call." Abigail was of a generation that considered long distance a hopeless extravagance.

Now she opened a drawer and pulled an envelope from

beneath some neatly pressed table napkins. "Your mother doesn't realize that I made this copy. Please keep this out of her sight, at least until we have more information."

We.

Lynne took the envelope and slipped it into her purse. This was going to be a very bumpy ride.

THE cats were howling and the basement entrances from both inside and outside were crisscrossed with crime scene tape when they returned to the Maple Leaf Inn. As the three generations of women settled in at the kitchen table for a round of Scrabble, Lynne found herself thinking words like BODY, MURDER, CONCRETE, JACKHAMMER, MORTGAGE, and SNAKE-OIL.

It was still quite early when they headed upstairs to bed, full of plans for visiting Lowell in the morning. Lynne found herself lying in bed by a window opened to allow an unseasonably warm breeze into the room.

She was far too keyed up to sleep. She had no idea what she could do about her mother's finances. Priscilla would not be happy if she discovered her daughter's meddling. And what if it was too late to fix this messy situation? What would happen to Priscilla then, if she lost the Maple Leaf Inn and the money she'd poured into it? Lynne allowed herself the uncharitable thought that if worse came to worst, Priscilla was far more likely to take up residence with her sister across town than to move to Southern California to stay with her daughter.

But none of this took into account the body in the basement, if indeed it *was* a body in the basement. Whether the Maple Leaf Inn could survive that notoriety was another matter altogether.

When she had tossed for nearly an hour and a half, Lynne went back downstairs to a bookshelf of travel books and New England authors that her mother had assembled for the Inn's future guests. Before she turned on the light, she glanced out the unshaded window into the backyard at the gazebo, which she realized now she hadn't even looked at first hand. As she watched, in a sliver of moonlight, she thought she saw a figure detach itself from the gazebo and walk farther back into the yard.

Who could be watching in the middle of the night?

She shook herself. Her imagination was working overtime. She turned on the lamp by the bookshelf. There were a lot of interesting choices—*Little Women, Walden, Ethan Frome, The Scarlet Letter*—but since sleep was her objective, she headed back up the stairs with *Moby Dick* in hand. She had only managed to get through the Melville novel in college by skipping the cetology chapters and buying *Cliff's Notes*.

Call me Exhausted. Five pages later she was sound asleep.

Chapter 6

IT had been so long ago that he had come to believe he was no longer in danger, no longer had any reason to believe those long-ago events might return to haunt—no, to injure—him. Life was good now, had been good for a long, long time. He couldn't go back there. Wouldn't go back.

There was no way to undo what had happened, and that he truly regretted.

But this was bad news. Very bad news.

Danger was a relative concept. So was safety. He'd learned those basic truths long ago and far away, at the hands of men who trafficked in danger.

His safety now was at issue once again.

This he knew: there was no statute of limitations on murder.

Chapter 7

THERE was no jackhammering going on when Lynne awoke the next morning to find Hester the cat again curled on her bed, this time a bit closer to her head. Another couple days and she'd probably be vying to share Lynne's pillow. Lynne reached out a lazy hand to pet the purring feline, then did her customary stretches, showered, and dressed. She was surprised to find, on her way downstairs, that Jenna's bedroom was already empty, the quilt positioned with military precision on her bed.

Following a slight burnt smell to the kitchen, she found a full house. Jenna and Cindy Jackson were seated at the kitchen table, while Cindy's little boy Bradley did something complicated with several toy trucks and some Tupperware just inside the kitchen door. Lynne carefully stepped around the rolling stock. She'd tripped on more than enough toys in this lifetime already, and reserved a special place in hell for the inventor of Legos.

Jenna seemed to be in the midst of breakfast, picking away politely at a lopsided tower of thick slices of bread, oozing strawberry jam and some white gloppy stuff that might be cream cheese from between the bread slices. The whole business was covered with a generous burst of whipped cream, though not quite enough to disguise the fact that the outside slices of bread were slightly charred and hastily scraped. Flecks of black on the plate might have been mistaken for pepper at another meal.

"Stuffed French toast," Jenna supplied. "Here's the paper." She handed it over and Lynne sat beside her to read.

The front page banner announced, "Bones Found in Local Cellar." State Police officers weren't commenting and the crime lab also remained mum. Detective O'Keefe from the South Hadford force, however, confirmed that the remains discovered in Mrs. Priscilla Jones's basement were most likely human.

A sidebar drawn from public records offered the history of the house's ownership, dating back to 1875 when it was built by Andrew Luddington. From 1968 through 1982, a boarding-house owned by former Golden Mills vice-president Charles Grant had been operated on the property. Charles Grant's widow, Louise, had told the reporter emphatically that her late husband had never been involved in any of the day-to-day operations of the boardinghouse. From 1982 until its purchase by Priscilla, it had been owned by Otto and Laura Saxton, who cared for dozens of foster children. Reached at their new home in Florida, the Saxtons replied very tartly that the youngsters in their care had always been accounted for.

Priscilla brought Lynne a cup of coffee, then placed a plate of stuffed French toast in front of her with a flourish. This portion didn't seem to have been burned, though the top slice had slipped almost completely off its base. It was starting to look as if Priscilla would need a cook as well as a good bakery. People who normally skipped breakfast or grabbed a latte at the Starbucks in their office building's lobby frequently changed gears altogether on vacation, stuffing themselves senseless on fat-laden B&B offerings that they'd never dream of eating at home.

Cindy sipped a cup of coffee. Either she'd been wise enough to decline the French toast or there wasn't enough to go around. Lynne was willing to relinquish her own share, though she sensed this would be a diplomatic blunder.

"They didn't leave here until just before you got back last night," Cindy said as Lynne set the newspaper aside. She wore shorts and a tank top, her russet hair hastily gathered on top of her head with a white plastic claw clip. Freckles covered every inch of exposed skin. "I kept an eye on things after you all left, and when they were leaving I came over to ask when they'd be back. They said this morning." She shook her head. "They weren't very friendly."

Priscilla put her hands on her hips and looked irritated. She wore a different ruffled full-length apron today, a floral print that coordinated with her burgundy outfit. Betty Crocker, circa 1956. "Well, then where are they?"

Lynne looked at the Regulator clock hanging on the wall beside the basement door, which was festooned with yellow crime-scene tape and tightly closed. "It's not even eight-thirty," she pointed out, "and aren't they coming from Concord?"

Priscilla sniffed. "Well, I'd think they'd want to get this all taken care of. I know *I* certainly want it taken care of. The thought of some poor soul down there all this time and me moving in here not even knowing about it—"

Jenna spoke up gently. "Grandma, I'm sure the police are being very careful to do everything right, to preserve evidence and all that."

"Evidence?" Priscilla's voice grew shrill. "There's bones in the concrete. What more evidence could they possibly want? They need to track down those ne'er-do-wells who lived here when this was a boardinghouse, and the delinquents in foster care, and see who turned up missing back then."

Lynne cautiously tasted her French toast. It was surprisingly good. Maybe all that her mother needed was some instruction on presentation. "I think that may be a bit more complicated than you realize, Mom. People were pretty mobile in the seventies, and if this was a boardinghouse, a lot of different people probably lived here. Generally I think that folks living in a boardinghouse aren't very settled in the community."

"I asked my mom about it last night," Cindy said. "She told me there was a regular parade of people through here, that she stopped even trying to keep track of them. I was pretty young then and I wasn't allowed to play over here. But I was friends with some of the Saxtons' foster kids."

Lynne regarded the young woman thoughtfully. "Your family lived in this neighborhood back then?"

Cindy nodded. "Right there across the street in the same house I live in now. We moved here when I was about five. My husband and I were living over in Nashua, closer to where Todd works, but then my parents started having all kinds of health problems. I was coming back and forth almost every day and it was just too much. Mama was the first one to move into the Washington Arms because she has this weird neuromuscular problem and needs a lot of special care. Daddy was lonely then, so Todd and I bought the house from them and he moved to an apartment at the Washington Arms where he can go see her every day in the nursing facility and they can have meals together."

"That must be really hard for you," Jenna said.

Cindy's voice quavered. "It's awful. And now Daddy's gotten so forgetful. I'm afraid he has Alzheimer's, but he refuses to be tested. Mama can only get around in a little motorized scooter, and lately she hasn't been able to even do that very much. Her doctor says before much longer, she won't be able to get out of bed. I don't know what I'll do then."

Lynne felt a wave of compassion that she could see mirrored in Jenna. "I'm so sorry," she said, glancing at Priscilla, who was loading dishes into the dishwasher and didn't seem particularly sympathetic. The mark of a true narcissist. "It must be terribly difficult for you to see them that way, Cindy."

Cindy sniffed and looked over at Bradley. "I've kind of

gotten used to it, but I wish there were some way he could know them both like they used to be. At least Brittany knew them before. Brittany's our fourteen-year-old," she explained.

Priscilla gave a yelp of pain and dropped a skillet into the sink with a clatter.

"What happened?" Lynne asked, jumping to her feet.

Her mother was already running cold water over her right hand. "I burned myself on that stupid skillet. I forgot it was still hot."

Lynne rummaged in the freezer and gathered ice cubes in a tea towel painted with autumn leaves. "Here, Mom. Sit down and hold this ice on it."

Priscilla obeyed. "I don't know what's happened to me. I've gotten so clumsy. I just wish we could get this all over with. Surely they can tell how long that body's been down there."

"Maybe," Lynne told her. "But a lot of people seem to have lived here, so it could be hard to figure out who went missing, or even when it happened. For all we know, it doesn't have anything to do with the boardinghouse *or* the foster home, either. Those bones could have been there for a hundred years. Hmmm." She considered. "Did they even have concrete a hundred years ago?"

"Concrete, yes," Jenna said definitively. "Indoor plumbing, less likely. This did all get started trying to fix a plumbing problem, didn't it?"

Priscilla nodded.

"Did the police say anything else about the former owners?" Lynne asked.

The question had been directed to Cindy, but Priscilla spoke up first. "Just that they'd be getting in touch with the Saxtons, who sold it to me, down in Florida where they retired."

Lynne paused for a moment to reflect on the irony that her mother was probably the only person in history who'd ever retired to New England from Florida. Even allowing for an eight-year stay in Buffalo, it was remarkable.

"Cindy?" Lynne asked.

"Not a peep," Cindy answered. "I tell you, they were downright rude."

"We just need to be patient, Mom," Lynne said. "This isn't television. These things take time. And face it, if there's a crime here, it's not a very recent one. We just have to assume that the police know what they're doing. It's their job, and they've got specialists to take care of it."

Lynne hoped she wasn't just spouting the standard law enforcement line. Murder wasn't exactly commonplace around here. Last night Aunt Abby had announced that apart from a domestic dispute in 1974, she could not recall a single homicide in South Hadford. Ever.

"I'm *tired* of having to be patient," Priscilla whined.

Lynne could certainly appreciate her mother's anxiety. During her first two marriages, Priscilla had been through plenty of tense periods, combat-related and otherwise, when she could only grit her teeth and wait. She had also endured the one experience every military wife most fears, the unbidden arrival of a military chaplain and notification officers. She certainly was entitled to a calm and carefree saunter through her sunset years, which wasn't likely to happen if the Maple Leaf Inn became known as the place with the bones in the basement.

Although—Lynne shifted focus for a moment—that might actually work as a macabre selling point, if you didn't mind attracting a slightly creepy clientele. Lizzie Borden's house down in Fall River, Massachusetts, was apparently thriving as a bed-and-breakfast. And as an added bonus, a creepy clientele might not mind having breakfast burned.

"You *are* going to come with us today, aren't you, Grandma?" Jenna, as befit somebody who had briefly embraced Buddhism and continued to practice yoga sporadically, remained the picture of equanimity. She'd eaten about half of her French toast and had managed to rearrange what was left so that it looked inconsequential.

"Well, I don't know . . . I mean, what if they need me for something here?" Priscilla asked.

"All they need from you right now is to stay out of the way and keep the cats out of the basement." Lynne realized she sounded harsh and softened her tone. "Now that the litter box is on the back porch, the cats will be fine. Pouty, maybe, but they'll get over it. And Cindy can keep an eye on the place while we're gone, can't you?"

"Of course," Cindy said. "They won't let me in, though."

"You probably won't need to get in," Priscilla said, "but I'll give you a key. I ought to have done that anyway, in case of emergency. Abby has a key, of course, but she's clear across town."

"Perfect," Lynne said. "And Cindy, you can call me on my cell phone if you think there's anything we need to know about that just can't wait."

JENNA settled herself comfortably in the front seat beside her mother half an hour later as Lynne pulled out of South Hadford. Some ongoing road work slowed them on their way out of town and Jenna noticed a police car parked nearby, lights flashing, for no discernable reason. If the police here didn't have anything better to do than watch day laborers repair roadways, maybe they *weren't* the best bet to figure out whose body was down in Grandma's basement.

As they threaded their way around the road work, a gray sky began to leak a light rain, just a gentle mist, really. Jenna had spent a couple of months up in Seattle once. This was the sort of precipitation that the folks up there never even seemed to notice.

Jenna was navigating, a task that really wasn't very complicated with her mother at the wheel. Jenna loved maps, and had used the ones from *National Geographic* to decorate more than one living space. She was also a pretty decent navigator, and even when she occasionally screwed up or the directions were wrong, she could almost always find a way back to the designated route. In any case, Priscilla had assured them that they'd have no difficulty whatsoever reaching the Lowell National Historical Park, just south of the nearby Massachusetts border.

Priscilla was, it seemed, mistaken, and became downright testy when her directions proved faulty.

"This doesn't make sense," Jenna said, frowning as she flipped through papers. "I've got two sets of directions here and they both want us to take a freeway exit that doesn't appear to exist."

"Of course it does," Priscilla chided.

Lynne glanced in the rearview mirror. "I thought you said you'd never been here, Mom."

"Well, I went to the Quilt Museum with Abby," Grandma snapped back, "and that's in Lowell, too. It certainly isn't my fault that she was driving and already knew the way."

Jenna hadn't seen much of her grandmother in recent years. There'd been a long period of limited communication after that business with Commander Tony coming on to her in the kitchen during the Del Mar racing season, when Jenna was in high school. But Priscilla had mended fences and come out to Jenna's college graduation with her last husband, a portly and florid fellow Jenna was instructed to call Grandpa Harvey. Grandpa Harvey had complicated a number of graduation plans, since he began to wheeze and grow faint if he had to walk more than a hundred yards. On their departure, her mother had celebrated by opening and diving headfirst into a particularly nice bottle of Ravenswood Zinfandel. That night she had told Jenna a bit about Grandma's Roller Derby days, a period of Priscilla's life that Jenna still had great trouble envisioning.

Back then, Priscilla had seemed competent if bossy, accustomed to ordering folks about and running the family show. Now she was physically much more frail, traded on helplessness, and frequently lapsed into pouting spells.

Finally they reached downtown Lowell.

"At last!" Lynne said. "This is why it's so important to check these things out in advance. Somehow it never registered with me that Lowell is a functioning city, and that the national historical park is smack dab in the middle of it."

They passed an imposing downtown Greek Revival edifice, with THE LOWELL FIVE CENT SAVINGS BANK carved in stone above two-story Doric columns. The downtown streets were busy despite the drizzle. A number of young people loitered about, kids who looked like they hadn't been in school for a while and hadn't gotten around to doing anything else.

They found the Boott Cotton Mill, a series of lackluster four-story faded redbrick buildings, on the north end of town at the river.

Lynne parked nearby and they hiked toward the bleak, seemingly deserted property. As they got closer, Jenna could see that some real effort had gone into sprucing the place up. The grime of a century and a half had been scoured away from the redbrick buildings.

As the rain grew stronger, they picked up the pace. Jenna and her mother wore lightweight waterproof jackets with hoods, while Grandma was decked out in a powder blue raincoat and matching umbrella. For extra protection, she wore clear rubber boots that slipped over her decidedly unsensible shoes and a fold-away clear rain bonnet.

"Well, whaddaya know?" Lynne pointed at a sign announcing that some 600,000 square feet of office space was available at Boott Cotton Mills. No wonder they'd worked so hard at cleaning the buildings up. They were looking to recycle the entire compound. The accompanying artwork showed a plaza crowded with smiling white-collar workers and busy refreshment kiosks.

Jenna looked around. "Guess we missed rush hour."

"Yeah," Lynne said. "By about a hundred and fifty years."

There were no kiosks. Nor were there cheerful workers on their way to offices in the buildings which had once produced a cheap, coarse cotton blend called "Negro cloth" that was sold by the carload to plantation owners in the South, where—in a semantic reversal—it was known as "white Lowell cloth."

Right now, the three generations of women were the only humans visible anywhere.

Because it was closest, they went first to the Working People's exhibit in the cultural center. A group of rambunctious schoolchildren was just leaving, and the docent seemed delighted to see some grown-ups.

"This building was once a boardinghouse for girls who worked in the mills," the docent told them. "The Lowell mills were something of a social experiment, a reaction to European industrialization. The idea was to avoid creating a permanent working class by employing girls from nearby farms and villages, girls who'd work here a few years and then go home and get married."

She waved a hand at a life-sized diorama of a dining room crammed with chairs and place settings. "They were required to live in these boardinghouses, but there really wasn't any alternative. The mills were built far away from other buildings out of fear of fire."

Jenna regarded the diorama. "This looks like pretty close quarters."

"It was," the docent agreed, "but even so, for many of them it was preferable to the lives they had left back on the farm."

"I'm surprised their families would let them come," Priscilla put in suddenly. It was the first she'd spoken since they parked the car. "I thought women in that era were supposed to stay at home and help run the farm. Churn butter and all that stuff." Jenna could hear a note of rebellion in her grandmother's voice. There were times when it was no trouble at all to picture the young Priscilla running off with the Roller Derby.

The docent nodded. "True enough. But here they could earn money to send home, and that money could provide things that they weren't able to produce on the farm. For many of these girls, moving here actually meant an increase in privacy, even though they lived communally in these boardinghouses. When they finished work, any time that remained belonged to them, whereas back home they were busy every waking moment. Have you all been to the cotton mill across the way yet?"

"That's our next stop," Lynne told her.

"When you get over there, you'll notice a bell tower with a clock on it. Everything happened according to those bells. From March through October the first bell was at four-thirty in the morning and the last one at six-thirty at night."

INSIDE the Boott Cotton Mill building, they found uniformed rangers who looked strangely out of place, as if they'd been airlifted from Yellowstone or Yosemite, then dumped in this dreary urban setting. Their primary function seemed to be handing out earplugs resembling pale green pencil erasers to everyone headed for the mill floor. Jenna was sure this was overkill, until they entered the mill floor and the machinery was turned on.

It was loud.

It was *really* loud.

Speech was impossible. The looms banged and clattered, roared and crashed. The entire building shook. Priscilla fled back to the lobby almost immediately, and after just a few minutes, Jenna's head was throbbing. How could anybody work in these conditions? No wonder nobody worked a long time here; they'd all go deaf.

And this was only a fraction of the noise that would have been generated when the entire building was in operation with looms running simultaneously on all four floors.

It would be like living in the mosh pit at a heavy metal concert.

Jenna thought about the hundreds of mill girls who had toiled in this cacophonous nightmare—day after day, week after week, month after month, year after year—because this was preferable to life back at home.

There was a lot to be said for the twenty-first century.

Chapter 8

WHEN they returned to South Hadford after a restorative visit to the New England Quilt Museum and a pleasant lunch at the American History Textile Museum, Lynne was pleased to see that her mother was in better spirits. A certain mind-set prevailed when she was leading a tour, even if the tour was a scouting expedition with her closest relatives. Without even thinking about it, Lynne was attuned to the behavioral nuances of her charges. Jenna seemed utterly relaxed and Priscilla had emerged from a day-long pout.

Mercifully, it had also stopped raining.

Lynne was pleased. She could easily build a full day's excursion out of Lowell. The only element they really hadn't explored was the Jack Kerouac connection, and only Jenna seemed to regret the omission. Lynne doubted that many of the people who took her tours would have much interest in Kerouac, and besides, even though the writer had been born in Lowell, he'd gone on the road at the first possible opportunity.

When they turned onto Barrington Road, the first thing

Lynne noticed was that the police vehicles were all gone. The street was quiet, with half a dozen houses on large deep lots and the Maple Leaf Inn at its end, where the street was wide enough to turn around.

It was, she realized now, seeing it without emergency vehicles, a truly beguiling building, and she could understand why Priscilla had fallen in love with the place. As they got closer, she saw Cindy waiting on the front porch in the swing, while Bradley dangled from branches of the apple tree. When they got to the porch she turned down a corner of the page, set *Family Circle* aside, and rose to greet them, smiling broadly.

"I've been watching out for you," she said. "I think they may be done in the basement." She dug in a pocket of her shorts, pulled out several business cards, and dealt them on the table beside her. "This is the state police guy who's in charge of things, I think. He wants you to call. And this is a lady from ABC TV news up in Manchester, and this guy is from CBS. You've got a bunch of phone messages, too. I could hear the phone ringing all the time while I was out here."

"Were these the only media people who came out, Cindy?" Lynne asked. It hadn't occurred to her before they left that the neighbors should have been warned against making offhand statements that could be regarded as newsworthy by the media.

Cindy looked mildly embarrassed. "The only ones I talked to."

"You need to be really careful," Lynne said gently. "You may not think you're saying anything that matters, but they might just twist around whatever you do say to make it fit their story."

"I only told them you weren't here and wouldn't be back until tonight."

Throughout this exchange, Lynne had watched her mother slowly shrivel in dread. She reached out and took the cards from Cindy. "I'll take care of these, Mom. Thanks, Cindy. Anything out of the ordinary happen today?" She realized as she spoke that the question was absurd. Nothing about this situation was ordinary, with the possible exception of Bradley and his truck armada.

Inside, the basement door was still sealed off and nobody mentioned the yellow crime-scene tape. It was starting to just seem like part of the landscape. They all headed, without much comment, in different directions, to kick back and relax a bit before dinner. At Priscilla's insistence, they were going to a Chinese restaurant over in the next town. Lynne thought it somewhat out of kilter to come from California to New Hampshire for Chinese food, but there seemed no reason to insist on "New England cuisine," which seemed pretty much an oxymoron anyway. Once you started boiling meat, you were usually in trouble.

While Lynne made herself a pot of tea, she listened to the messages and deleted all the ones from reporters without noting any numbers. She took the tea upstairs to her room, aware of how quickly the house had gone quiet, how swiftly they all had moved behind closed doors. Maybe it was just the contrast of the small town hush compared to the racket in the cotton mill, but it felt like more. She lifted Hester off the rocker and tossed the business cards from Jennifer Martindale of ABC News and Chet West of CBS into the trash. Then she sat down and called Detective Niles Burton, the State Police detective from the Major Crimes Unit, who was, according to the message, in charge of the investigation.

Detective Burton picked up his cell phone immediately.

"This is Lynne Montgomery. My mother owns the Maple Leaf Inn. We met yesterday." The meeting had been brief. Detective Burton had introduced himself and disappeared into the basement. He was still in the basement when they left for Aunt Abby's and he was gone when they returned after dinner.

"Is your mother available? I'd like to ask her some questions."

"She's very upset by all this," Lynne said, "and she's lying down right now. Maybe I can help you?"

"I appreciate the offer, but since you live in Southern California and just got to town, I'm afraid you probably can't help much. When would be a good time to talk with your mother?"

This was starting to get annoying. It was time to play the Police Family Connection card. "She's not avoiding you, detective. She really is terribly distressed. And I know it's important for you to speak with her. My son's a police officer out in California and naturally we want to do everything possible to help you."

"I see."

There was a pause. Lynne assumed he was digesting the police connection and trying to decide how hard to press on seeing her mother.

"Where is your son on the force?"

"Floritas, California. Our hometown. It's a beach town north of San Diego." After all these years it still gave Lynne a bit of a charge to realize that she lived in a beach town north of San Diego. It sounded so idyllic, and the wonder was that the reality wasn't all that far removed from the image.

"Well, never mind him for the moment," Detective Burton said. He'd check, Lynne knew, but that was fine. "About your mother . . ."

"My mother bought this property eight months ago from Otto and Laura Saxton, who were retiring to move to Florida. It was something of a spur-of-the-moment decision. Before that, Mother had been staying with her sister, who lives here in town. Maybe you know her? Abigail Chenonceau?"

"I haven't had the pleasure." His tone made it clear that other cops had passed on their own impressions, and that pleasure hadn't figured much in any of them. Few people got along well with Aunt Abby, and they already knew that Detective O'Keefe from the South Hadford P.D. didn't like her. O'Keefe, who'd been assigned as the local member of the investigative team, apparently because of his prior experience with the State Police, might well be merely the tip of an antagonistic police iceberg.

"Well, Aunt Abby has lived here most of her life. She retired as a supervisor at Golden Mills ten years ago. Anyway, my mother was living in Buffalo and when her husband passed away, she decided to come back to New Hampshire. This is where she and her sister grew up. Mom got the idea of opening a bed-and-breakfast and bought this place. She was trying to get it renovated so she could open by Christmas, and everything seemed to be pretty much on schedule until yesterday."

"When you found evidence of remains in the concrete."

Well, yeah. Time to go on the offensive. "Have you identified the person yet?" She assumed they'd been checking missing persons reports around the state and region.

Detective Burton hesitated once again. "When we're ready to make that announcement, we'll let you know. We're working with a forensic anthropologist."

"What does a forensic anthropologist do? Reconstruct a skeleton from those bones? How is that going to help?"

"Well, a skilled anthropologist can determine approximate age, sex, and time of death."

Approximate sex? Lynne bit her tongue. "Wouldn't it make sense to release that information if you're trying to identify somebody? Not that I'm trying to tell you how to do your job," she added hastily.

Detective Burton made a sound that might have been a chuckle. "No reason you should be different from everybody else."

"Well, now that you have everything cleared out of the basement, does that mean you won't need to keep coming back? I'd sure like to tell my mother she won't be bothered anymore."

"And I'd like to tell her that, too," Detective Burton said, "but I can't make that kind of promise just yet. And I really do still need to talk to her."

LYNNE went to her mother's room and relayed what she'd learned. Priscilla had been napping under a mohair afghan, but sat up and drew the soft fabric around her as Lynne spoke.

"Will those people never leave?"

"I think it'll just be hectic for a little while, Mom. I'm sure that things will quiet down once they identify whoever it was."

This sounded lame and Priscilla did not seem assuaged.

Lynne decided that as long as her mother was already upset, she might just as well bring up the mortgage. She didn't hesitate to put the blame on Abigail, either. The two sisters could mend fences later. Right now Lynne needed information.

"Aunt Abby tells me that you made a rather unorthodox deal to buy this place," she began.

Priscilla pulled the soft golden mohair tighter around her. "I don't know what she's talking about and I don't see that it's any business of yours."

The trick now, Lynne knew, was to get as much information out of her as she could before Priscilla dissolved in tears. Her mother had developed dissolving into tears into an art form over the years and it was next to impossible to deal with her once that happened.

"She mentioned a balloon payment that concerned her."

"It is none of her business." Priscilla's lip was trembling, but no tears yet.

"She's just concerned for the same reason I am, Mom. We want the best for you and we don't want you to have to deal with any unpleasant surprises." Like losing the place because she couldn't cough up that balloon payment. Or having it taken over by her "partner." "I was a bit surprised to learn that your mortgage was with an individual and not a bank."

"Mr. Colwhistle was able to give me a much better deal than the bank. He realized that this place will be a tremendous success, and that I'd need extra money in the beginning to get everything up and running."

"So the loan you made actually *was* more than you'd need for the mortgage?" This conversation was one piece of bad news after another.

"Well, of course it was! This place was a wreck. I had to

get furniture and accessories and there was a great deal of cosmetic work needed around the place. You may recall that it was part of the renovation that led to the awful problem in the basement."

Might as well go for broke. So to speak.

"Mom, how much do you owe this man?"

Priscilla swung her legs off the bed, shucked off the afghan and glared. "I cannot imagine how that would be any business of yours, unless you're counting your inheritance before it hatches."

Damn. There was no good answer to this. Lynne was well provided for right now, completely apart from the Booked for Travel agency, which broke even and sometimes turned a small profit. Monty, who had owned a Floritas insurance agency, had been ridiculously overinsured when he died. Even after buying the travel agency, Lynne had plenty of money left over.

"I'm not interested in any inheritance I might get from you," she answered evenly, "but I want to be sure that you're well provided for. I'd like to talk to this Will Colwhistle."

"Mind your own beeswax," Priscilla told her. Then she broke into the long-expected tears.

As Lynne quietly backed out of the room, she thought about all the life insurance Monty had carried, how stunned she had been to learn of her sudden wealth after his funeral.

All that money.

She would have turned over every penny of it to have him back.

Chapter 9

THE old man was easy enough to lure. A phone call, a vague promise of help. He seemed confused, and this was disconcerting. He didn't make the connection at first, and then he grew agitated. There'd been no hesitation or confusion all those years ago.

Meet me by the stream at sunset, he'd told the old man. *We need to get our stories straight.*

There was no reason to believe that the old man had broken his promise, but there was also no reason to believe that he could be trusted. Not anymore.

He arrived two hours early to position himself and get his materials in place. He chose a spot where he could easily slice through the cable if the wrong person arrived, or if the old man brought anybody with him.

Then he waited.

He was good at waiting.

He knew the layout well enough, knew the nearest buildings were for maintenance equipment and workers, people who would be gone by the time he'd set for the meeting. Nobody came. Nobody passed by. He had the streambed and its surroundings to himself.

Finally the old man came. His walk was hesitant, his steps unsure.

"Hello?" The old voice trembled. Maybe he was afraid, or maybe he was just confused. It didn't really matter.

From the vantage point that covered all the possible routes to the stream, he could see that the old man was alone when he approached. He moved back from the fail-safe position, carefully crossed the streambed on flat, exposed rocks.

The trees here by the stream were tall, the undergrowth thick, roots tapped into the everflowing waters. Leaves still clung to the branches of the trees and bushes. The tripwire, all but invisible, stretched across the path just below the rise on the bank.

"Over here." The words came out in a snarl as he stepped out into view.

The old man looked startled for a minute, then began his descent to the stream. He hit the tripwire on his third step, came tumbling forward, arms flailing. He opened his mouth as if to scream and swung his arms, but the only sound he gave was a kind of grunt just before he landed, headfirst, his forehead meeting the rocks below with a gratifying smack.

He watched the old man carefully for five minutes, ten. He wasn't moving.

Then he picked his way carefully across the stream to where the old man lay. His head was out of the water, resting on the rock where he had landed.

A bit of insurance here was probably a good idea. He grabbed the back collar of the old man's shirt and pulled him gently a few inches forward so that his face rested in the water. If the head wound didn't kill him—and head wounds, he knew, could be very problematic—the old man could drown.

Feeling infinitely better, he moved up the bank toward the buildings, careful not to leave muddy footprints, and removed the tripwire from the trees that had supported it. He coiled the filament and put it in his pocket.

Then he froze.

A female voice spoke nearby. "Let's just walk on down by the stream, Mother."

Damn! He stepped quickly into the underbrush. He couldn't be visible when they found the old man. He slipped back through the woods, retracing the steps he'd taken as he arrived. He had just reached the edge of the trail leading back to where he'd parked his car when that same voice spoke again.

"Look how the sumac's so pretty, Moth—Oh, my God! Somebody's fallen in the creek, Mother!"

From force of habit he made his way silently through the woods, his heart racing.

But he was pretty sure that nobody saw him leave.

Chapter 10

LYNNE turned to Jenna as they pulled away from the curb outside the Maple Leaf Inn the next morning, headed for Maine.

"I don't know about you," she confessed, "but I kind of feel like I'm playing hooky." She suffered a momentary twinge of guilt at the mental image of a fretful Priscilla trapped in the Maple Leaf Inn, with only three cats and Abigail the Ferocious to protect her from the wiles of the modern media.

But then she imagined a chunk of succulent lobster dripping with melted butter and the moment passed.

"You? Playing hooky?" Jenna cocked her head, looking doubtful.

"Oh my goodness, yes."

Lynne considered what to say next. Now that her children were adults, she felt more comfortable telling them some things than she might have ten years earlier. Back when David and Jenna, nee Jenny, were teenagers, she could never have been even remotely candid about her own adventures during the sexual revolution. Even now she doubted she'd ever offer much in the way of specifics, not that they were likely to ask. On the list of things that kids did not want to know about their parents, Evidence of Sexual Experience was right there at the top.

"Let's just say that in my wilder younger days, I found plenty of ways to slip off any number of military bases. With some guys that I know my parents wouldn't have approved of. Guys my father might have felt it necessary to shoot, actually."

Jenna chuckled. "You always make him sound like such a wild man."

"Well, that's what he was. You would have liked him, honey. I guarantee it."

Lynne thought about her dad, the impulsive daredevil. Greg Westbrook had worked very hard at being larger than life, and for the most part had succeeded. Handsome, arrogant, frequently charming, often inflexible, patriotic to a fault. He rarely had spoken of his war experience, though Lynne knew it was extensive and not all pleasant. He'd spent World War II in the South Pacific and after his sudden death, Lynne had watched the TV show *Black Sheep Squadron* with sorrow and fascination. The Black Sheep had been Marines, of course, and her father Navy, but she recognized the restless zest for life and for flying.

He had died doing what he loved, she knew, but she hated that he'd died too soon to ever know his grandson and granddaughter.

"I still can't believe he let you go to Santa Cruz for college," Jenna said. "With all you've said about him being such a tyrant—"

"Not a tyrant, honey," Lynne interrupted. "Just very strong-willed."

"Yeah, right. Very strong-willed. I just can't believe that someone so very strong-willed would let his only kid go to a school with no rules and no grades."

"Well, there were a few rules. But nothing that got in the way of having fun. Actually, he was off on active duty when

I was a senior in high school, so it was your grandma who agreed to let me go."

Jenna snorted. "As if she'd know what you were up to."

"No argument. And he wasn't happy when he caught on, either. But I was always careful not to get too publicly involved in antiwar stuff while he was in Vietnam, even though a lot of the kids I knew were antiwar protesters in a big way."

"But you've told me you opposed the war."

Lynne slowed to pass through Exeter, a charming small New Hampshire town dominated by the eponymous prep school. Oddly, there were big signs, right in the middle of the road by the school, warning of pedestrians crossing. Was this a new concept here?

Lynne knew that one reason why her father hadn't objected more strenuously to her college choice was that she'd been in one of the early classes at Santa Cruz, before the school had fully crafted its identity as rebellious or—in the parlance of the time—antiestablishment.

"I did, but very quietly. I think that what he really objected to was that he thought the place was populated strictly by draft-dodgers. But I was female and draft-exempt, and I had a pretty good scholarship. So he never really forced the issue." She turned on the radio. "Why don't you see if you can find some music?"

Jenna fiddled around until she found a radio station playing Simon and Garfunkel. The two of them settled into a comfortable silence.

Driving on two-lane New Hampshire highways offered a charming, all-but-idyllic vision of the region. Even without colorful foliage, the towns they passed through were steeped in proud tradition, the product of hundreds of years of residency by taciturn Europeans and their descendants. You could read a town's history in its architecture. Huge boxy houses with gables and steep roofs and multiple chimneys had been built for large families from once-abundant timber. Redbrick business buildings that followed, often as the forests were depleted, ushered in a new industrial and mercantile age, speaking of permanency and respectability, often with names set high above the ground in brick or stone. The stone buildings were usually the oldest and most pragmatic structures, dating back to a time when hardy settlers had only begun to wrestle the stones from ground they wished to use as farmland, one rock at a time.

For the United States, this constituted ancient history. In Europe it would have been laughably modern. But back home in Southern California, during the same time frame, the land had been tossed back and forth among Spanish and Mexican landowners and rancho patriarchs. Missions were built by Father Junipero Serra and his followers, who brought both Christianity and chicken pox to the native tribes.

In the brief period they'd been in New England, Lynne had already decided that her Fall Foliage trip would include as little history before 1800 as she could get away with. Bypassing Boston made it much easier to ignore the American Revolution, and also improved travel ambience dramatically. She considered it nothing short of a divine blessing that they could so easily fly in and out of Manchester, avoiding the nightmare of Logan Airport and the chaos of the Big Dig.

But if the trip was not going to cover Revolutionary history, the question was what to emphasize instead.

Jenna's fondness for New England writers made that an obvious choice, and her daughter had been brushing up on favorite writers ever since agreeing to come along. Lynne figured she could absorb all the relevant information from Jenna's research, which was probably extensive enough to build several tour days. She was more grateful than ever for Jenna's presence, having rediscovered the soporific effects of *Moby Dick*. She only hoped that other literary highlights would be more accessible.

Lynne had initially also hoped that New England women might prove an effective and simple topic to round things out, creating a trip that would appeal to strong older women who didn't mind learning something when they went on vacation. She'd even toyed with the idea of offering the trip on an exclusive basis to one of the local American Association of University Women chapters. The AAUW people she knew were bright and interesting and would be a lot of fun on a tour.

The problem, however, was that significant sites related to women were not centrally located, weren't even remotely close to each other. Lynne was accustomed to Western standards of distance, usually expressed in hours—five hours to Vegas, nine hours to the Bay area—and had somehow believed that because these New England spots were all so much closer in simple mileage that they'd be easily accessible. Nothing summed up the inaccuracy of that belief more handily than the locations associated with important New England women.

There was abundant material. New England had been the birthplace of impressive women from Priscilla Alden to Christa McAuliffe, with intermediate stops at Abigail Adams, Grandma Moses, and Louisa May Alcott. Lydia Pinkham had developed herbal remedies in Massachusetts while Margaret Rudkin opened Pepperidge Farms in Connecticut. Harriet Beecher Stowe, who lived all over the place, had written *Uncle Tom's Cabin* in a Maine house so cold that her children had to interrupt meals to warm their hands.

New England had it all covered in terms of women's education: the hoity-toity Miss Porter's School; the remarkable collegiate trio of Smith, Wellesley, and Mount Holyoke; and Prudence Crandall's Canterbury Female Boarding School in Connecticut. Prudence Crandall had the audacity to admit a black female student in 1832, creating a furor that cost her several arrests, three separate trials, and a mob visit to the school, which closed in 1834. Back in Massachusetts, Emily Dickinson had stayed in her room in Amherst while Lizzie Borden stepped out of hers in Fall River, proving there are any number of paths toward fame.

Lynne looked over and saw that Jenna's eyes were closed, her breathing slow and even. "Wake up, honey, we're coming to the Maine border."

"Huh?" Jenna's momentary confusion was confirmation that the girl had been dozing. Which wasn't such a terrible idea, Lynne thought. Maybe she'd take a snooze a bit later and Jenna could drive.

"This river we're about to cross," Lynne said, "is the boundary between Portsmouth and Kittery. Between New Hampshire and Maine."

"Very cool," said Jenna, sitting up and rolling her shoulders. "My first visit to Maine."

Lynne realized suddenly what it was she was so enjoying about this trip. It was the sense of hanging out with a girlfriend. Except that this girlfriend was also her only female child, her five-foot-ten, tan, blonde daughter, surely the prototype the Beach Boys had in mind when they sang of California girls.

No matter how old you became, Lynne believed, girlfriends were one of the most significant keys to enjoying life. She wondered now if her aunt and mother were tied together at all as girlfriends, or whether theirs was strictly a blood relationship, and bad blood at that. By the time you reached their age the situation was even more complicated. At their age, an awful lot of female friends—even here where longevity genes passed down from flinty loner to crusty hermit to self-sufficient curmudgeon—were . . .

Well, they were dead, that's what they were.

PRISCILLA Jones was in a real funk.

What had seemed like such a lovely idea—opening the Maple Leaf Inn and having Lynne bring some of her wealthy Southern California clients to stay there—was rapidly crumbling into unmitigated disaster.

Not half an hour after Lynne and Jenna left, Cindy Jackson had come across the street all panicky to tell her that her father had been seriously injured in a fall at the Washington Arms. Cindy had been at the hospital the previous night and was on her way back now. So far as she knew, Ralph had not yet regained consciousness.

Priscilla was ashamed to admit, even to herself, that she'd

been relieved when Cindy said she'd arranged for a girlfriend to watch Bradley. She took pride, rather, in her restraint in not calling Lynne, to spoil her day with news she could do nothing about. Abigail's day, on the other hand, she didn't mind disrupting, and Abby had promised to go to the hospital and report back to Priscilla.

Priscilla was growing more and more apprehensive about the whole Inn project. She had tried to read all those books Lynne sent her about how to open and run a bed-and-breakfast, but she really hadn't gotten too far with them. In some respects they were quite helpful, full of information like how to select toilet tissue, what size coffeepot to buy, and how to make your inn wheelchair-accessible. There was also plenty of information for those innkeepers foolish enough to permit children or pets or smoking.

Still, for every simple and cheerful decision—hot or cold cereal, tea or sherry in the afternoon, fresh or silk flowers on the dining table—there was plenty of much less palatable material. She grew queasy, for instance, at the admonition to remove stains from bedding as soon as possible. The books had detailed information on creating a business plan, whatever that was. They spoke of logos and four-color brochures and advertising, and all of them seemed to assume that you'd have a computer.

None of them, however, mentioned bodies in the basement.

That was something that was only supposed to happen in mystery stories, or on one of those nasty TV shows about crime investigation. It was not supposed to happen to an eighty-two-year-old woman just trying to scrape by after being widowed three times. And she didn't know what to make of this dreadful news about Ralph's fall. She'd grown reliant on his general knowledge of home repair and maintenance, his easygoing competence. How could she ever deal with all those others, the tile people and plumbers and all, without Ralph as a buffer?

The doorbell rang.

Priscilla found herself paralyzed. This morning it had

seemed like a blessing to have Lynne and Jenna off on their own, but this was the third time within the hour that somebody had rung her bell. The first and second had been reporters and she had told them through the closed door that she had nothing to say, just as Abigail had instructed her. This was probably another reporter. Surely it was too much to hope that Jason had returned to begin work on the gazebo, particularly if he knew Ralph wouldn't be around. As far as she knew, his tools were still quarantined in the basement.

The doorbell rang again, accompanied by an authoritative knock.

The porch was visible from the dining room window, so she slipped inside that room, moved around the stacked boxes of dishes and carefully opened the curtains just a crack. It was a policeman, that nice O'Keefe boy who had worked for Abby at Golden Mills, and he was alone. She took a deep breath and went to the front door, cautiously opening it.

"Yes?"

"Mrs. Jones, may I come in?" Detective O'Keefe asked. "I have some information that I wanted to share with you before you see it on the news."

Priscilla's heart fluttered. Suddenly she was back at China Lake in the cinder-block house with the cactus garden, stepping out to retrieve the mail one blistering afternoon when a car pulled up in front of the house and disgorged the chaplain and Greg's commanding officer. She had stood there beside the runty Joshua tree in her shorts and sandals, counting the seconds until they walked her up the path, ushered her indoors, then turned her world inside out and upside down. Twenty-three seconds it had taken, before they sat her down and told her that Greg wasn't coming home. Twenty-three seconds.

This couldn't be the same kind of bad news, however. She didn't have a husband, was finished with the marriage business, happy to have behind her the give-and-take of life with partners who mostly just took.

Then, as she let Detective O'Keefe in, she was struck by

another horrible thought. What if something had happened to Lynne and Jenny? Lynne had always been such a headstrong girl. Priscilla led the detective back to the kitchen, where the breakfast dishes were still piled on the counter. She felt only a flicker of embarrassment, as she fought to maintain her equanimity.

"Would you like some coffee?" The coffee was still warm, since she'd forgotten to turn off the coffeepot, but Detective O'Keefe had no way of knowing that the brew was four hours old. Policemen probably preferred it that way anyhow.

"Yes, thank you." He leaned in the doorway and watched while Priscilla found a mug and poured him a cup. Surely he wouldn't let her do this if he were about to tell her something terrible had happened to her daughter. Would he?

When she'd set the mug on the table and gotten the detective's assurance that he wanted nothing in it, she sat down at the kitchen table. He took the chair across from her.

"Mrs. Jones," he began, "I wanted to give you a heads-up on the latest information about what we found in your basement." He made it sound like he might have bad news about termites.

Priscilla turned to look at the cellar door with its yellow crime-scene tape. "You've identified that poor soul?"

He shook his head. "I'm afraid not. But they're going to be holding a press conference in Concord this morning that we hope will bring us closer to identification."

Priscilla shook her head. "You came over just to tell me you still don't know who it is?" There had to be a catch to this somewhere.

"No, I came to tell you that the forensic anthropologist has determined that there were actually two sets of remains down there."

"Two?" Priscilla felt suddenly queasy.

Detective O'Keefe nodded. "A male and a female, probably in their late teens or early twenties. We've also made some progress in narrowing the time frame, and an artist is working on possible sketches based on the imprints of the victims' faces in the concrete."

"You mean like"—she hesitated—"like a death mask?"

Detective O'Keefe nodded his head in agreement with what seemed like untoward enthusiasm. "Exactly. Now, neither of them was carrying any identification, at least none that survived all those years. But where we got lucky was that the male apparently was carrying a sealed metal case with some rolling papers and what seem to be a couple of marijuana cigarettes. The label on the papers identified them as Smokey Joe's brand. That particular brand was only available during a year or two in the late nineteen sixties."

"Rolling papers?" Priscilla had no idea whatsoever what he was talking about. She shook her head in confusion.

He nodded. "They're small thin pieces of paper that are used to roll cigarettes, or in this case probably to roll marijuana joints. Which we also found in the case."

She was growing more bewildered by the moment. "So they were drug addicts?"

Detective O'Keefe shrugged his shoulders. "This was a bit before my time. I was only a kid in the late sixties. But a lot of young people used marijuana back then. And in this case, it gave us a lucky break because we were able to concentrate on a specific period."

A lucky break. Somehow that didn't sound right. "You can tell their ages?"

"Approximately. My guess is that they were probably runaways. We're hoping that by making the public announcement that there were two victims in a probable time frame, somebody will come forward. I don't know how soon the artist's renditions will be ready, but those should help too."

Priscilla was sorry now that she hadn't called Lynne earlier, when she first heard about Ralph. She suddenly remembered Clara Day, whose husband had been Greg's CO in the late forties. "A burden shared is a burden halved," Clara would say in that molasses drawl of hers. If Priscilla had shared the burden of Ralph's accident with Lynne earlier, perhaps she'd be less distraught now. Or maybe not.

She experienced a sudden wave of emotion so intense that she had to sit down for a moment. Runaways. These young people had run away from parents, probably for no really good reason at all, and those poor parents had waited all these years, wondering where their children had gone, why they never heard from them.

Lynne had been a bit rebellious during that period, heaven knows, and there'd been times when her father had threatened to throttle her, but at least she'd never run away. Priscilla and Greg had always known where she was. And she was still alive.

She had decades of experience in maintaining composure in public, had not even allowed herself to shed a tear when they told her the jet Greg was flying had crashed. But the death of these two young strangers felt oddly personal.

Priscilla surprised herself by starting to cry.

Chapter 11

"SO what should I be watching for?" Jenna asked. Below them the Piscataqua River flowed into the Atlantic Ocean and straight ahead lay Maine. "A moose eating lobster?"

Lynne laughed. "Maybe later. Right now, I think we're more likely to see busloads of tourists from New Jersey, hot on the trail of bargains. One of the big outlet malls is right across this river."

Jenna scanned the horizon. Some women lived only to shop, but Jenna had only rarely fit that designation, and then usually at the end of a summer vacation when she'd earned a bunch of money and was about to return to school. Now that she'd been out of school for a while and was steadily under-employed, that sort of behavior didn't fit her lifestyle very well. She didn't have much disposable cash and it was harder to measure the passage of time without the framework of an academic year.

"This looks more like an outlet *town*," Jenna said, waving a hand from one side of the road to the other. She had envisioned Maine as a succession of rocky little bays with cold surf breaking and the occasional rustic house nestled in a forest clearing. That forest, this being fall, would be a blazing symphony in red and orange. While this fantasy image might be a reality somewhere—at least she hoped it was, since compared to its neighbors Maine was enormous—here every square inch of space seemed devoted to alleged bargains. The town of Kittery was chockablock with dozens, maybe hundreds, of upscale and semi-upscale retailers.

"True," Lynne agreed. "But they're fake outlet stores, just like the Carlsbad Company Stores back home. You know, not overstocks or factory seconds, just boatloads of stuff that's manufactured specifically for outlet malls, where there's no need to pay a middleman. However, if you look around in the backseat, I believe I brought along *Yankee Magazine's Guide to Real Factory Outlets.*"

Jenna didn't need to look hard. She'd organized all of the paper in the backseat before they were five miles out of South Hadford. "Found it," she said a moment later. "Skinny little magazine. And it only lists six genuine factory outlets for the entire state of Maine, one of which is the Maine State Prison Showroom in Thomaston. We going through there?"

"I don't think so," said Lynne. "Why? Do you want to make a detour? It's well beyond Freeport, but we might be able to get there if we hustle."

"No thanks," Jenna said. "Actually, even if we were passing right by it, I don't think I'd want to stop. Shopping at the Maine State Prison store is just a little too weird for my taste." She glanced at her watch. "Hey, we're making great time, particularly since we've been going on two-lane roads most of the time. Have you figured out exactly what you want to do when we get to Portland, assuming that we can find that Colwhistle guy's office?"

"This is your mission." Her mother deepened her voice in the *Mission Impossible* tone that she and Dad had always used, clowning around together. For a moment Jenna was so swept by grief and longing for her father that she could barely hear her mother's voice. "When we reach Portland, we'll go to Will Colwhistle's office. Once there, we will identify and neutralize the subject. This tape will self-destruct in ten seconds."

Jenna waited till she was sure her voice wouldn't catch. "I was actually wondering about some kind of slightly more specific plan, Mom. But if you don't have something worked out, I had an idea last night." Jenna explained the plan to her mother.

"Sounds good to me," Lynne said. "Now why don't you watch for someplace that sells lobster rolls so we can get some lunch."

"What's a lobster roll?" Jenna envisioned something along the lines of Chinese spring rolls or Filipino lumpia, both of which seemed out of place in New England. The Chinese food last night had been good but not remarkable, at least not to somebody who lived in LA and had many Chinese-American friends.

"Kind of like tuna salad," Lynne said. "On a bun."

Jenna leaned back and tested to see if there was enough room to put her feet on the dashboard. Not, it turned out, unless she wished to form her body profile into a letter N. But she was able to stretch her too-long legs out comfortably as she settled in for the not-exactly coastal drive. She was sorry she hadn't brought along some shorts on this trip, actually. It was absurdly hot for autumn in Maine.

After a brief lunch stop, which determined that lobster rolls were something Jenna could do without quite nicely, they continued up Highway 1. Jenna kept watch for weird highway signs for the list she was keeping. So far the best one was ENGINE BRAKING PROHIBITED, whatever that meant.

Despite the apparent prosperity of all those outlet stores, Maine itself seemed economically at a crossroad. Every time they came to a river, they passed more abandoned factories, with boarded-up windows looking down on the water that had once powered them.

They stopped briefly at a huge Maine Visitor Center between the old highway and the turnpike, where a larger-than-life Stephen King display greeted them. It was somewhat disquieting to find the King of Horror on board the state Welcome Wagon, but at least he wasn't hawking wares from the prison woodshop.

Back on the road they encountered a road crew ripping out vegetation that encroached on the road. This was no minor pruning, either. Gargantuan claws ripped out entire trees and shrubs by the roots, dumping them into huge trucks.

"That one was bright red," Jenna noted. "You'd think they'd leave it as part of the tourist display."

"They don't have much time for this kind of repair," Lynne answered. "You know what they say about the seasons in Maine. There's winter, still winter, almost winter, and construction."

They wound their way into Portland, Jenna managing the navigation chores with little difficulty. As they went deeper and deeper into the city, they passed huge frame churches and sprawling cemeteries, small stands offering pumpkins and cornstalks and chrysanthemums in a spectrum of fall colors. Many of the houses they passed were already decorated for Halloween, with tombstones and scarecrows and ghosts dangling from trees with foliage in a full spectrum of autumn colors. As they drew closer to the wharf area on 1-A, they passed huge piles of rusted scrap metal.

"We're getting close," Jenna said finally. The streets in the business district had resolutely Yankee names: Fore, Middle, Exchange, Commercial. No whimsy here. "Take a right up at that light, and then a left in two blocks. There are a lot of one-way streets where we're heading, so bear with me if we need to do some doubling back. The address we want on Silver Street seems to be right in the heart of downtown Portland. Next block . . . okay, that's it."

Jenna pointed to an old, redbrick building. Lynne parked and they walked back, passing a dolphin sculpture in the center of a rotary outside the old Armory building, now a luxury hotel.

Silver Street was cobblestoned and the interior of the building Will Colwhistle had listed as his Portland office was very trendy, very upscale, and very extravagant in a part of the world that prided itself on frugality.

"You ready?" Lynne asked.

"Of course." It surprised Jenna to see her mother so nervous and unsure of herself. Jenna had never quite gotten past her childhood belief that there was nothing her parents couldn't do. Maybe what was worrying Mom was the idea that Abigail had been brushed off by a secretary in the Manchester office. The idea of anyone putting off Aunt Abby seemed totally absurd. This guy must have a staff of retired master sergeants.

Upstairs they found Colwhistle Financial Services engraved on one of several brass plaques beside the entry to a suite of offices. Most of the plaques identified accountants or attorneys, nearly all in solo practice.

The reception they received was chilly, though not entirely ungracious. An efficient young woman smiled expectantly as they approached her desk. She was around Jenna's age, probably no more than twenty-five, but she had the air of a premature battle-ax. In a pinstriped navy business suit with a white silk blouse and small gold earrings, she was the essence of Yankee respectability. The name plaque on her desk read MISS LANCASTER *SECRETARY*.

"I'd like to see Mr. Colwhistle," Lynne announced.

Jenna had grown up calling most adults by their first names, an informality she was quite comfortable practicing. She doubted that many California secretaries—who were almost certainly called administrative assistants—identified themselves only by last name. Miss Lancaster's Southern California counterpart might even wear board shorts and flip-flops if the office were close enough to the beach.

"Mr. Colwhistle?" the woman said, frowning slightly.

"I'm Mrs. Montgomery. I understood he'd be in this office today." Lynne frowned back and cocked her head, looking perplexed but still very much in charge. It was all about attitude, her mother had said.

"Did you have an appointment?" Miss Lancaster asked doubtfully.

"Well, no," Lynne admitted, offering her most congenial

smile. "I was hoping he'd be able to slip me in for a few minutes."

Miss Lancaster shook her head. "There must be some kind of mistake, ma'am. Mr. Colwhistle isn't in town just now, and I'm not sure when he'll be back."

Show time.

Jenna moved to the end of Miss Lancaster's desk, forcing her to shift her attention from Lynne, standing directly in front of her. "I told you he'd be in Hartford," Jenna put in irritably, bad cop to her mother's good cop. "That he never came up here."

Miss Lancaster fell for it. "Well, that's not entirely true."

"Then he isn't in Hartford?" Jenna snapped, moving closer. Behind the desk, Miss Lancaster drew back. There wasn't enough room to really get into her personal space, but this wasn't bad.

Miss Lancaster whipped her head from Lynne to Jenna and back again, a much better groomed version of those silly little dogs people put in the back windows of their cars. "If you'd like to leave a message—"

"Perhaps you could just tell me where to reach him?" Lynne asked. "I always have trouble keeping track of when he's going to be where. If this isn't his week in Portland and he's not in Hartford, then I guess he must be in Montpelier."

"Forget it, Mrs. Montgomery," Jenna said crisply, realizing that she had never before referred to her mother by that name. "This girl doesn't know anything." She moved just a bit closer.

Bingo. Miss Lancaster's veneer of competent gentility cracked just a bit as pride triumphed over confidentiality. "I can't tell you because I don't know," she blurted.

"Is he here often?" Jenna asked brusquely. This role of annoyed companion was turning out to be kind of fun.

Miss Lancaster shook her head a bit, then stopped abruptly as if she'd realized the blunder she was making: Releasing Privileged Information to Strangers. Jenna moved back slightly, tossing the interrogational ball to her mother. Lynne asked a few more questions, ever-so-politely, then offered

Miss Lancaster a gracious smile and thanked her for her time. She left no message for Mr. Colwhistle.

OUTSIDE, Lynne turned to Jenna, genuinely impressed with her daughter's dramatic abilities. This was a side of Jenna that she hadn't really seen since seventh grade drama class. "Well?"

Jenna shook her head. "She doesn't know anything. I wasn't kidding when I said that inside. Though she seems like the kind of tight-ass who wouldn't tell you if she did. This is getting more and more interesting, actually. I think the guy just uses this place as a classy mail drop. I'm not sure that girl would even recognize him if he walked in the front door."

"This is all getting a little more complicated than I expected," Lynne admitted. "I guess the next thing is to leave messages at all his alleged offices. We can do that first thing in the morning. But right now, unless you can think of a good reason to stick around here, I say let's go eat some lobster and head on up to L. L. Bean."

"Actually, I can think of one good reason to stick around here for a little while," Jenna told her. "You know that place that always advertises capes in *The New Yorker*? The Casco Bay Wool shop that always has a picture of somebody who looks like Meryl Streep in *The French Lieutenant's Woman*?"

Lynne nodded. Of course she knew what Jenna was talking about. She had seriously coveted those capes for years.

"Well, we just passed their store," Jenna said, "and I happened to notice a sign saying that all of their shawls and capes are on sale."

Daughters were such a joy.

Ten minutes later as they were trying on shawls and capes, trying to ignore the fact that it was about eighty-five degrees and the natives were running around in shorts eating ice-cream cones, Lynne's cell phone rang.

She moved out into the street to answer, almost bumping

into a young man, naked to the waist, who should have kept his pasty body covered no matter how hot it was. She turned aside and answered. It was her mother.

"Hi, Mom, what's up?" Priscilla retained her generation's wariness of expensive long-distance calls, her sole area of frugality, now that Lynne thought about it. She must be seriously upset to be calling in the middle of the afternoon.

She was right.

"Everything's just awful. Right after you left this morning, I found out that Ralph took a terrible fall and he's in the hospital in a coma. A *coma,* Lynne! That poor old dear. And then that policeman came back. The one who worked for Abby." Priscilla's voice caught. Was she actually crying?

"Calm down, Mom. Take a deep breath. What happened to Ralph?"

"He fell into a creek at the Washington Arms and hit his head on a rock. But that's not all. I thought that the reason Abby's policeman came over was to tell me they'd identified whoever was in the basement."

"And did they?" Lynne asked.

"No," Priscilla wailed, "and it isn't just one whoever. It's *two* whoevers, a hippie boy and girl. Drug addicts."

Whoa.

"Hold on a minute there, Mom. Take it one step at a time. Just tell me what he said."

It didn't take long to clarify some of the main issues. Priscilla's own naivete was leading her to assumptions about drug use and abuse that Lynne didn't feel like trying to correct. But the notion of two bodies down there, much less two young bodies, was not good news.

One body was quite bad enough. Two bodies moved matters to a whole new level. It brought to mind serial killers, unsavory folks like John Wayne Gacy and Jeffrey Dahmer and that California woman who knocked off elderly boarders, stashed their bodies under quicklime in the backyard, and continued cashing their Social Security checks.

"But they don't know who they were?"

"No idea, I don't think. They're putting it on the news to see if anybody knows."

Lynne wondered how widespread the alarm call would be, how far it would move beyond the local and regional media. New Hampshire didn't normally contribute a lot to the national news scene, except every four years during the national political primaries. The local television and newspapers didn't strike her as particularly sophisticated. But the concept of two young people dug up in a New Hampshire basement might be enough to ricochet this story right onto national front pages, or shock TV, or the tabloids. Probably some combination of the three. They were a little too close for comfort to Boston and New York.

For the first time the photogenic nature of the Maple Leaf Inn seemed a detriment rather than an asset.

"Mom, why don't you go over to Aunt Abby's?"

"I'm too upset to drive."

"Then call and have her come pick you up, or come stay with you. I can call her if you want."

"I couldn't ask you to call her. This is already too much long distance," her mother said, with a faint but unmistakable whimper. "And I don't want to bother Abby."

"Nonsense. That's what family is for, remember? You always gave me a big song and dance about that when I was a kid. Family stands by and helps you when you need it." She had a sudden memory of Aunt Abby arriving in Florida by train when Priscilla had gallbladder surgery back in the fifties.

"I don't suppose you . . ."

It was a safe bet that Priscilla was going to ask them to rush right back, which seemed entirely unnecessary. And this seemed an imprudent time to tell her mother that she had just come from investigating that fabulous investment counselor, Will Colwhistle, in what looked like a very high-end mail drop. Better to just cut her off at the pass.

"Listen, Mom, Jenna and I are about to head out to Cape Elizabeth and get some dinner at the Two Lights Lobster Shack. Have you ever been there? It's near the Portland Head Light, out on Cape Elizabeth. Aunt Abby recommended it."

"I don't know."

"Well, I'm sure you'd recognize it, and next time we'll all go together. But we're actually a little bit behind schedule now. We're still in Portland, and after we eat Jenna has her heart set on visiting L. L. Bean."

Jenna, who had removed her *French Lieutenant's Woman* cape and stepped to the door to eavesdrop, rolled her eyes. She was not really an L. L. Bean kind of girl.

"Oh, please," Priscilla said. "Tell Jenna there's no reason in the world to go all the way up there. There's nothing you can't get out of the catalogue. Unless of course you want junk that people returned. Those things are relatively inexpensive, I've heard. But it doesn't matter how cheap something is if it's got somebody else's name embroidered on it, now does it?"

"Of course not," Lynne agreed, "but we need to get moving just the same, and I need to check out Freeport for my tour next year." The proposed tour was Lynne's only trump card here, other than hanging up, which seemed unsporting. "I figure we'll probably get home pretty late tonight, so give Aunt Abby a call and don't bother waiting up for us, okay?" She broke the connection and turned off the phone before Priscilla could sling any more guilt in her direction.

Back in the shop, Jenna was trying on a different cape, this one cashmere. Southern California never really got cold enough to warrant such warm outerwear, though it was fun to swirl around the shop in the capes. The shawls, on the other hand, seemed ideal, warm enough for cool winter nights without being stifling. The colors were wonderful, too. Lynne had already picked out a luxurious shawl of soft teal wool for herself and offered to buy one for Jenna, who was vacillating between cobalt and camel.

Now Lynne added a third shawl, in a deep rich purple, for her mother.

Purple was the color of royalty. Priscilla would like that.

IF it weren't for the weather, Jenna thought, the Maine coast would be a pretty spectacular place to live.

Of course that *if* was a mighty big qualifier. The Two Lights Lobster Shack, outside which she was currently scarfing down her second lobster dinner of the hour, would soon close for the season, on October twentieth at eight P.M. according to the posted sign. It seemed entirely possible that at 8:01 the whole place would be suddenly encased in ice.

She'd purchased two extra-long postcards of the Portland Head Light, the famous Maine lighthouse that stood nearby. The summer version showed placid waters and a bit of green lawn atop the rocky outcropping, the white of lighthouse and red-roofed outbuildings standing in stark relief against deep green forests visible beyond the deep blue bay. The winter version, taken from exactly the same angle, featured angry white waves breaking over ice-encrusted rocks, the lighthouse and its outbuildings covered in snow and blending into the landscape, with only a smudge of white suggesting land beyond the bay's cold gray waters.

A nice place to visit, but she sure wouldn't want to live here.

Still, it was actually a very nice place. The lobster was succulent, the informality of the restaurant ideal, and the bright red outdoor tables where she sat dunking bits of lobster into melted butter offered panôramic views. Nearby slabs of rock, scattered about willy-nilly, looked almost like the logs in the Petrified Forest in Arizona.

She momentarily considered ordering a third lobster, which she knew her mother would pay for without objection, but decided to exercise a modicum of restraint. Two would do.

Chapter 12

ABIGAIL Chenonceau cast a critical eye around her sister's parlor and off-limits dining room. There was much to criticize.

While the living room itself was in reasonably acceptable order, Priscilla had yet to make any headway whatsoever in the dining room. The mahogany dining table and sideboard were buried beneath boxes and the china closet remained empty. As far as Abigail was concerned, Priscilla had only drawn attention to the room's disrepair by tossing linen tablecloths over the table, sideboard, various boxes, and the chairs too deeply buried to be dragged into the parlor for guest seating. She probably thought it would resemble a summer home gone dormant, but the shrouding was too haphazard and the furniture beneath it all but unrecognizable.

"Abby?" Priscilla's call came from upstairs where she had gone to primp now that the majority of the party prep was finished. "Will you check and make sure I turned off the oven?"

It was typical of Priscilla to wait until the last minute to plan a gathering and then expect others to do most of the work. Correction. Priscilla hadn't expected assistance from *others,* not even her own daughter and granddaughter. No, she had called only her younger sister, knowing that Abigail couldn't possibly deny assistance, no matter how chaotic matters might be. To guarantee her sister's help, she had chosen not to make her plea until she had re-invited most of her guests for the other day's postponed afternoon tea.

Abigail moved to the kitchen and checked the oven, which was indeed turned off. She called reassurance upstairs. Was Priscilla more forgetful these days, or was it merely the stress of the bodies in the basement?

Lynne and Jenna were no help at all. They'd sauntered off to Salem this morning, promising to return in plenty of time to meet the neighbors. So while Priscilla sliced cucumbers and chopped hard-boiled eggs for little egg salad sandwiches, it was Abigail who picked up teacakes and scones at the downtown bakery, Abigail who gave a hurried last-minute press to the linen tablecloth, Abigail who provided an eleventh-hour polish to Priscilla's silver tea service.

And it was Abigail who broke through that silly crime-scene tape to bring the large folding table up from the basement. The table itself was remarkably light and easy to maneuver, unlike those heavy church tables Abigail had wrestled with over the years. Leave it to Priscilla to stumble onto something easier, without even trying.

The effort, Abigail conceded now as she surveyed the serving table, set up on a side wall in the parlor and covered with goodies, was more than justified by the result. Priscilla had put together a lovely centerpiece of fall leaves in a silver vase. There'd be cider offered as well as tea, and local apple slices, dipped in lemon juice and offered with caramel sauce.

She made some slight adjustments to a platter of muffins. She was grateful that the local bakery continued to produce baked goods in manageable sizes, none of these bagels big as inner tubes or muffins the size of ottomans. These were sweet rolls and small cakes the same size they had always been, as far back as Abigail could remember, from a bakery that had been on downtown Main Street since before she was born. The muffins, indeed, were even smaller than they used to be, kind of muffinettes, a perfect size for aging ladies. They said you could cut larger items up and serve them that way, but it always seemed inhospitable to take something sized for an individual, chop it into smaller pieces, then set it out for company.

"This all looks absolutely lovely," Priscilla said from the doorway, genuine gratitude in her voice. She looked quite lovely herself, in a purple cashmere twin set and black slacks, her white hair styled casually. She might easily have been mistaken for the younger sister, an error folks had been making for most of their lives. Abigail knew she ought to get over it, but it was a carefully nurtured grudge and she chose not to let it go.

Priscilla crossed and offered Abigail a hug. "It's so much fun to have you here to help."

As always, Abigail felt her irritation melt away. Over more than three quarters of a century, at least the parts of it that Abigail could remember, Priscilla had always possessed a quiet charm that her sister envied but could never emulate. Priscilla had been able to talk herself out of any scrape, had invariably looked beguiling as she explained how each new transgression was really just a question of interpretation. Priscilla always had her own interpretation at the ready.

"The sandwiches are all fixed," Priscilla reported now, "and I dressed the platter up with some parsley, but I think they'd better stay in the fridge till the last minute. We don't want anything to spoil." She shook her head. "Now where are the girls, anyway?"

"On their way back, I'm sure," Abigail answered without much conviction.

But even as she spoke, the front door swung open, letting in her niece and grand-niece, carrying bags of souvenirs and laughing.

"Wow!" Jenna exclaimed, stopping abruptly to take in the silver tea service, the Wedgwood cups and saucers, the platters of cookies and muffinettes and scones. "Now I feel guilty that we ran off all day. You two shouldn't have gone to so much trouble."

"It was nothing," Priscilla said.

Nothing for her, Abigail thought. Priscilla had mostly confined her efforts to trimming the crusts off bread and heating those little frozen quiche things.

"I couldn't have done it without Abby," Priscilla went on, and there it happened again. Abigail could feel her annoyance melting away, being replaced by a strange equanimity that could almost be described as contentment.

For all the trouble she could be, it was nice to have Priscilla back in New Hampshire. They might not have many years left, but who knew? When New Englanders passed a certain age in good health, they had a tendency to go on for a good while longer. Breaking a hundred was not uncommon. Sturdy stock had mated with sturdy stock in these parts, dating all the way back to the Pilgrims. The strong survivors had procreated some more. And so on and so on. The family bloodlines were strong, perhaps even strengthened by the addition of the Frenchman from Lyons, M. Henri Chenonceau.

Abigail sometimes wondered how it would end, whether one of them would simply keel over and be gone one day, or if they'd sit side by side in rockers on the porch out at the Washington Arms, waiting for somebody more mobile to bring by the feel-good companion dog. It seemed almost inevitable that they'd be living together at some point, that one of them would need to watch out for the other. It would be nice, when that happened, if Priscilla hadn't squandered every penny she had.

"So the neighbors are all coming by in"—Lynne checked her watch—"twenty minutes?"

"Or thereabouts." Sooner, probably. Punctuality mattered here in South Hadford, not like some places. "It's not just neighbors, though. We also asked a few others to join us," Abigail said. "The minister's wife and a couple of other ladies from church." Did Lynne attend church, Abigail wondered? Did Jenna?

"Guess we'd better spiff up then," Jenna said, vaulting up the stairs three at a time, her long legs flying.

"Have I met any of these people before?" Lynne asked. "I know it's been a long time since I've spent more than a day or two here, and I'd hate to embarrass anybody that I should remember." She swiped a brownie off the serving table. "This minister's wife, for instance. That would be a bit of a faux pas."

"She's only been here a few years," Abigail told her. "Our new minister is really just warming up." Pastors at the First Congregational Church of South Hadford stayed on for decades, generally leaving feet first for the short move to the graveyard outside. This latest one, Reverend Clement Booker, was a keeper, and Abigail genuinely liked his wife, Mary Beth.

First Congregational was the largest and best maintained church in town, always freshly painted a crisp white, its perfectly manicured churchyard filled with smooth white marble monuments and headstones dating back almost three hundred years. These days, you couldn't get in at all unless you were the pastor or had an old family plot. A few years earlier, when adjacent property went on the market, the church had bought it up, disassembled the frame house that stood on the grounds, sold the first-cut lumber the house had been built with to a hardwoods broker, then held a lottery for plots in the new area. Space was tight in cemeteries all over New England. Even Robert Frost had only managed to buy his plot in a Bennington, Vermont cemetery through a similar lottery.

Abigail and Priscilla's parents were buried there, along with the brother who'd died as a child and a marker for the other brother who had enlisted in the final days of World War II, only to die in Okinawa. His remains had never been returned to New Hampshire, and Abigail secretly chose to believe that John Jacob Chenonceau rested in the Tomb of the Unknown Soldier in Arlington National Cemetery.

"Well?" Lynne asked. "Who's coming?"

"All right, let's see. I don't know if they'll be coming, but

Cindy and her mom were invited." As Lynne's mouth opened to ask, Abigail continued. "Ralph's condition is unchanged, I'm sorry to say. Now, who else? Helen Vincent from down the block. Mary Beth Booker, the preacher's wife, and Dottie Connelly, who plays the organ Sunday mornings. Will you be joining us at church while you're in town?"

Lynne cocked her head. Abigail had done her best to make her question nonchalant, and if Lynne was annoyed, she didn't show it. But you just never knew with religion and Californians.

"We'll probably be in Massachusetts on Sunday," Lynne said. "Anyone else coming I ought to know about?"

"The McKinnon sisters, Louise and Charlotte. Charlotte's married name is Roberts. Both girls worked at the mill with me." Charlotte had been executive secretary to the two vice-presidents and Louise had worked directly for Abigail as assistant floor supervisor.

Lynne ticked them off on her fingers. "Cindy, Cindy's mom—what's her name?"

"Doreen. Doreen Tracy."

Lynne giggled. "The Mouseketeer?"

Abigail had no idea what Lynne was talking about, so she decided to ignore the question. "Doreen's in one of those little motorized scooter things. The poor dear has a degenerative muscular condition and she can't get around on her own at all anymore. Ralph tried to keep her at home, but since he had a little stroke of his own a few months back, he's had all kinds of problems." She lowered her voice. "I believe he's developing Alzheimer's, too, though how you can really tell in his case is a mystery. Even before his accident he was becoming terribly vague."

Lynne looked around. "It just now occurred to me that this place isn't even remotely ADA accessible. Is that something that Jason is supposed to be working on? Or Ralph? Or somebody? A wheelchair ramp?"

"That Jason boy doesn't seem to be working on anything," Abigail sniffed, "and he does that nothing on an hourly wage. But I'm sure we can take care of it, don't worry. Do you have clients who use wheelchairs? Is that likely to be a problem when you bring your group next year?"

"Not at the moment," Lynne said. "Right now I can't think of any clients with special needs who are likely to want to take this trip. Some travel agencies and tour guides specialize in handicap-accessible trips, but not me. One or two people with special physical needs are about all I feel competent to handle at one time." She waved at the stairs. "And all the bedrooms here are upstairs anyway. So it's really not an option. So. Is that it for the guest list?"

"Not quite." Abigail ran through another half dozen names and dossiers.

"Okay, then. I'd better go get cleaned up," Lynne said. "Don't want to make a bad impression on your friends."

Abigail didn't see how she could possibly be ready in time, but fifteen minutes later as the doorbell rang for the first time, Lynne was waiting in the parlor, wearing soft gray tailored wool slacks and a floral shirt. Both were part of a wrinkle-free travel wardrobe alleged to take all the hassle out of clothing maintenance on the road.

By the time the first guests had been introduced to Lynne, Jenna joined them as well, in a silk tank top and very short skirt, both in an arresting shade of turquoise. She looked tan and healthy and fit, with slender brown legs that went on forever. In this setting, she was the peacock accidentally penned up with a flock of guinea hens.

Abigail regarded her three generations of family with genuine affection. She knew that life was a series of decisions that often rested one upon the other in ways that made it impossible to go back and reconsider.

Forty-odd years ago, Abigail had realized with a resounding finality that motherhood would never be a part of her life. Yet despite her acceptance of spinsterhood, she had often wondered what it would be like to bear and raise a daughter. Not a son. She'd been around enough small children to know that she would never have possessed sufficient patience to raise a male.

But a little girl, now, that was different.

Lynne was the closest she'd ever come to having a little girl, at least in terms of bloodlines. Abigail's relationship with the young Lynne had been complicated by Priscilla's globe-trotting and the capricious duty assignments of the United States Navy, but between reassignments, her sister had sometimes managed to slip away and visit New England with her daughter.

Although Abigail could—and did—find fault in many of her sister's decisions and actions over the years, she remained convinced that Priscilla was a splendid mother who had raised an exceptional daughter. Seeing Jenna with them both now completed the circle.

And who knows what kind of wondrous daughter young Jenna might one day produce?

Chapter 13

LYNNE was making every possible effort not to be irritated by the forced conviviality of her mother's impromptu tea party. Priscilla had already been asleep when they returned from Maine last night, but she'd left a note on the kitchen table:

> *I've rescheduled my little tea party to tomorrow after-noon at 3. Hope this is all right.*
>
> *Love, Mom*

Well, there wasn't any way to dodge a command performance this like one, even though her mother clearly knew Lynne and Jenna had every intention of going in the morning to visit Salem. Indeed, Priscilla had lobbied strongly against visiting Salem at all.

"It's a silly waste of time," Priscilla had argued. "It's just appalling how they've taken that one tragic winter and used it to turn an entire charming town into the worst sort of tourist trap. Halloween stores open all year long, hokey exhibits, actual practitioners of Wicca, though I must confess I'm not altogether certain exactly what that means. And in all that, it's been entirely lost that Salem is actually more significant as a maritime center."

Well, she'd been right, but Lynne wasn't in any hurry to admit it. Rebellion against parental authority had a certain timelessness. And while the traffic in and out of Salem had been horrendous—they'd gotten back in time only by breaking a disconcerting number of traffic laws—she didn't regret the visit. She could now tell people firsthand that Salem was a tourist trap. Her favorite part of the day, actually, had been a row house they passed on the way out of town. Painted entirely black, with a pair of black griffins flanking the door, it had a sign that said: IT ISN'T A CHURCH. GET OVER IT.

In addition to allowing her to check off another tour group possibility (albeit in the NO column) visiting Salem had also let Lynne and Jenna avoid dusting and vacuuming the Maple Leaf Inn and readying the premises for company. And it was entirely possible that the gathering her mother had planned might actually prove useful.

Fifteen or so women were assembled here now, sitting in easy groupings around the parlor and sometimes spilling out onto the porch. Several others had dropped by briefly and then left. Cindy had brought her mother by on the way back to the Washington Arms from the hospital.

Having not previously met Cindy's mother Doreen, Lynne was surprised to find the woman tiny and dark, a quarter-inch of silvered hair showing at the base of her black coif, her olive complexion turned sallow by anxiety. She bore no likeness whatsoever to Cindy and Bradley. While clearly distressed that her husband remained unconscious, she made a real effort to be sociable and accepted her neighbors' expressions of concern gratefully.

Jenna and Cindy had taken care of the ADA issue by lifting first Doreen and then her motorized chair onto the front porch, with ease and grace and the strength that comes from youth. Bradley, briefly retrieved from whoever'd been watching him, was content for a while to play at the base of

Nana's chair. He seemed quite devoted to his Nana, and climbed into her lap for a ride at one point. When the chair stopped its travels—and Lynne could see that handicap accessibility could turn into a major problem at the Maple Leaf Inn—Bradley was sound asleep in Nana's arms.

While everyone was friendly enough, and carefully solicitous of the Tracy women, many of the guests carried an air of slight reserve, a caution that seemed more innate than intentional. Though the event had been deliberately labeled casual, nobody wore jeans. The Yankee idea of casual seemed to run more to denim skirts and tailored slacks. There wasn't a single unsensible shoe in the room, apart from Jenna's chunky, high-fashion footwear.

Lynne took her teacup and moved over to join the woman who'd been introduced as Helen Vincent, a lifelong South Hadfordite who lived two doors down Barrington Road from the Maple Leaf Inn. The sharp-eyed Helen looked to be in her sixties, though it was hard to tell with these New Englanders, who so often didn't bother with the cosmetic niceties that their Southern California counterparts relied on. Doreen Tracy was the only person she'd met whose hair was clearly colored. In this town, hair that had gone gray or white was allowed to remain gray or white, and plastic surgery would be accepted only to repair birth defects or to minimize accident scarring.

"That's wonderful needlework, Mrs. Vincent," Lynne said, indicating the woman's denim vest, which was covered with finely embroidered sprays of fall leaves. "Did you do it yourself?"

"Of course." Helen Vincent raised an eyebrow, perhaps at the notion that anyone might be so useless as to have to buy her clothing pre-embroidered. She also wore a khaki skirt, an Oxford-cloth button-down shirt, and slip-on leather shoes that looked exactly like the ones Lynne had considered last night at L. L. Bean. Her hair was a nondescript brown shot through with a liberal dose of steely gray and she wore no makeup.

"It's quite lovely," Lynne said, and she meant it. "Mother's really appreciated how enthusiastic you all have been about her plans to open the bed-and-breakfast." Lynne saw Helen Vincent's eyes narrow slightly and mentally regrouped. Maybe "enthusiastic" hadn't been the best choice of words. "I certainly appreciate your cooperation, Mrs. Vincent."

"It was a zoning question," Helen Vincent said, "and you may call me Helen. This place had been a boardinghouse once before, so there was precedent. And then the Saxtons had all those different children over the years. We've grown accustomed to not knowing who lives here, so I suppose having it be a bed-and-breakfast won't be too terribly different."

She shook her head. "There are certain innate problems when a continual parade of strangers moves through a secluded neighborhood like ours. But none of us here actively objected."

Inactive objection, however, seemed another matter. Lynne thought of Priscilla's assurances. Everybody was ecstatic, Priscilla had told Lynne repeatedly, thrilled that the Maple Leaf Inn would soon be open to guests.

"I understand you've lived here quite some time," Lynne went on.

"All my life." The statement was so matter-of-fact that it took Lynne by surprise. Among her friends in California, very few could claim to be lifelong residents of the state, and almost nobody she knew had been born and raised in Floritas. Even Monty, so firmly entrenched in the community that he seemed to have sprung full-grown from its sandy shores with a surfboard under his arm, had started out somewhere else. The Montgomery family had moved to Floritas from Santa Ana in the 1950s.

"And how long have you lived on this street?"

"Same answer."

Perfect. Lynne probably couldn't count on this taciturn woman to volunteer any information, but if she could figure out the right questions, she might be able to learn something that would help resolve the mystery of who was in her mother's basement.

Then somebody rapped at the front door and Lynne, who

was the closest hostess, moved to answer. A sullen teenage girl in tight jeans and a tank top stood there. She'd powdered over her freckles and hennaed her hair, but she still looked like Cindy.

"My mom left me a note to come get Bradley," the girl said, skipping social niceties.

"Do come in," Lynne told her. "You must be Brittany. I'm Lynne."

"'Lo," Brittany said, looking around the guests she could see from the doorway. None of them sprang to greet her. "Do you know where Bradley is?"

"Asleep in your Grandma's arms, last I saw," Lynne told her, just as Doreen came around the corner, still holding Exhibit A.

Bradley woke in mid-transfer, but remained sleepy and tractable enough to leave with his sister. Doreen leaned back in her chair when they left. Helen had fixed her a plate of sandwiches, but Doreen left them untouched in her lap.

"Such a shock about Ralph," Helen Vincent said when Doreen's grandchildren had left. "Is there anything we can do?"

"Pray," Doreen answered.

"What do they think happened?" Lynne asked. This had been bothering her, a lot. "Did he faint again? Have another stroke?"

"The doctors aren't sure," Doreen answered, "and nobody knows what he was doing down by the stream in the first place. He's got a skull fracture and they're worried about bleeding in his brain. . . ." Tears began to flow down her cheeks and she made no attempt to stop them. Helen handed her a tissue, then cleared a spot on the table beside Doreen to set down the tissue box.

Doreen just sat and cried.

Lynne slipped away to find Cindy. "I think your mom is pretty upset."

"If you can find Jenna to help me with the stairs, I'll bring her back home. She shouldn't have come, but she insisted.

And thank your mom for me. I'll run along with her. She'll probably want to go right back to the hospital."

When Cindy and Doreen had gone, Lynne returned to Helen Vincent, who was filling a plate of her own with three small sandwiches and three cookies, placed at even intervals, none touching.

"I suppose the police talked to you about this house," Lynne began.

Helen nodded. "I don't think any of us were much help." She sipped her tea and took a cucumber sandwich off her plate. "The place has turned over quite a bit, even since I was born. And of course the structure itself dates to the late nineteenth century."

But the plumbing didn't. And parts of the plumbing system had been covered by the concrete that also had covered the bodies of the two strangers in the basement floor. Concrete from cement that couldn't have been poured before 1969, when the rolling papers had first been manufactured.

"I've been wondering a lot about when it was a boardinghouse. Do you know how long that went on?"

"Around ten years," Helen said. "Pretty much right through the seventies, at least until the first Reagan administration. I remember there was a big John Anderson poster hanging in the front window for a while in 1980, and that some of the neighbors weren't happy about that. Ralph Tracy was one who was furious. Very conservative, Ralph. But of course Charles Grant was the owner and he'd become something of a political liberal over the years. His son spent years in the hospital after his military service. For all I know, Mr. Grant was the one who hung the poster. Anyway, not too long after that, the place went on the market. It sat empty for a while, and then Otto and Laura Saxton bought it."

They'd come full circle then. Otto and Laura Saxton had sold the place to Priscilla Jones, before it even officially went on the market.

"Could we back up a little?" Lynne asked. "Tell me more about the boardinghouse period. Who were the boarders?"

"Well," Helen began, "I think it mostly was folks who

came to attend the junior college or to work at Golden Mills. Sometimes both at the same time. There always seemed to be a lot of young men, now that I think about it, and there was a lot of turnover."

Helen nibbled a cookie. That perfectly arranged plate was empty now. No waste.

"I was raising my children then, and I must confess I was never terribly comfortable with the parade of people who seemed to come through there." She frowned, seeming to hear what she'd said for the first time. "I had no reason to be concerned," she amended. "Just a mother overreacting, I suppose. But I wasn't terribly sorry when they sold the place."

"Some time after 1980?" Lynne asked.

"Thereabouts. My youngest daughter graduated from high school in 1981 and it was empty then, I think. People might have made more of a fuss about the boardinghouse if it hadn't been owned by somebody so respectable. Charles Grant owned the property all through the boardinghouse period." At Lynne's puzzled frown, she continued. "Mr. Grant, rest his soul, was one of the vice-presidents at Golden Mills. He passed away oh . . . four, maybe five years ago."

"Did he live here?" Lynne asked, with a sweep of her hand.

The question brought a little chuckle. "Goodness, no. The Grants had a lovely home over on Wilmington Street. Louise Grant lived there until a few years ago, when she went to live with her daughter down in Connecticut. And to be perfectly honest, I didn't really know the man, other than to see him at church. And of course he sat on the Town Council."

Of course. "But he did own the boardinghouse?"

"Oh yes, and quite a bit of other property as well. I believe there was money in his family, though he was the sort of man who could fall into a cistern and come out with a diamond bracelet."

Helen Vincent flushed, suddenly aware that she was being extremely indiscreet. "I'm talking out of turn here, I'm afraid."

Lynne had the sense that she'd carried this topic as far as

Helen Vincent would allow. But as Helen began to collect her plate and cup, she tried for one last question. "Did Mr. Grant come around often?" *Mr. Grant.* This was starting to sound like reruns of *The Mary Tyler Moore Show.*

Helen remained silent a moment. Then she shrugged as if she'd won a minor battle with her conscience. "He'd come by on the first of every month and get the rent from the manager who lived here. Sometimes there'd be a problem if somebody couldn't pay, and once or twice I remember some shouting. Mr. Grant had a bit of difficulty keeping managers, which was rather ironic since he was in charge of personnel at the mill. There was a whole succession of managers, usually in couples. The wife would do the cooking and the husband would do the yard work, snow shoveling, that sort of thing."

Lynne tried to imagine a circumstance under which boarders upstairs might not notice that down in the cellar a couple of young people were being entombed in concrete. Could it be done without the residents being aware? Possibly. The way the bodies were curved around the circular well would have minimized the amount of cement and effort required to bury the bodies. A motivated workman—and surely whoever had done this was *highly* motivated—could have managed the whole business in a few hours, once the bodies were down the stairs.

"Were there a lot of managers because the job didn't pay very well or because Mr. Grant was difficult to work for?"

"I really have no idea," Helen said, "though it probably didn't pay at all. I think somebody told me once that free lodging and board was all Mr. Grant offered. That might explain the turnover. You know what they say about getting what you pay for."

"And you think most of the boarders who lived here worked at the mill?"

"Most is probably an exaggeration," Helen said. "*Many* would be more accurate. And you know, now that I think about it, I do believe that mill workers had some kind of priority, and a special rate for room and board."

Shades of Lowell and the boardinghouse dioramas. This homegrown version might have been smaller and served a more varied clientele, but in both cases the roomers had come from somewhere else and probably moved on afterward to still another location.

"The one who'd know about that is Charlotte Roberts," Helen said, craning her neck to find the woman. "She was Mr. Grant's secretary for years and years. There she is. Oh, Charlotte!"

A plump little woman turned at the sound of her name. "Yes, Helen?"

"Could we bother you for a moment?" Helen asked.

"Certainly." Charlotte Roberts was probably close to seventy, round and cheerful, with rosy cheeks and pure white curls. With the exception of Cindy Jackson, Lynne realized suddenly, nobody from the neighborhood—or the community, for that matter—seemed particularly young. What would happen to South Hadford when these stalwarts passed on?

"I was just talking with Lynne here about the period when this place was a boardinghouse," Helen said.

"I was wondering what happened to the records from back then," Lynne said.

If Lynne hadn't been looking right at Charlotte Roberts, she would have missed the slight tightening of the woman's shoulders, the brief narrowing of her eyes. Then she smiled and the moment passed. "Mr. Grant was always a bit proprietary about the boardinghouse," she said apologetically. "He kept all the records in his office in a separate file cabinet of his private affairs. I never had anything to do with them, apart from making up the deposit slips and putting the rent money into his special account."

"Would those records still be around?" Lynne asked.

"The police have already asked me that very question," Charlotte said, with just enough of a lilt in her voice to suggest that she rather liked being part of a murder investigation. "I told them that Mr. Grant retired eleven years ago and when he did he took all of his personal records with him. I packed the banker's boxes and there were at least a dozen of them. If Mrs. Grant didn't keep those records—and I can't imagine why she would, actually, what with downsizing everything to move into her daughter's place in West Hartford—I don't know how the police can ever hope to track down all the residents from that period."

Lynne had no idea herself.

Chapter 14

HE wouldn't have believed how anxious this waiting was making him. He'd never been much good at it, under any circumstances. Over time he'd gotten better but this, now, was like being ricocheted back through time.

It would all have been much simpler if Ralph had drowned. Still, the coma was buying time, and people sometimes lingered in comas for years.

The amount of publicity was terrifying. Surely they'd identify the bodies soon. It seemed incredible that they hadn't already, with all the forensic testing available.

He had truly believed all this was behind him, that all he had to do was look forward.

How dreadful to have been so wrong.

Chapter 15

PRISCILLA had given hundreds of parties in the course of her life.

Bridge parties, baby showers, wedding showers, welcomes to new officers' wives, farewells to wives who were being transferred. Children's birthday parties. Luncheons, brunches, afternoon teas. Cocktail parties before important base banquets and dinner dances. Seated dinner parties with multiple courses and vast quantities of liquor. Hen parties during periods of personal danger to the husbands who tied them all together, even a slumber party of sorts once during Vietnam when the Tet Offensive had everybody so worried.

By all accounts and in historical context, she regarded this afternoon's gathering as a clear success.

A sense of detente seemed to have been reached between Priscilla and her now-wary neighbors. All had rallied in support of Cindy and Doreen and nobody seemed to fault Priscilla personally for the notoriety that had overtaken this quiet residential neighborhood. Indeed, everybody had been politely reassuring. She wasn't entirely sure about Helen

Vincent down the block, but Helen's resentment seemed so long-standing that Priscilla doubted anybody could do much to change her mind.

But she'd worry about Helen Vincent later. Right now Priscilla felt tired and raggedy, ready to collapse into bed till morning. She might still be capable of throwing a good party, but the fact of the matter was that doing so wore her out.

Abby had helped with the cleanup and taken some of the leftover sandwiches home for her supper. Lynne and Jenna had shooed Abby out, finally, promising to finish up tidying the parlor, sending Priscilla upstairs to rest, saying they might go out for a drive later.

Where they could possibly need to go Priscilla hadn't been told, but Lynne had never been one to share information unless specifically prodded. Even then, getting anything out of her was impossible unless she wanted to share.

Up in her bedroom, Priscilla kicked off the shoes that were starting to pinch her feet, then stared at her reflection in the dresser mirror just long enough to determine that she looked every bit as worn out as she felt. Maybe Abby was right. Perhaps trying to run a bed-and-breakfast was more effort than she was capable of. Lynne seemed to be maintaining a deliberate neutrality, but Priscilla could sense that her daughter shared Abby's concerns.

And Jenna—well, Jenna was a child, really, and it didn't matter much what she thought. Jenna ought to be getting married anyway, finding some nice young man to share her life and give her some children. Priscilla felt perversely proud of being a great-grandmother to David's children, though she'd barely seen them and certainly hadn't developed any kind of real relationship with them.

She wasn't sure what to think about Jenna. Her granddaughter was a beautiful young woman, poised and well-mannered, but she seemed surprisingly wishy-washy about having a career, not like so many of those young girls today, acting as if they'd come right out of the womb ready to take over as somebody's vice-president of marketing. If Jenna had majored in something useful instead of English, then gotten a real job, she'd probably already be married. It was obvious that she'd be a good mother. Priscilla had watched her surreptitiously with young Bradley. Jenna didn't seemed to mind entertaining the youngster, and Bradley was a handful, no doubt about it.

Priscilla sighed, propped herself on a mountain of pink and white pillows, and picked up the TV remote. She needed to figure out something about how to handle television for the Maple Leaf Inn, yet another entry in the seemingly endless list of Major Decisions for Innkeepers. She certainly wasn't going to put televisions in the bedrooms. That would mar the sense of pleasant isolation she was hoping to foster among her guests, the illusion that they had gotten away from whatever rat races they ran in their daily lives. The Maple Leaf Inn was to be a retreat, and as such, really shouldn't have any modern communication at all, though Lynne had warned her against too much media isolation. There had to be, Lynne told her, a couple of daily newspaper subscriptions, as well as at least one good-sized television available for guest use. That TV, regrettably, would probably need to be in the parlor, though it could be camouflaged there by putting it in some attractive piece of furniture. She'd have to think about that some more.

She clicked the TV on and found the local evening news just beginning with Jennifer Martindale. Jennifer was one of her favorite local reporters, at least partly because she shared Priscilla's granddaughter's name and hair color. Come to think of it, Jenna would probably make an excellent TV reporter. Priscilla would have to think of some casual way to suggest this.

Jennifer Martindale wore burnt orange tonight, her blonde hair thick and curly, her deep brown eyes staring intently at the camera.

"A shocking identification of one of two bodies discovered earlier this week at South Hadford's Maple Leaf Inn," the anchor teased, as a picture of Priscilla's home and future business flashed behind her in the corner of the screen. "We'll be right back with details on this sensational story."

Shocking? Sensational? Whatever that meant, it couldn't be good. As the picture changed to a commercial for a headache remedy, Priscilla yelled for Lynne and Jenna. She felt a headache of her own begin radiating at her temples.

LYNNE reacted instinctively to her mother's urgent scream, racing up the steps to Priscilla's bedroom with Jenna at her heels. They found Priscilla hyperventilating on her bed, staring wide-eyed at the television.

"They identified one of them," Priscilla said, between gasps. "You know, from—" She pointed downward. "Oh, my goodness, I feel like I'm having some kind of a fit. My heart is just racing."

"Take it easy, Mom." Lynne put a protective arm around her mother's shoulders. "Whatever's happened, we can deal with it. Take a deep breath now. Easy does it." She sat beside her mother on the bed as Jenna sprawled on the floor. Lynne could feel Priscilla's slight body quiver as she took her mother's hand in her own. She wondered if she had become so inured to her mother's histrionics that she would fail to notice if she actually ever did need an ambulance.

The commercial ended, and the picture changed to a blonde anchorwoman with too many teeth staring into the camera with what appeared to be genuine excitement. The now-familiar photograph of the Maple Leaf Inn was behind her in the top right corner of the screen.

"I'm Jennifer Martindale," the woman announced, "with the award-winning Channel Three News. This afternoon, police made a shocking identification of one of two bodies found earlier this week in the basement of a South Hadford bed-and-breakfast."

The picture of the Maple Leaf Inn was replaced by a color portrait of a young woman. Lustrous black hair fell straight past her shoulders from a middle part, and straight bangs brushed her eyebrows. She was pretty despite a rather large square jaw, and she was made up in the style of sixties Carnaby Street, with thick black eyeliner and silvery white lipstick. It was clearly a professional portrait, though it didn't have the mass-produced look of a graduation shot.

The anchor continued. "Dental records confirm that the long search for shipping heiress Sydney Shackleford is finally over. Shackleford was last seen in late 1970 and was the subject of a widespread search the following year when she failed to appear for an annual family meeting at the Shackleford family compound in the White Mountains. Channel Three's Misty Davis reports."

Misty Davis began with a voice-over as the scene switched to a press conference in front of a government building. "Here in Concord this afternoon, police made a shocking revelation about the identity of a young woman found entombed in a South Hadford basement earlier this week."

Lynne recognized Detective Niles Burton, standing behind a large cluster of microphones, a massive electronic bouquet. He looked neither happy nor comfortable.

"This afternoon," Detective Burton said, "we notified the family of Sydney Shackleford that dental records confirmed her identity as one of the two victims recovered from the South Hadford site."

Good. He hadn't mentioned the Maple Leaf Inn by name. Lynne crossed her fingers as he continued. At least four or five people in New England were unaware of the precise location where all this had taken place. If Sydney Shackleford was from a prominent family, as they were hinting, this might well become a national story. Then everybody would know. Maybe it was time to pack up Mom and take a road trip.

"At this time," Detective Burton continued, "we still have no identification of the male victim. We hope that anybody who might have information which might help identify him will contact the New Hampshire State Police." A number flashed on the screen.

Now the newscast cut to Misty Davis, a tiny woman with black pixie-cut hair and distinctly Asian features. She stood beside a group of white-barked birch trees spilling golden

leaves near a covered bridge. A sign just behind her read: PRI-
VATE PROPERTY. NO TRESPASSING. Lynne watched a lazy leaf
flutter to the ground beside the reporter as she began to
speak.

"Jennifer, a prominent New England family found closure
today after wondering for three and a half decades where
their daughter and sister, shipping heiress Sydney Shackleford, had gone."

Closure? Lynne had trouble buying that statement, even
without knowing anything more. Surely the identification of
a child missing for so many years would rip open deep and
painful wounds. And what exactly did it mean to be a shipping heiress? Had her family founded UPS?

"Shackleford was twenty-two and a recent graduate of
Radcliffe College when she missed her family's annual
Christmas gathering here at this scenic White Mountain re-
treat," Misty Davis continued.

Another photograph filled the screen. Sydney didn't look
quite as artfully pretty in this one. The thick eyeliner and
white lipstick were gone, and the bangs had grown out into
wings of straight ebony hair. She wore a black graduation
gown and held a matching mortarboard in her left hand. A
white peace symbol decorated the top of the mortarboard.

She was flanked by an unhappy looking middle-aged couple who seemed to be her parents. The man wore a three-
piece suit and fairly oozed controlled anger, clenching what
seemed to be the family jawline and looking as if he'd prefer
to be hiking up Mount Washington in midwinter. The woman
wore a floral dress, white gloves and a pillbox hat with a little veil. She offered a tentative smile, one that did not signal
any sort of enjoyment. A girl of perhaps twelve or thirteen
stood next to her mother. Off to the side, looking alienated in
the studied fashion of the young Marlon Brando, stood a
young man with a prominent jaw and a shock of unruly black
shoulder-length hair. All of them—except for the mother,
whose chilly demeanor suggested she was probably the type
to insist on being *called* "Mother"—looked as if Dick Tracy

or Clutch Cargo had perched on a branch of the Shackleford family tree.

"This afternoon, Roderick Shackleford spoke for his family," the reporter continued in a voice-over as the visuals switched to a middle-aged man who stood beside the NO TRESPASSING sign and spoke into half a dozen broadcast microphones.

For a moment, Lynne thought it was the father, trapped in time. Then she realized that Roderick must be Sydney's brother, the one reflexively rebelling in his sister's graduation photo. His hair was short now, salt and pepper, and he was dressed in woodsy casual, wearing a red plaid flannel shirt.

As he began to speak, he seemed genuinely moved. "My family has hoped and prayed all these years that Sydney would one day come home. We are brokenhearted to have found her this way. We ask your indulgence and respect for our loss."

Indulgence and respect. Roderick Shackleford was comfortable in front of the bank of microphones, held himself with an easy confidence. When he stopped speaking, shouted questions filled the air, lapping over one another.

"Who was Sydney with?"

"Did you ever meet her boyfriend?"

"When did you last see your sister?"

"What was the family quarrel about?"

"When did you first learn this was Sydney?"

"How is your mother holding up?"

"Do you have any idea who she was with?"

Shackleford raised a hand to silence the reporters. "We know no more than you do at this point. If anyone has any information that will help to identify the young man who was with my sister, please contact the New Hampshire State Police, for the sake of his family." He glanced around, then spoke quickly, heading off another round of questions. "That's all. Thank you very much for respecting my family's privacy."

As if they had a choice, Lynne thought. That gate across

the entrance to the covered bridge looked sturdy and substantial, and surely a family that could afford property referred to as a "compound" could also afford to post a guard or two.

She still had absolutely no idea who Sydney Shackleford might have been or why she'd run away from what seemed to be substantial wealth, but it was clear that this story was getting larger by the minute.

As the news moved into another commercial break, Lynne turned to her mother.

"Jenna, hit the mute button, would you?" The TV went silent. "This is good news, I think, Mom. We'll probably have a bunch of looky-loos here again tomorrow, but now there are other areas for them to follow up on, so with a little luck we'll be pretty much left alone. In any case, I think it's time we all went away for a few days."

"How can we possibly go with all of this going on?" Priscilla wailed.

"How can we *not* go?" Lynne countered.

"I thought that tomorrow was supposed to be the day we went to Concord," Jenna put in. She'd been sitting quietly on the floor through all of this. Lynne wondered what she was thinking.

"It is indeed," Lynne said. "We have a room for two at a very nice B&B down there, and I'll call to see if there's room for one more. If need be, I can stay in a nearby motel and the two of you can stay at the B&B. That'll give you some experience at the other side of the inn keeping experience, Mom. The place is called the Concord Arms and it's supposed to be very nice. It was recommended by one of my clients. And it's not too far from Orchard House and all the other transcendental sites."

"I couldn't force you into some shabby motel," Priscilla protested. Without much emphasis.

At the moment the idea of being in a room of her own with her mother housed elsewhere was remarkably appealing, no matter how Spartan that room might be. But Lynne put on her game face and squeezed Priscilla's shoulders once again.

"That probably won't even be necessary. Just let me make a phone call or two. I wouldn't be surprised if we can all stay together." Actually Lynne *would* be surprised, this being October in New England, when hostelries were jammed to the rafters with out-of-towners. But who knows? They could get lucky.

Priscilla closed her eyes and gave a deep sigh. "If you're sure I won't be a burden."

Chapter 16

LYNNE grew alarmed at how agitated Priscilla became as they prepared to leave the Maple Leaf Inn the following morning. Already there'd been three reporters out to the house and Priscilla was dithering about, wringing her hands like Lady MacBeth on speed. So Lynne called Detective O'Keefe, whom she'd begun to think of as "their" law enforcement officer, in what was rapidly becoming a multi-cop situation. He answered immediately and seemed to understand when she asked for help.

"I'll post a patrol car at the entrance to the cul-de-sac," he promised. "We're seeing a lot of outsiders already, and I think you people are wise to go off for a few days. Is there somewhere I can reach you?"

It didn't seem an optional request. Lynne gave him her cell phone number and allowed herself a secret smile as she added, "Of course you can always reach us through my aunt Abigail." She could practically feel him tensing over the phone. What *had* happened between the young William

O'Keefe and the never-young Abigail Chenonceau, anyway, Lynne wondered as she hung up the phone.

"Okay," she announced finally, as Jenna reorganized the box full of guidebooks that would be sharing the backseat with her. "Time to hit the road."

They passed through Nashua, which was surprisingly big and busy, full of light industry and mail-order businesses taking internet advantage of New Hampshire's sales tax, a nice, precise, easy-to-compute zero percent. West of Nashua they crossed into Massachusetts in a light but chilly rain, then continued on a little-traveled and heavily wooded back highway.

Soon they found themselves alone on the road beneath a canopy of trees that met across the two-lane highway. There was less color in the foliage as they moved farther south, and Lynne crossed her fingers that the northern peak would last until she got up to Vermont and northern New Hampshire.

Long before she bought the Booked for Travel agency, Lynne had been noted for collecting random bits of information. This habit was serving her well in this new line of work, giving her the opportunity to appear knowledgeable about areas where she in fact had only the sketchiest awareness. Superficiality had its benefits in the business world.

The bit of trivia that clung to her as the three generations of women headed toward Concord had to do with New England's forests.

When the Pilgrims arrived in the seventeenth century, about three-quarters of New England had been wooded. Over the next few hundred years, relentless clear-cutting reduced that percentage to somewhere around one quarter. At that point, the settlers had looked around and realized that the prosperous farming they had envisioned when they cut down all the trees would never be a reality in this harsh and rocky soil. So they'd switched course once again. Systematic reforestation over recent decades had swung the balance back to three-quarters forested land once again, though these woods would never be the same as the old-growth forests they replaced. Hence the booming trade in recycled hardwoods from dismantled buildings, like the house on the lot that had been appended to the First Congregational cemetery in South Hadford.

At a full-service back-road gas station, a taciturn fellow filled the rental car's tank at a rate some sixty cents less per gallon than the current price in San Diego County. Stretching her legs, Lynne asked the attendant how he was doing in the rain.

"Can't complain," he answered. "I'm not freezing yet."

And there you had it, the stoicism that had settled and maintained this region for so long. Somebody—Alistair Cooke, perhaps—had once remarked that if America had been settled from west to east, New England would still be uninhabited.

Small signs along the way told of Christmas tree farms, handmade doll shops, antique stores. One claimed THICKLY SETTLED, though it seemed hyperbole. Even on back roads, it didn't take very long to reach Concord. And as they arrived, they had their first serious disagreement of the day.

While planning the trip back home, Lynne had orginally hoped to stay at Longfellow's Wayside Inn in nearby Sudbury, a hostelry in business nearly three hundred years. When she learned that the place was booked solid for the entire month of October, she'd gone to Plan B. Once she saw the charming grounds of the client-recommended Concord Arms, a short distance from the equally charming Monument Square in Concord, she was quite content to be right there in town. Even better, she had managed to finagle a second room because of a last-minute cancellation when she called that morning.

This should have led to group exultation, but then Priscilla kicked up a fuss about who should be bunking with whom. As they squabbled outside before checking in, Lynne finally grabbed *The Story of the Wayside Inn*—how many hotels had entire books written about them, anyway?—and announced that the single would go to the person who picked the single digit closest to the last number on the last page of the book.

The book's index ended on page 338 and Jenna, who guessed eight right on the button, won a room of her own.

JENNA had been rereading Henry David Thoreau's *Walden* in the car today, doing her best to ignore the bickering between Lynne and Priscilla. By the time they finished with lunch, she was ready to throttle her grandmother, and was fervently grateful to have her own room.

Priscilla surprised her, then, by announcing that she'd stay in this afternoon and rest. "I'm sure you'll have a much nicer time at Walden Pond without having the albatross of a grandmother hanging around your neck."

As Jenna struggled to think of some kind of diplomatic response to this, her mother spoke up.

"You're never an albatross," Lynne said. "I think of you as more of a swan."

And they were off.

Jenna had feared crowds at Walden Pond, a commercialism that would destroy her appreciation of a place she had long regarded as mystical. To her enormous relief, the parking lot was nearly empty and there was nobody else in sight.

A replica of Thoreau's ten-by-fifteen-foot cabin stood near the parking lot, and she studied it with a sense of wonder. She could understand the grief at the loss of a beloved brother that had driven Thoreau to seek simplicity here, and she'd seen enough of her friends take up occupations they didn't really like to know exactly why he had sought respite from the family pencil-making business. When Thoreau wrote about "lives of quiet desperation" he knew what he was talking about.

"You say he suffered from depression?" Lynne asked, breaking what had already become an agreeable silence.

"How ever did you guess?"

Desolation and depression permeated the tiny, hand-built cabin and its simple furnishings. Today's drizzle, which had probably kept a lot of tourists from visiting, only under-

scored the sense of loss. The most famous picture of
Thoreau, made years after his two-year sojourn at Walden,
showed a sad-eyed fellow indeed.

"'I went to the woods,'" Jenna quoted now, "'because I
wished to live deliberately, to front only the essential facts of
life, and see if I could not learn what it had to teach, and not,
when I came to die, discover that I had not lived.' That's
from *Walden*. He lived out here for two years, but he wasn't
in seclusion all the time. He'd go into town a lot to see Emerson."

They crossed the highway and followed a brief trail to the
shores of Walden Pond. It looked more like a small lake, actually, with a sandy beach at one end. Most of the foliage
was still green, with hints of red and yellow differentiating
the shapes of individual trees.

As far as they could tell, they were the only humans
around. Jenna could almost feel her concerns melting away
as a strong sense of peace overtook her.

"I'm going to walk all the way around," she announced.

Lynne smiled. "I think that sounds like a splendid idea.
Would you mind some company?"

Jenna was surprised, but only for a moment. "Of course
not." She realized too late that she had hesitated, and worried
that her mother would feel hurt.

"I won't jabber," Lynne promised as they set off, "though I
have to say that if I see something wonderful I'm going to
pipe up."

"I wouldn't recognize you if you didn't," Jenna told her
easily. "And I'm happy to have you along."

"I just wish you could have had your sunset over the gold
and red foliage. I know how much that meant to you."

"I don't mind," Jenna said, surprised to realize that she
really didn't.

LATER, as they browsed in the gift shop after circumnavigat-
ing the pond, Lynne said, "You know, I think maybe your

grandmother had the right idea. I'm half tempted to go take a nap of my own."

Jenna could see that her mother was a bit ragged around the edges, and not without cause. "Then maybe I'll go on the tour of the Old Manse this afternoon. I know Grandma won't want to do that, and you didn't seem too terribly enthusiastic either." Lynne rolled her eyes in confirmation. The Old Manse, longtime home to various Emersons and the newly-weds Nathaniel and Sophia Hawthorne, overlooked the North Bridge where the "shot heard 'round the world" had been fired. Location, location, location.

"Then we can all go to Orchard House tomorrow morning," Jenna went on. "I know Grandma did say she particularly wanted to see Louisa May Alcott's home."

"That sounds perfect." Her mother sounded almost relieved. "Tell you what. Drop me off at the Concord Arms and leave me your room key so I won't bother Grandma. I'll see if I can get any out-of-town newspapers and find out what kind of coverage the Sydney Shackleford story is getting."

Jenna groaned. "Thanks a heap. I'd actually managed to forget about all that. But you can probably find out more than you want to know online. Help yourself to my laptop."

She returned her attention to the gift shop, stocked with every imaginable take on Thoreau and Walden and transcen-dentalism. She felt splendidly at home here, where the most important decision to be made was whether to buy the sweat-shirt saying "Simplify, Simplify" or the one for the "Thoreau Sauntering Society." She rejected out of hand the shirt for the Walden Woods Project, despite its cool logo. Somehow it felt too glitzy, too Hollywood, though she was grateful that con-temporary celebrities had succeeded in thwarting commercial development here. But when she tried to imagine Henry David Thoreau at a Hollywood benefit, or even conversing one-on-one with some rock musician out in the woods, she came up empty.

Eventually she settled on "Simplify, Simplify," picking up an application for the Thoreau Society and a bumper sticker that read: "All Good Things are Wild and Free." She wasn't sure she qualified as either, and she certainly wasn't making any significant moves in those directions. Thoreau probably wouldn't have objected to a job in a West LA bookstore, but who knows what he or any of his compadres might be like in the twenty-first century?

She stopped for a moment to consider.

None of the Transcendentalists would be particularly employable, not even Emerson, who'd had the good fortune to live at a time when a writer could still carve out a significant living lecturing and producing philosophical essays. Today he'd probably be teaching at Harvard or Princeton, publishing the occasional learned tome through a university press. The handsome Nathaniel Hawthorne might be living in Malibu with his lovely wife Sophia, doing screen adaptations for his own novels. The intellectual adventuress Margaret Fuller could be the chair of the Women's Studies Department at Smith or Wellesley and a regular contributor to the *New York Review of Books.*

Bronson Alcott would still be wistful about the end of the 1960s, when he'd have been at the helm of some commune with an experimental school, but he'd be comfortably supported by his hardworking and prolific daughter Louisa May.

Louisa May would likely be the most commercially successful of the lot. With her talent for creating captivating and accessible fiction, she could literally write her own ticket. Her books would debut at Number One on the bestseller lists, and she'd appear on only the best talk shows, explaining just how the antics of that wacky Alcott family had found their way into her fiction once again.

And what of Thoreau? It would all depend, Jenna decided, on where he happened to be born. Back in the nineteenth century he'd been born in Concord and had never strayed too far from home, preferring his own two feet as a mode of transportation. To find the same degree of isolation that had fed his soul in Concord, he'd need a way of steering clear of the trappings of modern society, no small accomplishment in a global community. Folks who went off to live alone in the woods these days were considered crackpots or worse, and often with ample reason. The Unabomber, after all, had lived alone in a one room house he built himself, writing long philosophical treatises; modern society might never again trust a self-sufficient forest loner. But whatever Thoreau's shortcomings—and there didn't seem to be many of them—a contemporary version would be a peaceable man, whose stand on civil disobedience might lead to the occasional op-ed essay or NPR interview.

And, except for Thoreau, the entire gang would probably be reachable via links from http://www.transcendental.com.

Chapter 17

LYNNE added the local *Middlesex News, The Boston Globe,* and *The Boston Herald* to the *Manchester Guardian,* which she had surreptitiously brought along when they left in the morning, and settled herself on the covered balcony of the second story of the Concord Arms. All the papers had Sydney Shackleford on page one. Lynne started with Manchester and then moved on to Massachusetts. She hadn't been able to find the *New York Times,* but she figured she could get that online using Jenna's laptop.

At the moment, she didn't even want to think about how widespread the news of Sydney's identification might be. Certainly the story would have gone out on all the wire services. By now it was probably on junk TV and in foreign papers from Istanbul to Ho Chi Minh City.

The basics were the same in all accounts.

Sydney Ann Shackleford was the second of four children born to Reginald and Helene Shackleford, and she made her first appearance on November 25, 1948—Thanksgiving Day. The union of Reg and Helene had consolidated two significant New England fortunes. He was a war hero and she was a debutante. Helene Blanton was descended from the banking Blantons of Boston and Reginald Shackleford's family had dominated New England ports for centuries: slavers from Africa, whalers to all corners of the globe, explorers to the Arctic, all distilled down over time to the current fleet of multinational cargo ships.

The scions of both families had been shrewd in their investments, so shrewd indeed that Shackleford Shipping had briefly attracted the attentions of Teddy Roosevelt and the trustbusters, who reluctantly moved on to fry larger fish. By the time Sydney came along, the Shacklefords had extensive landholdings in the White Mountains and Nantucket, while the Blantons wintered on Beacon Hill and summered on the Cape. The two families had produced bankers, lawyers, and executives scattered all over New England, including several Shacklefords who were presently full-time employees of the Shackleford Foundation.

A dozen cousins from the two families had grown up together through the fifties and sixties, a less political, more Protestant version of the Kennedys. The boys prepped at Exeter and the girls at Miss Porter's. Some went to Harvard and others to Yale, but nobody left New England and even the low achievers somehow managed to muddle their way through prestigious schools and retain those all-important student deferments during Vietnam.

Not all had aged gracefully, and some hadn't aged at all. For every one who toiled with the Peace Corps, somebody else had OD'd in an inopportune location. Most had eventually grown into responsibility, including several lawyers, a federal judge, and a preeminent neonatologist.

But even adulthood hadn't saved them all. Jack Blanton, Sydney's closest family ally growing up, became a Cantor Fitzgerald vice president and left final messages on his wife's cell phone and their home answering machine from the World Trade Center on the morning of September 11, 2001. He was above the flames, he told her, there was no way out, he loved her and the kids, and he had chosen to jump rather

than burn. And Sydney's youngest sister, Sarah, had taken a
leave of absence from her work in Houston with NASA to
follow her sailing heritage and cross the Atlantic solo. Sarah
left from Nantucket on the misty morning of her fortieth
birthday and was never heard from again.

And Sydney—well, nobody really knew what had happened to Sydney, until yesterday. She'd been reportedly spot-
ted in locations from Puerto Vallarta to Bangladesh, and the
Peace Corps cousin in Malawi had been certain he'd once
seen her briefly in a Johannesburg airport.

"IS this a private party, or can anybody attend?" Priscilla's
voice came from behind Lynne, who'd become so engrossed
in reading about Sydney and her family that she'd all but forgotten her own relatives.

"Pull up a chair," Lynne urged. "I've just been reading
about the Shackleford family. Seems we really stepped in it
this time."

Priscilla shuddered. "I don't know *what* I'm going to do
about all this. Abby just looks down her nose at me and
somehow manages to make it seem like all this is my fault. I
wish Harvey were alive. He'd know what to do." Harvey was
the heating contractor from Buffalo, the third and final Mr.
Priscilla.

"I know. It's tough to have to suddenly make all your own
decisions when you aren't used to it. That was really a problem for me when Monty died. So where do you usually get
your financial advice these days?" Lynne hoped she sounded
offhand, maybe even a little bored.

It worked. "Well, Mr. Colwhistle, of course," Priscilla
said.

Once her mother opened this door, Lynne decided to drive
a tank through it. "How do you get in touch with Mr. Colwhistle when you need to talk to him?"

"I leave him a message, of course."

"Where?"

"At his office." Priscilla's tone was growing clipped, her defenses raised. She was starting to realize just what she'd done here.

"Would that be the Manchester office?"

"It would. And don't you get any ideas about going behind my back, missy."

Oooh. She *was* upset. Time to change the subject. Or, more correctly, to return to the subject.

"I've been reading all about Sydney Shackleford and her family and I can't come up with any reason in the world why she would be in your basement." Lynne gestured at the newspapers.

"Well, maybe she got lost on her way to Mont Blanc. You know the police said they were drug addicts. Those people frequently overdose and kill themselves."

But they didn't often cement themselves into other people's basement floors. In any case, there was no evidence that Sydney and her male companion had done anything more than roll and smoke a little weed.

"Mom, Mont Blanc is way up in the White Mountains and the commune where she lived is up north too."

"Well, maybe the boy was from around South Hadford."

"And nobody in the area would make the association? How could that be?"

Priscilla shrugged. "They die, they move away, who knows what happens?" She looked at her watch. "I spoke with the woman who runs this place and she told me there's a very nice television room in the basement."

They both let that one pass. The basement of the Maple Leaf Inn would not become a television room, ever.

"She also told me the local news begins in"—she checked her watch—"forty-five minutes."

"I'll be there," Lynne promised. "But right now I want to finish reading all this coverage, and go online to see what else I can turn up."

Both Boston papers ran sidebars about Mont Blanc, the White Mountain compound where those Shacklefords not summering in Europe spent black fly season and where all family members gathered for holidays. Sydney's mother had been making cranberry sauce for forty-five, the story went, when she went into labor with Sydney.

The press was almost never allowed across the covered bridge leading to Mont Blanc, though WGBH had once convinced the Shacklefords—several of whom were on their board—that a tour of the place would make splendid public television for a PBS fund-raiser. That program was being re-broadcast tonight.

Mont Blanc's large central lodge, the *Globe* reported, was filled with dead animals, some standing (the grizzly from Alaska), some lying (favorite dogs permanently curled by various firesides), scores of miscellaneous beheaded mammals, and at least one coiled rattlesnake. A dozen surrounding "cabins" were the province of various families, and each was large enough to comfortably house at least eight. Communal facilities included various swimming pools, saunas and tennis courts, cross-country ski trails, and a year-round ice-skating rink, though this was no longer used on a regular basis. An indoor arcade offered a world-class collection of antique pinball machines and enough modern versions to keep even the most jaded contemporary youngsters satisfied.

The *Herald* made it sound like Pleasure Island, the young cousins and their descendants being the jackasses.

The *Globe* concentrated more on Sydney, who had been, by all accounts, an extremely intelligent and headstrong young woman. She had donated some of her stock in Shackleford Shipping to the Black Panther Party in 1968 as partial retribution for her family's undeniable complicity in—no, absolute reliance on—the African slave trade. Slaves, molasses, and rum. For over a century, the Shacklefords had them all in motion, all the time.

But while Sydney might have suffered passing guilt over slavery, her overriding political concern in her young adulthood had been opposition to the Vietnam War. She was active in the Student Mobilization against the War and almost didn't graduate because she had spent so much time working for Mobe. But she did get a diploma from Radcliffe, soon to be totally subsumed into Harvard, in June of 1970. She had considered entering the Peace Corps, as her cousin Marshall had, but told friends that since the Peace Corps represented the corrupt American government, it was therefore unacceptable.

She moved instead to a commune in northern New Hampshire, a place that made and sold candles to support the group's various activities. Incredibly, White Mountain Candles, the corporate entity that had grown from this haphazard hippie commercial venture, was still in business, a respectable earth-friendly company that made a wide range of candles sold mostly through high-end gift shops and tony mail-order catalogues. White Mountain Candles, the *Guardian* reported, had started embedding pine needles and berries in holiday candles long before their competitors.

The last time any of her family members saw Sydney Shackleford was at Thanksgiving dinner at Mont Blanc in 1970, one day following her twenty-second birthday. She had brought a male guest with her who was introduced only as Weezer and had announced plans to spend Christmas in California. Several months later when Sydney failed to appear at an annual family meeting, the Shacklefords attempted to locate her and trace the mysterious Weezer, but none of the people at the New Hampshire commune admitted knowing him, and they all said Sydney had left for good before Christmas.

The *New York Times* online carried the story in their business section. Sydney Shackleford had, the *Times* reported, been spearheading a movement among her generation of Shacklefords to sell off some of the extensive family holdings in real estate. In particular, she favored donating several hundred acres of the family property in the White Mountains to Open Door, a Boston-based group working to remove racial prejudice from education. In her absence, the idea had been tabled and eventually abandoned.

AUNT Abby called Lynne's cell phone just before the news came on. "They've identified the boy," she told her. "He was a military deserter. Be careful how you tell your mother. You know what a patriot she is."

"Indeed," Lynne agreed. "Was the boy local?"

"I don't know, and I don't want to tie up your line," Abigail said, which actually meant that she had direct dialed this call herself and felt it had gone on quite long enough. "I suspect the police will be calling you shortly."

"Did the police call and tell you?"

"No," Abigail said. "That O'Keefe boy came by. He's put a roadblock at the turn to your cul-de-sac to keep out the riffraff and reporters. I told him he should speak to you directly."

Lynne's phone beeped, the polite little sound it made when there was a call waiting. "I think that's him calling right now," she told her aunt. "Let me get this and I'll call you back later."

"No need," Abigail said, and hung up.

IT was actually Detective Niles Burton of the Major Crimes Unit on the line, and once again he wanted to talk to Priscilla, who waved her arms frantically to signify that she did not want to talk to him now or ever. She couldn't quite bring herself to leave the room, however, and listened attentively as Lynne spoke with the detective.

"His name was Eldon Weibeck," Detective Burton said. "He was AWOL from the Army dating to September 1970, when he failed to return from leave to see his family in New Bedford, Mass." So he'd already been an official deserter at Thanksgiving dinner at Mont Blanc. No wonder he and Sydney had been evasive about his identity.

"How did you identify him?" Lynne asked.

The detective hesitated a moment. "Dental records, after his mother came forward. Apparently he and Sydney visited her around the time he was supposed to report back, and he told his mother he wouldn't go back to Nam. He said he was going to Canada. That was the last she ever saw or heard of him. She recognized Sydney from the pictures in the papers yesterday, but she said her son had only introduced her as Minerva, and that Sydney didn't say much."

Minerva, the goddess of wisdom? And a silent Minerva at that? Uncharacteristically shy behavior for the outspoken young Ms. Shackleford. What had her relationship to the deserter been? Girlfriend? Fellow activist? They might never know.

Lynne thought of poor Eldon Weibeck's mother, waiting patiently for a third of a century to finally learn the awful fate of her son. She'd have been afraid to report him missing, back then, knowing he was AWOL and would be arrested if he showed up publicly. There had been a general military amnesty back in the late seventies, but Lynne wasn't sure if that applied to deserters or only to draft dodgers.

"Is his mother still in New Bedford?" Lynne asked. "Because that's actually where we were headed next. And I'm sure that my mother would like to convey her condolences personally."

"That's up to Mrs. Weibeck," the detective said. "All I can promise to do is pass along your request."

Chapter 18

ALL these years, he had never known who they were, that boy and girl, only that they had been where they shouldn't be.

He had come to realize, over time, that they certainly weren't who he'd thought they were back then, but his awareness went no further than that. Their anonymity had soothed him into believing that nobody would ever miss them, that nobody would come looking, that nobody cared.

Now that belief was blown to pieces.

As he read and listened to the reports about them, he felt a sinking sense of despair. No longer anonymous, they were somehow more alive now than they had been before.

He had bumbled it back then and he'd bumbled it with Ralph. He couldn't have the old man waking up, that was for sure. He'd blown his chance in the privacy of the streambed. Now he'd have to risk something much more public.

He could almost feel his blood pressure rising . . . but wait! That might just be what would save him.

Chapter 19

LYNNE wasn't surprised to find the Weibeck story all over the following morning's papers.

Priscilla buried her pretty little head in the sand and urged Lynne to set them aside until after the visit to Orchard House. "Such a lovely morning," Priscilla said, over a delicious breakfast of airy waffles served with apples poached in cinnamon, and nary a burnt anything. And it was actually the truth. The drizzle seemed to have stopped and the sun was shining. "Why spoil it with this nasty business?"

They were seated at one of several small tables in a cheerful, brightly lit breakfast room. Freshly cut bronze mums were in little vases on all the tables and the innkeeper herself freshened coffee mugs and teacups.

"Because we're smack in the middle of this nasty business," Lynne reminded her. "Although if we were back there in South Hadford, it would be even worse. We'd have all kinds of press and police bothering us." It was starting to feel a bit as if she and her traveling companions were also on the lam. "But never mind. Why don't you finish packing up while I read the papers? Then as soon as Jenna gets back and showers, we can check out and head for Orchard House."

So while Priscilla busied herself in the room she and Lynne had shared, and Jenna ran through the historic streets of Concord, Lynne learned that police were actively investigating the possibility that Eldon Weibeck had died in the process of assuming a new identity. The commune that evolved into White Mountain Candles, the *Globe* alleged, had served as a sort of informal Underground Railroad for Vietnam deserters, somehow providing them with new identities. That would certainly fit with Sydney's known history as an antiwar activist.

And maybe she'd combined business and pleasure with the AWOL Private Weibeck. It wasn't possible to tell if he was a good-looking boy, since the picture of him that was in all the papers was a standard military portrait, designed to strip any semblance of individuality from the young soldier/sailor/marine. In this case, draftee Weibeck was with the U.S. Army, or had been until he decided to take an early departure. Lynne would not have recognized him from that picture if she'd run into him on the street, and she assumed that once he decided to desert, he had immediately begun growing his hair. Young men with short hair in 1970 were highly conspicuous outside of the military.

If he'd been linked romantically—or merely sexually, this being the anything-goes sixties—with Sydney, all sorts of interesting questions arose. Where, for instance, had the Radcliffe econ major encountered the working class draftee? And how on earth had they ended up in the basement of the Maple Leaf Inn?

Lynne gathered up the papers and went back to her room, where Priscilla was repairing some problem with the manicure on her left pinky. She hadn't yet gotten around to packing up the three bags she had brought, claiming that since they would probably be gone several days, she would need all sorts of things, including five pairs of shoes.

Lynne, however, always traveled light and took as little out of her bags as possible when she stopped. Packing up took only a matter of minutes, long enough to zip her cosmetics bag and put it and her nightshirt into the bag. As she zipped the suitcase, Detective Burton called on the cell phone.

"Mrs. Weibeck says she'd like to talk to you," he told her, sounding frankly incredulous. "I said that you were likely to be in her area within the next few days."

"Have you learned anything more about what he was doing with Sydney Shackleford?" Lynne asked. "Apart from what's in the morning papers?"

"Haven't seen them, so I don't know," he told her.

BUT he was fibbing, it seemed. The phone rang again as they parked at Orchard House, where they intended to take the first tour of the day so they could move on as quickly as possible to New Bedford.

"Ms. Montgomery?" It was a female voice, very self-assured. Also totally unfamiliar.

"Yes?" Lynne answered warily.

"I'm Marita Freeman from the *Boston Globe*."

Swell. Her byline was on the lead story about Sydney and Weezer and the Underground Railroad.

"Could you hold just a moment?" Lynne turned to Jenna and Priscilla. "You guys go on in and get tickets. I'll be right with you." As they headed indoors, Lynne sat down on a weathered wooden bench and resumed the conversation. "How did you get this number?"

"I called your travel agency in California," the woman said. Give her a few points for persistency and spadework. More than a few, actually, if she'd uncovered the alleged underground railroad so quickly.

"I see. And why are you calling?" As if Lynne didn't know.

"I was hoping to get your mother's reaction to the identification of the bodies in her basement, and to the probability that Eldon Weibeck died because he was a fugitive."

"I'm afraid my mother isn't speaking to the press," Lynne told her. "Sorry."

"Perhaps you can help me, then." Before Lynne could cut her off, the reporter went on. "I'm sure you've heard that Eldon Weibeck was an Army deserter. Well, I'm looking into the possibility that he was one of a number of military deserters who were associated with Sydney Shackleford's commune in the late sixties and early seventies."

"Excuse me?"

"There were a number of very political people living there at the time," Marita Freeman told her. "A few years back, a woman who was running for state office in Vermont had an opponent who claimed she had been part of a group who smuggled draft dodgers into Canada."

This sounded strange to Lynne. Why would anybody need to be smuggled? The Canadian border was relatively open and thousands of miles long. The people who had gone to Canada to escape the draft had generally been young white men of means, guys who could slip in discreetly and not attract attention.

"And did the woman deny it?"

The reporter chuckled. "But of course. It opened an interesting dialogue, however. And the commune where she had lived is the one in New Hampshire where Sydney Shackleford also lived."

"It sounds like you ought to be talking to that woman, not me," Lynne said.

"I have, of course. But she hasn't been willing to contribute much."

Hmmm. Was this because she didn't know anything or because she was afraid of being considered an accessory to some kind of crime? "Did she win that election?"

"No."

"Did she lose because of those allegations?"

"It's possible," Marita Freeman said, "but it's more likely that she lost because her opponent outspent her ten to one. Vermont is a poor state, and a little bit of campaign financing goes a long way."

"I don't think I understand what any of this has to do with the Maple Leaf Inn," Lynne said.

"That's the big question," the reporter said. "What was Sydney doing with the Weibeck guy in South Hadford?"

"If I knew I'd tell you," Lynne said. It was starting to occur to her that a friendly reporter could become an asset, particularly since the police were so uncommunicative. "I'd tell you to ask the cops, but I daresay you already have." Something else occurred to her. "When was that commune started?"

Lynne wasn't sure if communes *started,* exactly, or if they morphed out of groups of people who were already living together. She'd known some people from UC Santa Cruz who went off to live communally, though she hadn't known them well. It had always been extremely informal and that was, she thought, the point.

"The summer of 1969," the reporter told her. "That was in a different location. They moved to the place in the White Mountains where Sydney lived in the spring of 1970. And that's the location they've used ever since. The candle factory is still there today."

"Was Sydney's money running that commune?"

"Good question. I don't know. It probably wasn't in the beginning, when she didn't live there, but I wouldn't be surprised to learn she was a major contributor. Problem is, nobody wants to talk about it."

JENNA had loved the card game *Authors* when she was young, and it had served as her introduction to many of the writers whose paths they were crossing on this trip. She could still tell you the four titles included for every author in the game, though she wouldn't pretend to be familiar with all of their work. James Fenimore Cooper (*The Deerslayer, The Spy, The Pathfinder, The Last of the Mohicans*) had bored her silly, and she'd managed to avoid Sir Walter Scott (*The Talisman, Ivanhoe, Kenilworth, The Lady of the Lake*) altogether.

What had drawn her to Louisa May Alcott (*Little Women, Little Men, Eight Cousins, An Old Fashioned Girl*) was, of course, the fact that she was the only girl in the deck. In this manly company, she was distinctly feminine, her soft gray hair pulled back in a curly chignon, white collar rimmed with lace, a cameo at her throat. This image was far removed, however, from other pictures Jenna had seen of Louisa as a dark and brooding young woman.

Of all the authors in the deck, Louisa May Alcott was the one Jenna had first read and loved.

Other writers featured on this trip weren't as striking, though Nathaniel Hawthorne had cut a dashing figure, with long blonde curls and a drooping moustache. Longfellow looked like Santa Claus and Mark Twain seemed downright scary. She realized now that the Twain shown here was the older fellow with bushy white hair sprouting everywhere, thrust repeatedly onto the lecture circuit because he was flat out of money, again and again. She was looking forward to seeing his house in Hartford, but for the moment, she was enthralled to be at Orchard House.

Jenna had watched the various film versions of *Little Women* before leaving, discovering, not to her surprise, that she preferred the most recent one. This was partly because the casting of Winona Ryder as Jo felt so accurate and partly (though she'd never admit this to her mother) because it was in color. Jenna had friends who'd been film majors at UCLA and they were always carrying on about their favorite classic black-and-white films, but Jenna had trouble appreciating them because they were so—well, colorless.

Their tour group gathered in the parlor where the young Alcotts had frequently hung a curtain to separate the dining room, which then became the stage for their many play productions. Jenna could almost feel the psychic energy.

"Louisa was twenty-five when her family moved here," the docent, a soft-spoken woman in her sixties, began. "The Alcotts lived in Orchard House from 1858 to 1877, which was much longer than they'd stayed anywhere else. Louisa's father Bronson was an educational reformer with a bit of a crackpot image. Typically he'd start teaching somewhere with his newfangled ideas and everybody would be impressed. Then the parents would start to get nervous and withdraw their children. This happened twenty-three times, and they were all ready for a bit of continuity when they came here."

Orchard House's exterior as viewed from the road was unremarkable, a boxy two-story wooden residence with a front door and gable in the middle and a chimney up top. The Alcotts being a spectacularly idiosyncratic family, however, this public facade disguised a jumble of two houses that Bronson had cobbled together to meet his family's various needs. Indeed, Jenna realized, the Alcotts would probably even be considered eccentrics in contemporary Southern California. In nineteenth-century Massachusetts, they must have seemed like Martians.

"When did Louisa start to write?" an older woman asked.

"When she was very young," the docent replied. "She had a number of other jobs when she was younger, trying to help the family stay afloat financially. Her early publications were often very melodramatic and sensationalist, and she didn't want to write *Little Women* at all. Her editor asked her to write a book for girls in response to *Oliver Twist*, which was aimed at boys. She said she didn't know about anything other than her own family and any book about them would be too boring. Well, *Little Women* was published in 1868 and it made her a fortune, two hundred thousand dollars."

This brought a gasp from Priscilla, who brought her fingers up to her mouth in exaggerated surprise. Jenna caught her mother's eye and grinned. Grandma had her entertaining moments.

Up in Louisa's room, the docent pointed out the tiny semi-circular desk between two windows where Louisa wrote. The sheer volume of verbiage that she had produced there was awesome: dozens of novels, including a number of lurid ones published under pseudonyms, endless essays and short stories, much poetry and extensive journals. There were no word processors in the nineteenth century, no typewriters for the common man or woman.

"The March family in *Little Women* is a half-generation younger than the Alcott family, but otherwise is based very clearly on her own family," the docent told them. "Anna was Meg. Elizabeth, who was known in the family as Lizzie, was Beth, and she had actually died before the family moved here. May was Amy, an anagram. Marmee was Marmee, named by one of the sisters. And Louisa, of course, was Jo.

"When Louisa was thirty, she went to Washington to nurse during the Civil War, but she almost immediately contracted typhoid. The medication used for treatment then was calomel, which contained mercury and had dreadful side effects. And that, in turn, created lifelong health problems and painful joints that led to genuine writer's cramp. But none of this kept her from being so amazingly prolific. It was Louisa who supported this family by her writing."

Jenna thought, for the first time in a long time, of Rob Cleary. The bookstore where she worked was adjacent to a coffee shop frequented by a number of aspiring young screenwriters who brought their laptops and stayed for hours, sipping lattes and making the occasional keystroke. One fellow in particular had caught her eye, a dark, sad-eyed guy with thick, curly black hair and a wardrobe that consisted entirely of black. He showed up most days around ten and usually stayed for several hours.

She found an excuse to talk to him and discovered that he was Rob Cleary and he was *not a screenwriter.* He wrote *fiction. Literary* fiction, fiction that *mattered,* fiction that was *profound.* He spoke of his writing as if it were a separate entity, and he spoke in italics. Screenwriters were *hacks,* he'd say, commercial novelists beneath contempt. They started going out and on their third or fourth date went back to his apartment after a pricy dinner at a trendy restaurant. She expected a hovel and several roommates, but it turned out he lived alone in a Santa Monica condo with an ocean view, leather furniture, and a huge Jacuzzi. He clearly wasn't supporting himself by his writing, and Jenna had drunk enough wine with dinner to really push him on how he paid his bills. Finally he admitted that he was living off a trust fund.

But only, he assured her, until his novel was finished.

They stopped seeing each other without really discussing it, and she still saw him now and then at the coffee house, sitting with his laptop open, waiting for the muse. So far as she knew, he had published nothing. She wondered what he would make of Louisa May Alcott. He'd probably call her a hack, she realized.

Jenna would argue that Louisa used her talents to provide for the people she loved.

And they'd both be right.

Chapter 20

IT was late Saturday afternoon by the time they reached the Weibeck residence in a grim little neighborhood of New Bedford, which had never, even in its commercial heyday, been known as a particularly safe place to visit.

Lynne had locked everything in the trunk after their fast-food lunch on the way down from Concord, and wasn't really concerned, but she could sense her mother growing more nervous by the moment as Jenna drove them to the little brick house. Lynne half-expected to find reporters camped out on the Weibecks' tired, browned-out patch of lawn, but apparently the media had come and gone. She could picture them shuddering, recalling that New Bedford was the town where Jodie Foster got raped on the pool table in *The Accused,* a film based on true events.

Lynne did not mention *The Accused* to Priscilla.

The door was answered by a stooped man in his seventies, dressed in a white shirt and navy blue jacket over old cotton trousers, with a clip-on necktie. He didn't look comfortable in any of it and had probably donned the dress-up clothes expressly for the purpose of facing the press. Lynne wanted to tell him to take the fool coat and tie off and relax, but this was not her show.

"I'm Frank Weibeck," he told them, extending a hand as the three women came inside. "Eldon's uncle." It was already getting dark, even though the end of Daylight Savings Time was still weeks away. The dusk carried a distinct chill. "Thank you for coming."

He led them into a living room dominated by a large crucifix occupied by a bloody, suffering Jesus. The crucifix was surrounded by a mix of religious paintings and formal portraits of towheaded children at various ages. The boxy brown upholstered furniture did not seem to have been selected with comfort in mind and was covered in heavy plastic slipcovers.

A large lamp sat on a table directly in front of a picture window, with a large framed copy of the military picture of Eldon that had been in all the papers propped against its ceramic base. Mustard-colored draperies covered all the windows, including the one behind the lamp. Lynne wondered if they were usually open to let in light, if Eldon's family had reacted to this widescale invasion of their privacy by closing out the world in the only way possible.

A pale, plump woman with carefully curled white hair sat in the chair facing Eldon's portrait. She wore a black dress and leaned slightly toward the oxygen tank beside her, its clear lifeline extending to her nostrils. Her fingers twisted a tissue, then carefully deposited it in a wastebasket under the end table beside her. A box of Kleenex sat on the table over the wastebasket and it was obvious that she had been crying, probably nonstop since the word of Eldon's death finally came to her.

"This is Eldon's mother, Margaret," Frank Weibeck told them.

Margaret Weibeck's fingers were cold as she extended a hand to Lynne, then waved the others to the plastic-covered sofa. "Thank you for coming," she said, as a younger version of herself, in black jeans and a dark blue turtleneck, came from the back of the house. "This is my daughter, Susan."

Lynne realized with a start that this woman was her own contemporary. Susan's eyes were blue, her shoulder-length hair a mix of dark blonde and silver, an Eastern European variant on salt-and-pepper. She offered a smile and nodded at the visitors. "Could I get you folks something to eat or drink?"

As Lynne started to shake her head, she heard Priscilla pipe up. "I'd like a glass of tea or lemonade, if it's not too much trouble."

Susan looked expectantly at the others, and Lynne realized that her mother's experience with this sort of situation was vastly wider than her own. The kitchen was probably crammed with casseroles and plates of cookies.

"Whatever's easy," Lynne said, as Jenna nodded and added, "Me too, please."

There was a moment of uncomfortable silence as Susan left the room.

Then Priscilla took over again, all her military mourning experience rising to the situation. "I'm so sorry that we had to meet under these circumstances," she said, as if there was any likelihood of their being acquainted under any other circumstances. "This must have been such a dreadful shock."

Frank Weibeck hovered near the door that connected the living room to what seemed to be a small but very formal dining room. Lynne had taken the other armchair and Priscilla and Jenna sat on the couch. The plastic slipcovers squeaked when any of them moved. After a moment, Frank reached into the dining room and brought out a chair for himself.

"What I don't understand is how you happened to find Eldon," Margaret said. "Or even how he happened to be with that Shackleford girl, for that matter. I met her that once when she was here with Eldon, but I had no idea she was wealthy. He introduced her with a different name. Minerva."

Lynne thought of Sydney Shackleford in this working-class living room, incognito. Had she viewed Eldon and his family as a sociology experiment?

"Did they visit you for long?" Lynne asked. "That—what was it? September?"

Margaret nodded. "It was just after Labor Day when she came here with him. Eldon had been home since early August, actually. I had major surgery in August, and because Mr. Weibeck had passed away and Eldon was my only son, the Red Cross was able to bring him home for it. He was in Vietnam, you see, had been there since the March before."

Susan returned with four glasses of tea and a platter of cookies that she placed on the coffee table. She distributed the tea, passed around sugar, then plopped to the floor beside the platter of cookies. "He had no idea what was going on with Mom," Susan said, picking up her mother's story. "I went to pick him up at the airport in Providence and he was still wearing his jungle fatigues. He said they were just about to set out on patrol when somebody came and pulled him out and said it was a family medical emergency. He didn't know about Mom's surgery, that it was planned, and he said he thought for sure one of us was dead. He just threw some stuff in a bag and got on the first plane they had coming back."

"Susan brought him to see me in the hospital," Margaret continued. "He looked so handsome in his uniform. I had no idea he was unhappy about his service. He'd complained a bit about being drafted, but there weren't any draft dodgers in New Bedford. The boys around here went and served when they were called." A note of pride crept into her voice. "Actually, most of them tended to enlist in the Navy or the Coast Guard if they were going to be called, but Eldon said he'd get out faster if he went into the Army as a draftee. He'd tried going out on the fishing boats once or twice, but he got seasick. He'd been going to the junior college for a while and was thinking about learning a trade in the Army and then maybe going to college on the GI Bill when he got out."

"What kind of trade?" Priscilia asked.

"He was considering several possibilities," Margaret answered.

Which meant Eldon probably had no idea at all, Lynne thought. Not so remarkable for that moment in history—or any moment, when you got right down to it. Lots of kids were clueless about their futures in the years right after high school. Though maybe in this blue-collar community he'd have been under greater pressure to find employment.

"Once Mom was back home and doing all right, Eldon took off," Susan said. "He said he was going to hook up with some Army buddies in Boston. His leave was supposed to be over the second week in September, but he told us he'd gotten it extended and . . . well, we were stupid enough to believe that."

"When did he bring Sydney Shackleford here?" Lynne asked.

"After Labor Day, I remember that," Margaret said, "because I was hoping he would be here for the neighborhood barbecue. But he didn't come back until a few days after that. He'd been growing his hair and he had a moustache." She shook her head in annoyance. This version of Eldon clearly didn't fit her mental picture of the dutiful military man, or the picture propped on her lamp.

Susan smiled. "He looked like a hippie," she said, "with faded jeans and tie-dyed t-shirts and sandals, the whole bit. I remember thinking it was a good thing that Dad wasn't around to see it because he'd have just been livid."

Frank Weibeck spoke up for the first time, pride in his voice. "My brother Tom was a Navy man, and he served in the Pacific theater during World War Two. We Weibecks were all Navy men."

"And so was my late husband, Lynne's father," Priscilla put in. She was on firm ground here. Lynne hoped she wouldn't muddy the waters by mentioning her second late Navy husband. One was quite enough. "He was a Navy pilot in the South Pacific."

Frank Weibeck's smile widened. "Then Tom might have been part of his ground crew."

Priscilla beamed. "What a small world this is!"

Lynne reached for a cookie, a jam thumbprint that looked made from scratch. She fully expected a chorus of "Anchors Aweigh" to break out any minute now. "I guess it makes sense that a town with the sailing history of New Bedford would have a lot of Navy men. It didn't bother Eldon that he was Army in the midst of all that?" And where the hell had he gotten the name Eldon, anyway? The rest of the family had nice normal names.

After a moment of silence, it was Susan who spoke next, and she avoided looking at her mother.

"He didn't care so much whether he was Army or Navy," Susan said. "He told me the last time he was here that he thought the war was wrong and he should never have gone in. He made it sound like he'd had a choice—I mean, he was *drafted,* and around here that meant you went, no questions asked."

"It was that Minerva girl who poisoned him against his country," Margaret put in suddenly. "I could just tell he was up to no good with her. Why, he was actually intending to have her sleep in his bedroom when they were here. I told him that no matter what immoral behavior he might engage in away from home, in this house he would respect the laws of Jesus." She nodded toward the crucifix. "That Minerva girl slept with Susan in her room. There was an extra bed because her older sister had gotten married and moved out."

Lynne caught a twinkle in Susan's eye. She'd have bet anything that Sydney slipped into Eldon's room once the household turned in for the evening. Though in a place this size, they'd have to be mighty quiet if they were getting it on. *Getting it on.* She couldn't remember the last time she'd used that expression, even in her mind. There was something about this sudden immersion in the late sixties and the draft and the Vietnam War—not to mention long male hair and tie-dyed t-shirts—that was making her downright nostalgic. Maybe things hadn't turned out quite the way young people had hoped they would back then, but it had sure been exciting trying to change the course of history.

Which was not a sentiment she would have uttered in front of her own parents at the time, either. And certainly not one she would bring up here and now.

"So Sydney was here with him in September," Lynne said. "What was she like?"

"Snotty," Susan answered immediately. "Like she thought her you-know-what didn't stink. She had this attitude to her that I could tell Eldon liked, but I thought she was just some rich girl slumming."

Interesting observation. "What made you think she was rich?" Lynne asked.

Susan considered for a moment. "Well, she was driving a cute little MG that I know was worth a lot of money because I was going out with a guy at the time who was really into cars. She had a watch that looked like it had diamonds all around it and when I asked her about it, she said oh, no, those weren't diamonds but she liked the watch because it kept her in touch with her roots. I thought that was *very* strange."

Susan took a sip of her tea. "Mostly I think it was more how she just didn't fit in here at all. Like, I was going to business school at the time and we had to dress up for class, you know, heels and a nice outfit like you'd have to wear to work in an office. It was part of the requirement. She said something like 'I can't believe you're doing that' as if I was just too weird for words. I really wondered if Eldon knew what he was getting into with her. I mean, he was really cute and I could certainly see what she would like about him. But she had kind of a horsy face and she was really bossy."

"To Eldon?" Lynne asked.

"To everybody. And she kind of expected to be waited on. She never threw away her own soda cans or offered to help with the dishes or anything. One time I was vacuuming in here and I got to where she was sitting on the couch and she just lifted her feet as I went by."

"How long did they stay?"

"Just a couple of days," Susan said, "and then they left again." She looked at her mother apologetically. "I never told you this, Mom, because there didn't seem much point, but before he left that last time he told me he just couldn't go back to Vietnam. He was sure he was going to be killed if he went back. I told him he didn't really have a choice, that he was in the service. He gave me a real fierce hug and he said, well maybe he did have a choice. But then he wouldn't talk about it anymore. Minerva came in and she wanted to go somewhere."

Susan looked over at the picture of Eldon in his Army uniform. "And the next day he was gone."

Chapter 21

"I cannot imagine," Priscilla said in her most patrician tones, "what makes you believe that quality tourists are going to want to visit this nasty little town. Nantucket is so much nicer."

They were strolling through the historic district on Johnny Cake Hill in New Bedford, a part of town that admittedly could use a bit of polish, though renovation was in progress in several spots. Scaffolding covered many of the old brick buildings, with doors and window frames being sanded down to the original wood through layers of ancient paint. On Sunday morning, the business district was all but deserted, and they'd easily found parking on the street.

Lynne was doubly grateful now that she had followed her instincts last night and checked them into a blessedly nondescript chain motel outside of town, off the interstate. A cursory check had revealed no bed-and-breakfasts in New Bedford that Lynne wished to gamble on, and AAA didn't list any motels there. While Fall River was technically in the neighborhood, she couldn't quite bring herself to stay at the

Lizzie Borden B&B. She hadn't even dared mention it to her mother, for fear of an out-and-out tantrum.

"This nasty little town," Lynne told her, "was the center of the world whaling industry for years, and it was one of the wealthiest cities in America in the 1850s. Herman Melville sailed out of here. Frederick Douglass lived here. You're right, Nantucket initially had most of the whaling fleet, but then nature intervened. Nantucket's harbor developed a sand bar that kept the bigger ships out, and when that happened, New Bedford was ready and waiting."

Priscilla heaved a mighty sigh.

Lynne ignored her and kept walking, stepping away from some unidentifiable debris on the sidewalk beneath the scaffolding. "The whale oil produced by the New Bedford whaling fleet lit the lamps of the world, Mom, and it oiled the machines of the industrial revolution. Right up till the discovery of petroleum in 1859 in Pennsylvania."

Priscilla did not seem impressed, and she had registered absolute astonishment at the discovery that this dreary neighborhood was a part of their National Park Service, complete with the same improbably dressed park rangers they'd encountered in Lowell at the cotton mill. The Visitor's Center was located in a renovated bank building, which had gone through a brief incarnation as an auto parts shop, pre-gentrification.

"Surely your clients won't be interested in that sort of thing. And even if they were, couldn't you take them to Nantucket? Or Mystic Seaport? That's so much nicer."

"My clients will be interested in whatever I decide to include in this tour," Lynne said evenly. "If the Whaling Museum turns out to be a bust, then no, I probably won't bring them down here. But I'd much rather visit a genuine historical location than a recreation like Mystic Seaport." She held up a hand to stop her mother's protest. "No matter how nice that recreation might be. As for Nantucket, that involves ferries and ferries are a hassle I try to avoid wherever possible."

"Hmph," said Priscilla.

"Can you do anything about the Underground Railroad connection?" Jenna asked. She'd been reading through various guidebooks last night after dinner. "That seems to be popping up a lot as we move around. New Bedford had a strong Abolitionist movement, and all kinds of fugitive slaves lived here. Some of them actually had stowed away on ships coming up from the South. And remember, they said the Alcotts harbored at least a couple of fugitive slaves in Concord. From what we've been learning, it seems like maybe there was some kind of Vietnam era counterpart at Sydney's commune and maybe also at the Maple Leaf Inn. . . ." She seemed to realize what she had said and stopped speaking abruptly.

But Priscilla jumped right in. "Are you trying to suggest that draft dodgers were regular visitors to my hostelry?"

Where to begin? Lynne decided to skip the reference to her mother's "hostelry," even while registering that this was the first time she had ever heard the word spoken out loud. And without a dictionary at hand, it seemed pointless to suggest that it probably was not accented on its second syllable.

"It seems possible that something like that was going on," Lynne said. "We know that Eldon Weibeck was AWOL from the Army and that Sydney Shackleford lived in a White Mountain commune that may have helped draft dodgers and deserters get to Canada. And we know that both of them ended up dead in your basement."

Then a thought struck her. "But what if they *didn't* send the deserters and draft dodgers to Canada? What if they developed new identities for them so they could stay right here?"

"You mean like the Weather Underground and the SLA?" Jenna asked.

Lynne shook her head. "The things you know about. Where on earth did you hear about the Weather Underground and the SLA?" She herself had all but forgotten the leftist political figures who had changed identities and quietly resurfaced as new people in different locales. Usually they were under indictment when they vanished, and as far as she knew, most of them had returned to their original identities by now. Few had even been prosecuted, though now that she thought about it, she recalled that a Minnesota soccer mom, whose worst crime seemed to be having a big mouth, was serving about eight hundred years in California.

"I had a course on the sixties, remember?" Jenna said. Actually Lynne didn't remember, though it sounded vaguely familiar.

"At UCLA?" Priscilla asked incredulously.

Jenna shrugged. "That's the only place I went to college, Grandma."

"Hmph," Priscilla said again.

Lynne stopped on the sidewalk. "If I could have your attention, ladies?" Jenna and Priscilla both stopped and looked at her expectantly. Lynne waved an arm at the entry way of a large and surprisingly modern looking building on the corner. "This is Eighteen Johnny Cake Hill, my friends. The New Bedford Whaling Museum, which recently celebrated its one hundredth birthday."

THE two whale skeletons suspended from the ceiling inside the Whaling Museum were so enormous that Jenna thought at first they must be fake. When she thought of whales, which admittedly wasn't often, her primary frame of reference was the various Shamus at Sea World. Any Shamu killer whale she'd ever seen could fit tidily inside the jaws of the sixty-six-foot-long blue whale that was floating above the open, airy lobby.

As they climbed the stairs to the second floor, the whale skeletons looming even larger, Jenna realized that what she had never appreciated before was the incredible effort involved in whaling. These creatures had been *enormous*.

And when she stepped into the room that housed the Purrington and Russell panorama, she noticed that even her grandmother seemed interested.

Priscilla cast her eyes around the large room. The painting was on huge rollers. "It says this is a quarter mile long. Can that possibly be true?"

"You're only seeing a small part of it, Mom," Lynne said. While a nice chunk of the eight-and-a-half-foot-tall painting was revealed, showing some fairly idyllic South Pacific island experiences, most of it was rolled up and only displayed as it moved around the room on its perpetual journey. "This used to travel around and be displayed onstage. The painting would be hand-cranked all the way through with a live narration. Panoramas were an art form in the nineteenth century, usually about something historical, like the Battle of Gettysburg. Or this one, 'A Whaling Voyage Around the World.' All for a quarter's admission."

"Like a movie," Jenna added. "Back before there were movies."

"Or like the Roller Derby," Lynne added. "Entertainment that came to the people."

"That was different," Priscilla said. "They could *see* us. We were out there all day, skating. We even had our cots in the middle of the arena in some places, to rest during the day and sleep at night."

This was something Jenna made a mental note to pursue later. Priscilla had bunked down in the middle of skating rinks? With hundreds, maybe thousands of people watching? With other young people whose parents were willing to let them go on the road with total strangers?

"I'm sure this panoramic painting seemed incredible to the people who didn't know anything about whaling," Lynne said.

"But they aren't letting *us* see it," Priscilla complained. "Just this little part."

"It's probably too fragile," Lynne said, trying to smooth things over.

"Well, it seems silly to paint something that nobody's allowed to see." Priscilla sounded peeved. She was starting to sound peeved all the time, Jenna realized.

"Most things that people paint don't get seen by anybody, Grandma," Jenna answered mildly. Her grandmother seemed to be needlessly hounding her mother, and they all still had a lot of time to spend together, in some very small spaces.

"Artists paint because they want to, or because they feel compelled to, but that doesn't necessarily mean that anybody ever sees what they do, and for sure they mostly don't sell much." Jenna had been to a lot of gallery openings in LA, and she knew the incredible odds against getting even that far with an artistic career. Even having the show wouldn't do any good unless the artwork sold well. Gallery owners knew they could pick and choose from a never-ending field of talented and desperate artists.

Jenna moved on to the next room, where the half-scale whaling ship *Lagoda* sat in all its proud glory. When an earlier incarnation of the museum had been damaged by a 1977 explosion and fire nearby, spectators had reported the *Lagoda*'s sails billowing in the night winds, in what appeared to be a futile and utterly surreal attempt to get away. And it had survived the fire.

A spry male docent who looked to be about sixty-five was hovering near the *Lagoda,* eager to share his knowledge about the ship in particular and whaling in general. The first thing that Jenna noticed was that even at twice the size, this would not be a large vessel. The extensive crew required to capture and render enormous whales would be living in each other's pockets most of the time. Whaling expeditions typically lasted four or five years, until every possible cubic inch of storage space was filled with whale oil. Five years on a pitching, heaving boat could be a very long time.

"That old saying about police and fire work applies to whaling as well," the docent said. "Long periods of boredom punctuated by brief periods of sheer terror. Finding the whale was only the first part of the process. Once a whale or school of whales had been sighted, the whaleboats were lowered and almost everybody raced to the scene."

A father with two young boys came up then and the docent bantered with the kids for a moment. Once he had their attention, he went on. "When the whaleboat got close enough to the whale, the harpooner would aim an iron harpoon at the whale. He wasn't trying to kill it, just to attach it to the boat.

The harpoon is basically just a huge fishhook, and the harpooner's arm was critical to the success of the hunt."

"Like a quarterback's arm," the dad put in. The boys nodded enthusiastically. Plenty of male bonding going on here and what could be a more perfect setting?

"Once the harpoon was in the whale, things started to get interesting. What do you suppose the whale would do?" The question was addressed to the kids.

"Run away?" the older boy suggested.

"Dive?" the littler one added.

"Good job, sailors," the docent told them. "You're both right. There'd be a three-hundred-fathom line attached and it would come whipping off its holder so fast they'd have to pour water on the rope to keep it from bursting into flames. Sometimes the whale would take off and pull that little boat behind him until he got worn out. They used to call that a 'Nantucket sleigh ride.' If the whale dove, or 'sounded' instead of running, they might have to tie more lines on, if the ocean floor was deeper than three hundred fathoms. A fathom is six feet, so you can see those whales could go really deep to try to escape. Being attached to several tons of angry whale by a harpoon was dangerous and difficult."

"So they just raced around then?" the father asked.

"Until the whale got tired. Or got away. Or died, though that usually required another step. Once the whale was worn out and the boat was close enough, the harpooner would come in for the kill. After the whale finally died, then the *really* messy part would start. The whole carcass needed to be processed into oil very quickly before the sharks could get at it. They'd tow the whale back to the ship and lower a platform off the side. Sailors would go down there and cut off big chunks of whale fat, or blubber, and those would get hauled up to the ship. There more sailors would cut them into smaller and smaller pieces. The littlest ones were called Bible leaves because they resembled an open book. Those would go in a huge copper pot like this one here"—he pointed to the tryworks on the deck of the ship—"over a fire to render the oil. As the process went on, they'd use what was left of the Bible leaves to fuel the fire. So the whale was essentially processing itself."

"Cool!" the older boy said. The younger one, getting bored, was trying to swing from the rigging.

"All that oil was packed into barrels that would be assembled as needed by a cooper, or barrelmaker, who traveled on the ship for just that purpose. The rendering went on around the clock until the whole whale was processed. And while they were doing that, they'd cut off the whale's head and haul it onto the ship, because it had something even more valuable in it."

Jenna was beginning to feel a little queasy about all this, though the older boy's attention hadn't flagged for an instant. If anything, he was becoming more bloodthirsty. His eyes widened as the docent continued.

"A sperm whale's head has a sonar organ so it can find food on the bottom of the ocean. Three or four gallons of a special oil called spermaceti surround that organ. They'd barrel that oil separately because it was much more valuable than the regular whale oil. Spermaceti was made into candles that burned very cleanly. In fact, it was so valuable that after most of the oil was bailed out, somebody'd get down inside the head to make sure they had every drop."

Yuck, and yuck again.

How could anybody romanticize whaling? Jenna thought this all sounded like the worst possible punishment. And if they were lucky enough to locate an area with a lot of whales, they might have to repeat this process again and again. Who knew when there'd be another whale, particularly after the oceans began to be fished out? It wasn't so much a sense of adventure that had brought whalers to the Pacific and then to the Arctic Ocean. It was systematic extinction. They kept wiping out whale populations and being forced to search wider and wider.

Not long before this trip, she'd read about a DNA study of the world's current whale population. Using scientific methodology that Jenna didn't pretend to understand, they had determined that during the whaling era, many more whales had probably been killed than previously believed. Tremendous genetic variations in the modern humpback population, for instance, suggested that there might have been ten times as many humpbacks as shown by unconfirmed whaling records dating to the mid-nineteenth century.

One whale whose capture had been joyously noted throughout the whaling world was the legendary rogue bull, Mocha Dick, who terrorized Pacific whalers for half a century. Mocha Dick, generally considered the inspiration for Moby Dick, was credited with dozens of attacks on ships, often unprovoked. He survived countless attempts to capture him. He came to the defense of other whales. He played dead.

Finally, when he had grown old and slow and blind in one eye, he was captured, with nineteen rusty harpoons lodged in his body. The year was 1859, when Edwin Drake was discovering petroleum in Pennsylvania.

PRISCILLA had wandered off into other parts of the museum and they found her at an exhibit of island artifacts brought back to New England by sailors. She seemed much more cheerful than she'd been earlier.

"This reminds me of the kind of stuff they used to sell around the Pacific naval bases," she said, with a distant gleam in her eye.

Lynne pointed at a "Sailor's Valentine," intricately crafted floral patterns made from delicate pastel shells. There was nothing authentically native about these souvenirs, which were made by Barbados natives expressly for the sailors to take home to their loved ones. "I'd swear we made something just like that in Girl Scouts in Guam."

Priscilla smiled. "Now that you mention it, you did."

"I don't suppose you still have it?" Lynne said.

"I wish I did," Priscilla said in a tone that suggested she'd eighty-sixed the doodad at the first possible opportunity. "But you know how your father was whenever we moved."

Jenna perked up at this. She found her grandpa Greg, who'd died years before she was born, a fascinating character, grown larger than life through his various legends. She remembered watching *The Great Santini* with her mother, who sat quietly sobbing at the video's end. *That guy could've been your grandpa,* Lynne had told her, a few minutes later when she'd regained her composure. *Except for the basketball.*

"Ruthless," Lynne agreed now. "But he always ended up doing whatever you wanted, Mom. I always used to wonder how that happened. He'd bluster and holler and carry on and then the next thing I knew, you'd have that little smile going and whatever it was you wanted, it would be happening."

"Men," Priscilla said with a shrug. "You just have to know how to handle them, that's all." She turned to Jenna. "You pay attention, Jenny. It's time you got yourself a husband."

Chapter 22

PRISCILLA made herself comfortable in the backseat, where she was seriously considering taking a nap.

It disturbed her that she tired so easily on the road these days. She'd spent most of her lifetime in motion, much of that motion moving from one location to another. Truth be told, she'd found those last years in Buffalo with Harvey pretty boring. She would not, of course, ever mention this to any of her relatives, even if they begged for the information. Lynne would shrug her shoulders and Jenna wouldn't care and Abby would just sniff in that superior way of hers, suggesting she'd known all along that Harvey was a mistake.

He hadn't been. He just hadn't been very interesting. But he'd provided Priscilla with stability, a lovely home and carte blanche to decorate that home. Most of those sets of dishes that Abby was always cluck-clucking about, for instance, had been acquired during the Harvey years. And the dining room furniture, and Priscilla's sleigh bed, which Harvey had only visited rarely. He snored, and set up camp in a guest bedroom without complaint.

"How long till we get home?" Priscilla asked now.

"Three hours if we're lucky," Lynne said. "Four if we run into serious traffic."

"It's Sunday afternoon," Priscilla said. "How much traffic can there be?" Suddenly she wanted desperately to be back at the Maple Leaf Inn.

"Actually, I don't have any idea," Lynne admitted. "All these distances are so much shorter than what I'm used to in California but they always take longer than I expect. I just don't have any frame of reference, except to say things here aren't quite as close together as they seem when you look at a map."

"That's 'cause all the roads in New England are winding old cow paths," Jenna said. "I haven't seen a straight line yet. Hey! I think that's a cranberry bog!" She pointed out her window.

Priscilla turned her head. Sure enough, they were passing an undulating red ocean of brightly bobbing cranberries. "They're all over Southern New England these days, Jenna. Cranberries are a big business now that everybody drinks cranberry juice, but the berries have been here since before the Pilgrims came."

"Cool." Jenna continued staring, looking behind her as they drove on past the corralled cranberries. "So these are the berries they have in those little bags at the grocery?"

"No," Priscilla said. "*Those* berries are harvested by hand. These floating berries are the ones that get canned or made into juice. First they flood the bogs, then they go through with machinery that knocks the ripe berries loose. It's kind of like an old manual lawn mower, or a paddlewheel on a steamboat."

What was she thinking? Jenna had probably never seen a manual lawn mower *or* a paddleboat. Oh, well. "The berries float, so they're easy to collect." Having grown up in New England, Priscilla prided herself on cranberry sauce made fresh on Thanksgiving morning, resorting to canned product only when she was in a part of the world where cranberries of any sort were a novelty and you had to make do with what you could get at the Exchange.

The light danced on Jenna's face as she brushed back a wing of her tousled golden hair. Her granddaughter was a beautiful girl, though this was scarcely surprising, considering her bloodlines. Lynne had always been lovely, save for a brief gawky period during puberty, and Monty had possessed almost Nordic good looks, with blonde hair, blue eyes, and a perpetual Southern California tan. Priscilla had always worried that he'd develop skin cancer. Whoever would have thought it was his heart that would kill him, and with no warning whatsoever?

It was all so unfair.

The Navy pilots and other military daredevils she'd known—those were guys you half-expected to go down any day, though when it actually happened, it still was an enormous shock. But Monty had been an insurance salesman, for pity's sake, in a beach town where his lifestyle seemed to offer no stress beyond deciding which Hawaiian shirt to wear to the office. There's no dress code, he'd once told Priscilla with a flashing grin, when you're the boss.

The bog behind them, Priscilla settled back into her seat again. Suddenly Jenna turned around, looking inquisitive. "I know this really isn't any of my business," she began.

Priscilla hated conversations that began that way. "But?"

"But I've always wanted to hear more about when you were in the Roller Derby. And since you brought it up this afternoon. . . ."

Of all the things Jenna might have said, this was the last one Priscilla would have expected. Truth be told, she rarely thought about the Roller Derby years. "I didn't bring it up. Your mother did."

"Because it's interesting," Lynne put in.

Priscilla sighed. "There's not much to say. I did it for a while and then I stopped."

"Grandma, c'mon!"

Lynne tilted her head to catch Priscilla's eye in the rearview mirror. "I always told her that when she was older she could ask, Mom. She seems plenty old enough to me."

"Oh, I suppose," Priscilla said, "and when you put it like that, it sounds like I was some kind of painted lady, or prostitute or something. Just don't bring this up around Abby. She always thought I shamed the Chenonceau family by being what she called a gypsy." Gypsy was probably the most complimentary term Abigail had used, now that Priscilla thought about it. And Abby hadn't known the half of what Priscilla was up to on the road. She paused. "I don't know what to say. Ask me something."

"Okay," Jenna said. "How did you get into it in the first place?"

"Well, I'd heard about it," Priscilla told her. "It was during the Depression, you know, and most folks were desperately poor. They'd do anything for money. There were all these marathon things where people would dance until they collapsed, or ride bicycles for six days. Then a guy in Chicago got the idea to have people do a marathon skating show. They'd skate in shifts and end up doing three thousand miles in a couple of weeks, same as the distance from New York to Los Angeles, without ever leaving the skating rink. It was called the Transcontinental Roller Derby."

"And people came to watch it?" Jenna sounded incredulous.

"Oh, mercy yes! You'd think it would be kind of boring, particularly around day seven or eight, but people would come day after day and they'd cheer for the white shirts or the red shirts. Don't forget, there wasn't much else to do, and this was cheap entertainment, a quarter or less for about eleven hours a day. Folks would develop an attachment to different skaters. I had fans just about everywhere we went, kids who'd ask me to autograph a program. Maybe youngsters today would find it dull, but there was no TV or those computer games or whatever back then."

"So did you join up when the Roller Derby came to New England?" Jenna asked.

Priscilla laughed merrily. Suddenly she was enjoying these

memories much more than she would ever have expected.
"Goodness gracious, no! I went to it. You see, I graduated
young from high school and there wasn't much going on in
South Hadford. I wanted to go someplace else, but my parents wouldn't hear of it. And then I got a lucky break. Or actually, it was somebody else's break and my luck. There was
a woman from Chicago who'd been visiting her family in
town, and she fell and broke her leg. She had this huge cast
and couldn't manage very well on crutches, and she needed
somebody to go along with her to Chicago. Take care of the
luggage, bring her meals from the dining car, that sort of
stuff."

After all these years, Priscilla could still picture her perfectly—a heavy, dyspeptic shrew with a hooked nose and a
bad word for everyone. But she couldn't for the life of her remember the woman's name. Not that it mattered. The woman
was certainly dead by now, complaining about the amenities
in heaven, and could some angel *please* open a window because it was really unbearably stuffy.

"You mean like the rich pretentious woman in *Rebecca*?"
Jenna asked.

Priscilla returned abruptly from heaven and chuckled. "I
guess you could make that comparison. But there wasn't any
Max de Winter in Chicago. She had me stay for a few weeks
after we got to Chicago, because she still couldn't get
around, and she lived in a beautiful house near the lake in
Hyde Park. But it really was dreadful work and when I saw
an ad looking for skaters for the Roller Derby, I figured I had
nothing to lose. I knew how to skate and I was a pretty good
athlete. And wouldn't you just know it, they took me. I can
still see the look on that old bat's face when I told her I was
moving out. They had us training for months to get ready,
just skating for hours and hours and hours. My feet were
covered with blisters and they got infected, so they took me
to the hospital and the doctor painted them purple. I got a
few days off then, but after that it was right back on the
track. I swear there were times I would have given it all up if

that woman hadn't been so certain that I'd quit and come back to fetch her tapioca pudding."

As Priscilla continued her tale, the Massachusetts miles melted away. She rather relished telling the story, and Lynne and Jenna were an excellent, albeit captive, audience. Once she'd started talking about it, it was as if she'd opened a hallway to an entire portion of her life that had been sitting there patiently, perfectly preserved, since the 1930s.

She remembered faces and names, traveling by rail from town to town, the sound of "Deep Purple" played nightly near their quarters at the Texas State Fairgrounds in Dallas. She remembered the girl who got pregnant and went back to Detroit, the sixteen-year-old who came from Omaha to Fort Worth to track down a sweet-talking skater who'd done her wrong, and the four-day quarantine while they waited to see if one of the boys really had scarlet fever. She remembered staying up all night playing blackjack with the girls on the train while the boys played poker at the other end of the car. She remembered dreadful pileups on the track, arms and legs intertwined, elbows and shoulders bashed, and it seemed a miracle that most of them had escaped serious injury.

As she talked about it now, it all seemed innocent and entertaining, charming and wholesome, a slice of bygone Americana.

And by the time she reached the part of the story where she parted ways with the Roller Derby and went to Boston where she met the dashing Lieutenant Greg Westbrook, late of the US Naval Academy, they were turning onto Barrington Road in South Hadford.

The first thing she noticed was a South Hadford police car parked at an angle to block easy access. Young Officer Chapman, who'd been the first on the scene the morning the bodies had been found, got out of the car, recognized them, and waved them on into the cul-de-sac.

The second thing she noticed was that in the three days they'd been gone, the maples in front of the Inn had turned a vibrant, pulsating scarlet.

And the third thing she noticed was a state crime-scene van in the driveway, right next to Abigail's Buick.

Would this nightmare never end?

ABIGAIL was exhausted.

She had brought an overnight bag and moved into the Maple Leaf Inn shortly after the girls left town, when Cindy Jackson called, all upset. Cindy was spending much of her waking time with her mother at the hospital, waiting for poor Ralph to regain consciousness. But she was worried about strangers roaming the neighborhood. Reporters were trying to interview neighbors when nobody answered their knocks and rings at the Maple Leaf Inn. And emboldened by the apparent absence of inhabitants at the Inn, they were also wandering around the grounds and disappearing behind the building.

This invasion of privacy was not acceptable, and Abigail had immediately phoned William O'Keefe, who claimed he'd just ordered police guards stationed around the clock. He did, however, note that the local police force had been stretched quite thin by recent developments.

"I am a taxpaying citizen of this town," Abigail had told him, speaking each word slowly and distinctly, "and I have been a South Hadford taxpayer for more than half a century. This unfortunate situation demands police attention. Until you and the state detectives are able to determine what happened here and why, the safety and security of this piece of property is your responsibility."

"I'll take care of it, Miss Chenonceau," he finally answered, and she knew that he was remembering that summer long ago when he was working his way through school at Golden Mills. She had discovered the boy necking with one of those trashy Whipple girls in a supply closet during their lunch break. If William O'Keefe hadn't been such a good worker, and if they hadn't been technically off duty, she'd probably have fired them both on the spot. Instead she assigned them to particularly unpleasant duties. The Whipple girl quit two days later, but O'Keefe stuck it out, and she'd always admired that.

She only hoped he was putting that same tenacity into this mess with the bodies in the basement.

Twice this weekend she had been startled by noises outside, once the sound of footsteps crunching in the underbrush behind the house and the other some kind of crash at one of the wells for a basement window. Last night after that happened, she'd seen a tall figure loping away into the darkness when she went to investigate.

Now Priscilla and the girls were back, jabbering about their adventures. When they'd called to announce their return by dinnertime, Abigail had surveyed the pantry and refrigerator, then planned a cold dinner buffet from the leftovers that remained from the neighborhood tea. Even though time seemed to be moving at glacial speed just now, it had only been three days since they'd last eaten this food. She discarded the mushy cucumber sandwiches and some questionable tuna salad, but there were still deviled eggs and mini-quiches that could probably be heated one last time.

The girls had taken the remaining cookies when they left, so Abigail had gone outside, picked some choice apples, and baked a pie. Priscilla hadn't seemed to really notice, but Lynne and Jenna had both come into the kitchen, beaming and sniffing appreciatively.

As they were setting out the food, the pair of crime scene technicians came up the basement stairs. The woman had been here every time, but the man was new to this case, or so Abigail thought. She was alarmed at how murky her thought processes were becoming.

"Smells great," the man said, with a nod at Abigail. "You ladies have a nice evening, now." As he went out the back door, carrying a brown cardboard box, Abigail decided that he looked as tired as she felt.

The woman stopped for a moment and set down the case she was carrying. It looked heavy. "We're done for the day," she told them. "I'm sorry we keep inconveniencing you."

"We've been out of town," Lynne answered, "so it's just my aunt here who's really been inconvenienced. Are you done yet?"

The technician cocked her head. "I think so. But I couldn't swear to it. We took out some more of the concrete floor yesterday." She smiled apologetically and nodded at Abigail. "Poor Miss Chenonceau had to leave, it got so noisy. But I think we're finished with the jackhammering, and possibly with the rest of it."

"When will you know?" Lynne asked.

"Maybe tomorrow." She picked up the case and Lynne opened the door for her. "Night, all."

"They've been back here twice," Abigail said, when they were gone. "I have no idea what they think they're going to find at this late date, and it seems to me that they've already broken up and analyzed every square inch of that basement." Though they hadn't seemed to notice that she'd brought up the folding table for Priscilla's party.

Lynne shrugged. "There's a prominent family involved now, so you've got to figure they'll be working extra hard to solve this. But I must say I didn't expect to find anybody here on Sunday."

Over dinner, Lynne reported what they'd learned at the Weibeck residence in New Bedford. "It's not much, really, but it seems clear that Sydney Shackleford had some kind of plan to help Eldon avoid going back to Vietnam."

"It can't have been a very good plan," Abigail said after a moment, "if they both ended up dead in the basement here."

Chapter 23

AFTER Abigail had gone home and Priscilla had shuffled off to bed, Lynne and Jenna spread the maps and guidebooks over the living room floor.

"My schedule is all shot to hell," Lynne said, "and God only knows what else will happen the rest of the time we're here. If I'm going to put together a trip, we need to really hustle around to check out all the other locations I have in mind. Plus trying to track down that scoundrel Will Colwhistle. Thank goodness he was thoughtful enough to put his mail drops in interesting places."

"So you think they're all mail drops?" Jenna asked.

"Don't you? And while we're in the White Mountains, I'd also like to squeeze in a stop at the commune-turned-candle-manufacturer where Sydney Shackleford lived."

"Surely the police are doing that."

"Well, I certainly hope so. And I don't want to get in their way. But I'm really intrigued by the Sydney story."

"Are you going to try to get into the Shackleford compound up in the White Mountains?"

"Mont Blanc? I'd sure like to, but it looks impenetrable. Besides, I don't think Sydney's family had any idea what she was up to, or where."

"I don't see how we can possibly cover it all." Jenna smoothed a New England regional map lying on the floor and leaned forward to look at it. "There's too many locations and they're spread all over the place. And don't forget, I have to be back at work a week from tomorrow."

This was the kind of opening that Priscilla would drive a truck through, cross-examining Jenna about her various deficiencies: husband, career, children. Lynne was grateful, not for the first time, that her mother had gone to bed.

"We'll just have to race around for a few days," Lynne said. "It'll be fun. If we leave your grandmother here, we'll be able to move much faster, and I think she's too worn out to travel right now anyway." She examined the map for a moment. "Maybe we can do a clockwise circle starting here and heading down through Amherst to Hartford. Or go straight to Hartford and hit Amherst when we head north. I assume the Emily Dickinson house is still on your must-see list."

Jenna nodded. "But there doesn't seem to be that much to see there. She was a recluse and most of what happened in her life happened in her mind. Which I assume is not available for tourist inspection."

"After Amherst," Lynne said, "we could drive through western Massachusetts, hit the Berkshires quickly, and from there go on up to Vermont."

"I probably shouldn't bring this up," Jenna said, "but do you honestly think that there'll even *be* a trip next year? I know Grandma has her heart set on it, but just watching her this past week, I don't think she's got the stamina to run a bed-and-breakfast. A place like this takes a lot of work."

"I know, I know. But nobody's ever been able to tell her anything. Once she gets her mind set on something, it's like she's wearing blinders to anything that might detract from her mental image. She's always been that way."

"I guess so," Jenna said. She glanced toward the stairway

and lowered her voice. "I absolutely couldn't believe what she was telling us about the Roller Derby."

Lynne laughed. "Indeed. And you have to figure she was really sanitizing it for us. She's always looked at the past through—well, I'd say rose-colored glasses, but it's really more like a selective filter. Whatever doesn't fit with what she wants to remember, she just dismisses."

Jenna smiled. "Digital photo enhancement."

"Exactly, though she'd never get the analogy." Lynne stood and picked up her empty glass. "Can I get you anything?"

Jenna shook her head. "I'll just keep plugging at this map, trying to figure out how to get a month's worth of travel into a week." She grinned. "What a great problem to have!"

In the kitchen, Lynne refilled her glass with Diet Dr Pepper and looked around. What *were* the odds that this cockamamie plan would actually come to be? Though her mother would have been horrified at even the thought that she might not be healthy and strong enough to run this operation, she was eighty-two. People of eighty-two got sick. They went into nursing homes. They died. And generally when these things happened, they weren't setting out on a business venture that would be risky for somebody half their age.

Aunt Abby wouldn't want to move to the Maple Leaf Inn. Though the house she lived in now wasn't the one the sisters had grown up in, she'd been living there for the past fifty years. Lynne had wonderful memories of the old house, with its porch swing and attic full of old furniture and trunks crammed with dress-up clothes from long ago. It was there that she'd raked leaves, rolled in the piles, and learned to tend the aromatic fires that disposed of fallen leaves in that less ecologically oriented age.

Unfortunately, that house had burned to the ground in the fifties in a fire that rose from electrical problems rather than leaf disposal. Abigail had bought the house she lived in today shortly after that fire, and she was so comfortably at home there that it was pointless to even consider the possibility that she'd move into the Maple Leaf Inn.

In any case, it would be disastrous if she actually did move in, out of some misguided sense of family loyalty. Abigail had never suffered fools and it seemed clear that she regarded the Maple Leaf Inn as a project that went far beyond quixotic, straight into idiotic. Lynne had observed nothing on this trip, she realized, to dispel her earlier suspicion that the sisters were the sort of blood relations who never really become friends.

So if the place opened, and if her mother became unable to run it for whatever reason, there was no reason to assume that Aunt Abby would automatically step into the breach. It would be Lynne who'd need to drop everything and come sort out the mess. And dropping everything was becoming increasingly difficult. The travel industry had been in questionable health even before 9/11 and things since then had mostly just gotten worse. She could no longer justify having two full-time employees at Booked for Travel back in Floritas, and it was a stroke of luck that Leslie actually wanted to go part-time after the birth of her baby.

Back in the living room, Jenna had organized various piles of paper and was making lists on a legal pad.

"Do we need to stay at specific places to check them out, like the Concord Arms in Concord?" Jenna asked. "Because that might complicate things beyond the realm of possibility. The best shot we have at getting everything done is to move till we drop and then check into whatever fleabag happens to be handy."

Lynne laughed. "We're pretty much set on reservations, which is a good thing because during Leaf Peeper Season, any fleabag that's handy is likely to be booked solid. I've read about people without reservations who wound up sleeping in their cars. Though we do have an advantage in being on the road mid-week. Most of the New Yorkers and Bostonians who take pleasure drives to see the foliage do it on the weekends." She waved a hand in the general direction of the piles of paper. "All the suggested foliage driving tours are about one weekend's worth of travel. Whereas my tour, if it ever happens, will probably run about seven to ten days, portal to portal."

"What's the place in northern Vermont that you're so excited about?"

"The Inn at Shelburne Farms," Lynne answered, without a moment's hesitation. "And we've got reservations there Wednesday and Thursday night so we can go to the Shelburne Museum all day without having to worry about getting to our next destination. I consider that my little gift to myself on this trip."

"And our reservations haven't been screwed up by all this mess here?"

"Nope. I was able to change them and we're fine. They may even have some vacancies. The place is up on Lake Champlain, practically in Canada, and it gets cold early up there. The Inn is only open through October twentieth, so we're really just getting in under the wire."

"Wasn't October twentieth when the Lobster Shack closed, too?"

"Good memory. If it weren't for the foliage, everything would probably button up tight after Labor Day, like it does in other northern tourist areas."

Jenna nodded. "And what about the other nights?"

"Friday night we're booked at a lodge in the northern White Mountains, a place that's supposed to be a lot like what your grandmother envisions here. I'm thinking of that as a kind of reality check. And along the way, there are some B&Bs that I want to check out, but we don't need to stay at them."

"So tomorrow and Tuesday night are open?"

"Uh huh. Tomorrow is totally open. Tuesday I was hoping to get a room at the Equinox in Manchester, Vermont, but they still claim to be full."

Jenna shook her head. "They sure weren't very imaginative naming these New England towns, were they? Seems like just about every state has a Salem and a Manchester and a Concord and a Plymouth. Not to mention all those Middle-burys and Middleboros and Middletowns."

Lynne laughed. "It all depends on who settles an area, doesn't it? I bet there isn't a single San or Santa Anything in the whole region."

Lynne watched Jenna roll the little circular metal doo-hickey along the highways from South Hadford to Hartford. It was a mileage calculator designed to transfer twisting highways on maps into reliable mileage projections. Jenna peered at the face of the instrument, which resembled a compass, then scribbled on the legal pad.

"It's a bit more than a hundred miles from here to Hartford on the interstate," Jenna reported. "Worcester's the only really big city between here and there, and we can even avoid that if we stay on the 495 Beltway till it meets up with the Mass Turnpike."

"So if we left by eight or nine tomorrow morning, we could easily get there in time to go to the Mark Twain house and also visit Mrs. Grant?" Louise Grant was the widow of Charles Grant, the Golden Mills VP who had owned the Maple Leaf Inn during its boardinghouse incarnation. After her husband's death a few years earlier, she had moved to West Hartford to live with a daughter and her family. Lynne had gotten her address and phone number from Charlotte Roberts, the woman at Priscilla's tea party who had been Grant's secretary.

"I don't see why not," Jenna answered. "Of course there's no telling what kind of roadwork we'll run into, but it looks like a pretty straight shot. Is there anywhere you want to stop between here and there? Sturbridge Village is right on our path."

Lynne shook her head. "If I ever need to use Sturbridge Village, I know it will be just fine. Any of the restored towns in this part of the country will work all right as a fallback, but I don't need to actually see them all."

Jenna chuckled. "You've seen one lady in a long skirt grinding corn, you've seen 'em all."

"True enough, I guess. I do like those places, but it's really a time issue now. Is there anything else that you'd like to see?"

"The stuff I'd like to see is mostly way off our path. I'd love to see the Edward Gorey house out on Cape Cod, or Cape Cod itself, for that matter. But the stuff you need for the trip is more important. And it's not like I've never seen any beaches."

"I was thinking if we had any time left over at the end, we could go down to the Gorey House," Lynne said. "I'd kind of like to see that one too. But that was before . . ." She waved a hand toward the basement. "As it stands, we barely have enough time for what we've just been talking about."

"Think this one through, Mom," Jenna said. "I think something nice and macabre, Gorey-esque, would be just the ticket for ending this trip."

IN the morning, Jenna was up earlier than usual. Despite all the hassles related to the Maple Leaf Inn, this trip was a wonderful adventure, a look at a part of the country she had never really given much thought. She could now understand her mother's wanderlust a bit more clearly, too. There was a wonderfully sensuous freedom to be moving down roads you'd never traveled toward destinations that had previously only been dots on a map.

So many of the pleasures of this trip had been unplanned. Unplannable, really. The bog of floating cranberries. The Maine coastal bunker they discovered on their way to their lobster dinner, built in 1905 to watch out for anyone planting offshore mines. The "Falling Leaves, Fallen Lives" quilt at the New England Quilt Museum in Lowell, a tree with 3,023 leaves, one for each victim of 9/11. The remarkable clam chowder in an otherwise unremarkable Massachusetts restaurant. The wacky 3-D camouflage hunting clothing at L. L. Bean, replete with rips and tears and matching headgear, for the hunter who wants to look like a dead bush.

They were on the road by nine, having gotten permission to visit Louise Grant at her daughter's house at twelve-thirty, which presumably was after Mrs. Grant's lunch. She'd been bright and alert on the phone at eight-thirty, assuring Lynne that she'd been up for hours.

And she was still bright and alert when they reached her house.

The neighborhood was the kind of comfortable, spread-out place that you see in Hollywood depictions of middle class suburbia, with expansive lawns, huge shade trees that were still mostly green this far south, and houses that managed to be both boxy and sprawling. It was another unseasonably warm day, and both Lynne and Jenna had shed the outer layers of their go-anywhere outfits.

Mrs. Grant had asked them to come around to her ground-level entry in the rear, since her daughter would be at work and she didn't like to take unnecessary trips on the stairs. Her door, which really was the entrance to the basement, bore a cheerful wreath of fall leaves with planters of chrysanthemums in bronze and yellow hanging alongside the stairs. Given the circumstances of their visit, Jenna decided, the less gratuitous mention of basements the better.

Mrs. Grant seemed genuinely puzzled by their presence. She also seemed a bit ill at ease. "I'm happy to meet with you," she said, "but I honestly don't see what I can tell you. I've spoken with the detective from the New Hampshire State Police several times and told him over and over that I really don't know anything. They even made a special trip down here to see me."

"Well, we were passing through town anyway," Lynne said, "though I'm glad to know they're being so thorough."

Louise Grant wore wool, blithely ignoring the weather. Her softly gathered gray plaid skirt hung below her knees and the beige twin set she wore above it would have been suitable for any fall in any of the past hundred years. Her shoes were no-nonsense lace-up black leather brogans and her stockings looked to be some kind of support hose. Jenna realized, as they came inside, that it would be unthinkable to call this venerable woman anything but Mrs. Grant.

Mrs. Grant brought them into a sitting room furnished with solid old furniture and sturdy chairs that promised little in the way of comfort. A faint aroma of soup hung in the air.

"I'm sorry about what's happened to your place," she said when they were settled, "but I don't see what it is that you want from me. I already told the police that the boarding-house was Charlie's bailiwick. He liked the idea of having a place where mill employees could live as they got situated in town. There's always been some portion of the mill worker population who are transients, and South Hadford didn't have much in the way of housing for those folks. Charlie was a bit of a visionary." There was unmistakable pride in her voice. "He believed in giving a chance to people who were a bit down on their luck, and having lodgings for them was part of his plan."

Jenna was seated on a love seat beside a small table, posi-tioned to give her a view of the entire room as her mother spoke with the older woman. The living area was compact but homey, and she assumed that behind the doors on the op-posite wall, one would find bedroom, lavatory, and some kind of kitchenette. Mrs. Grant had found herself a pleasant compromise between the independence of living alone in an oversized house and the reassuring presence of others in a re-tirement facility. And in this newer suburban construction, the basement was built to be livable, to be used. Not like the creepy basement of the Maple Leaf Inn, or Aunt Abby's, which actually was worse, with a dirt floor.

The furniture here looked used and loved, and there wasn't a speck of dust anywhere. Wall-to-wall beige Berber carpet was covered with several area rugs, sumptuous Oriental car-pets in colors that coordinated perfectly with each other and the rest of the room. The impression was of genteel good taste, the kind you had to be born with.

On the table beside Jenna stood an arrangement of pho-tographs in gleaming silver frames. She looked closer. The largest was an eight-by-ten studio portrait showing a much younger Louise Grant, a stern man with silvering hair who had to be Charles Grant, and three teenage children. The two girls favored Louise, and the boy was a taller, thinner version of Charles. Charlie, Mrs. Grant called him. He didn't look like a Charlie. He looked like a Mr. Grant.

"When you talked to the New Hampshire detective," Lynne said, "did he ask about records from the boardinghouse?"

"He did indeed, and I told him there weren't any. Charlie was always a bit secretive about business in general and the boardinghouse in particular. He kept the boardinghouse files in his office, but after he retired and brought all those papers home, he put them in the fire. He said it was past the seven years he needed to keep them for tax purposes and that they were wasting space."

"Did he burn other papers?" Lynne asked.

"Some," Mrs. Grant said.

"Were there a lot of them?"

"Oh my, yes. It seemed like he burned papers for days."

"When he owned the boardinghouse, did he spend much time over there?"

Mrs. Grant shrugged. "I don't really know. He worked long hours in general, and I never knew if he was at the mill or checking on some of his rental properties. He was kind of a hands-on landlord, though he didn't do any of the fix-it work himself. I do know that he had difficulty keeping couples to manage the boardinghouse, though usually somebody would turn up pretty promptly when he needed new help. There seemed to be a great many young people floating around back then."

"Was there ever a period when the building was empty?" Lynne asked.

They'd talked about this on the drive down. Jenna felt certain that if a group of young mill workers and students lived at the boardinghouse, there was no way that anybody could have killed two people and buried them downstairs, and her mother tended to agree. The cul-de-sac was situated so it would be difficult to drive a car full of bodies down Barrington Road without being noticed, though if somebody had legitimate business at the boardinghouse, that person probably wouldn't seem out of place. Once at the boardinghouse, it was technically feasible to drive around to the back door, almost to the basement entrance. But you'd still need to get the bodies down the basement stairs, and be certain that nobody'd be roaming around down in the basement looking for the fuse box or a missing sock.

Mrs. Grant nodded. "I've been trying to remember. He had a lot of work done at one point, but I don't remember if there were boarders living there at the time. They came and went, you see. Some of them stayed for several years and others were gone in a week."

"Do you remember when that was?" Lynne asked. "When he had the work done?"

"I told the police I didn't," Mrs. Grant said, "but now that I think about it, I'm pretty sure it was the fall that Charlie had his emergency appendectomy. That was Amelia's senior year, and I remember it because she had the lead in the school play that fall. *Our Town.* She was Emily. She and I were just talking about all this the other day."

Amelia was the daughter with whom Mrs. Grant lived now, the one who was off at work somewhere.

"Our kids were always heavily involved in drama," Mrs. Grant continued. "Johnny even went and studied acting in New York for a while. Anyway, Charlie was really frustrated then because he wasn't supposed to be up and around and he wouldn't hear of using a wheelchair or even a cane, for heaven's sake. Men are so silly about those things. Of course we worked out a way to get him in to see Amelia in the play, but Charlie couldn't supervise what was happening at the boardinghouse and he fussed a bit about it."

"Who was doing the work?" Lynne asked.

"Mostly Ralph Tracy, I think. Charlie had owned some rental houses in that neighborhood and he sold them around the same time to put the money into the boardinghouse, because it needed so much work. I believe he sold one of them to Ralph, as a matter of fact. Across from the boardinghouse.

The girl the Tracys adopted lives there now. Cindy something. I forget her married name." She frowned.

"Jackson," Jenna supplied. "I didn't realize she was adopted."

"Oh yes," Louise Grant said. "It was so sad. Her mother so desperately wanted children, and she had stillbirths over and over again."

Jenna remembered the several tiny markers she'd seen that first day in town at the First Congregational Cemetery for "Baby Lucinda Tracy." She hadn't made the connection then, but she hadn't yet met Cindy. Who looked nothing like her mother. Her adoptive mother.

"I believe Cindy actually married one of the young men who lived at the boardinghouse when Charlie was running it," Mrs. Grant went on. "Anyway, Charlie sold that rental house to Ralph."

"Todd was one of the boarders?" Lynne asked, sounding surprised. "Nobody ever mentioned that."

"Probably because it's common knowledge around town. It was interesting, though, because so many of those workers in the mill move on, you know. I thought it was lovely when that boy married Cindy. Though I only knew the Tracys through church, of course."

Of course? The implication was that the Grants didn't move in the same social circles as Cindy and her family. Jenna supposed this made sense if you considered that Ralph was a handyman and Mr. Grant a mill VP. She was more interested, actually, in the news that Cindy's husband was one of the guys from the boardinghouse. Jenna hadn't seen much of Todd Jackson, a lanky, middle-aged fellow who worked long hours at some kind of computer company over in Nashua. Nice but bland, he'd seemed. And very devoted to Bradley.

"It must have taken quite a while to get the boardinghouse in shape," Lynne said. "I know that my mother's been overwhelmed by all the work that's needed now, and that's after it was owned by the Saxtons for twenty years. Not that they abused it or anything," she added hastily, "but apparently they took in a number of foster children over the years and the place got a bit run down. Ralph tells my mother that whenever there was a choice between fixing something right or making do, they always opted for making do."

"That's the Saxtons all right," Mrs. Grant said, nodding her head. "I must say I admired Otto and Laura for all they did with those foster kids, though. They had four of their own, after all, which would be more than most folks could handle. But they just kept opening their hearts to those poor youngsters. I believe one of them actually married one of their natural daughters." She smiled. "It was all I could do to raise my own three kids, never mind anybody else's." Her eyes moved to the portrait on the table by Jenna.

Jenna picked up the picture. "These are your children?"

Mrs. Grant nodded. "Amelia's on the left. She's the youngest. Then Sandra and Johnny. He's the oldest."

"Do your other children still live in South Hadford?" Jenna asked.

Mrs. Grant shook her head and a flicker of sadness crossed her dark brown eyes. "They're both in Boston. Sandra's an attorney with a large firm and Johnny has a very successful business. I don't get to see them as often as I'd like."

Jenna picked up another picture of Mrs. Grant seated at the center of a group of well-scrubbed children, with a smattering of adults standing behind her. "These are your grandchildren?"

"They are indeed." As Mrs. Grant identified the children and matched them to parents, she offered the universal Grandma Grin, the one that turned the most competent, level-headed women into gushing, dithering idiots. Interesting to see that even the most totally proper women were not exempt. Jenna figured it was probably hormonal.

"If we could get back to when your husband had the place renovated," Lynne said carefully. "That was Amelia's senior year? When did she graduate?"

Mrs. Grant closed her eyes and lowered her head for a moment as she thought. "She was in the class of seventy-one," she said, opening her eyes, "so that would have been the fall of nineteen seventy."

The fall of 1970.

When Eldon Weibeck and Sydney Shackleford visited Eldon's family in New Bedford, then disappeared.

Chapter 24

THE neighborhood was quiet this time of day, which wasn't surprising. Suburbs emptied out on weekdays. Parents were at work, usually both of them toiling so they could make the payments on the too-big houses. The kids attended schools where lunch was served, not like it used to be when moms were home, fixing noonday nourishment for their offspring. A few maids or cleaning ladies, maybe, but little chance anyone would be looking out the windows.

And if they were, they wouldn't see much.

She had too much of a conscience, and she was too damned smart. It was a shame he had to do this, but sometimes bad things couldn't be helped. A late-model white Chevy sedan was parked right in front of the house. What the—?

He decided to wait and settled himself comfortably in the back of the borrowed van. Seemed like every time he had to tidy something up lately, it involved waiting. He'd "borrowed" the van from an owner who was in the Bahamas, because it was generally nondescript, bearing only the vague

company name "Bright Horizons" and an 800 number on its
windowless sides. Precautions were important.

A few minutes later, his patience was rewarded.

Some reward. It was worse than he'd ever imagined.

Two women came up the path from the rear of the house.
He froze in horror as he realized that the older one he'd seen
on the news, telling some reporter she had nothing to say
about what had happened in her mother's basement.

As if she had any idea what actually had happened in her
mother's basement. He allowed himself a small smile.

But why was she here, and who was the tall young blonde
with her? The girl was a real babe, too. They were laughing
and talking. Both looked healthy and happy and uncon-
cerned.

Which meant that they hadn't learned anything. He hoped.

He had no way of knowing what had happened in there.

Should he follow the women, or go inside? Too bad he
hadn't tagged the car when he had the chance while they
were inside. But how could he have known?

Best to stay with the women and wait for another opportunity. He let them pull away, then started the engine and followed at a discreet distance.

Chapter 25

LYNNE turned to Jenna as they left Louise Grant's daughter's house. "So what comes first? Track down that Colwhistle office or the Mark Twain house?"

"Whichever," Jenna said, checking her watch. "Why don't we get the Colwhistle thing out of the way, since it's not too likely that he's going to be there anyway. Then we won't have to race out of the Twain house."

"Fair enough, navigator. Get us to Pratt Street."

About twenty minutes later they'd found the address in downtown Hartford, not far from the Connecticut Capitol Building, one of the few buildings described as looking like a wedding cake that actually *did* look like a wedding cake. It was white with lacy turrets and arches and gables, all liberally decorated with squiggles of something that might well have been frosting. Gold piping abounded and the gaudy gold dome looked like a gazebo that should be harboring statuettes of a bride and groom.

Pratt Street seemed downright modest and unassuming after that, though in fact it was much nicer. Will Colwhistle's

Hartford address was on a little downtown road with brick pavement, quite charming and as sophisticated in its own way as the Portland office.

"He's got a taste for the old and understated," Jenna muttered as they entered the stone building.

"Maybe that's why he wanted to finance the Maple Leaf Inn."

"Yeah, right. Of all the old houses in New England, he had to finance this one."

Inside the lobby, big glass cases were filled with displays for various state agencies and other tenants in the building. The woodwork was rich and smooth, but Lynne didn't truly appreciate the building until she happened to glance upward.

"Good God. Jenna, look." She pointed upward. "I think you may have spoken a bit too soon about understated."

Jenna dutifully peered up at a heavy dark wooden ceiling painted with geometric patterns on heavy beams and cross beams. It looked a bit like the interiors of California missions. "What on earth is this doing in a town like Hartford?"

"I can't imagine," Lynne told her.

For all she knew, the ceiling might actually have *been* from some Spanish mission, presumably located elsewhere than Connecticut. William Randolph Hearst certainly wasn't the only rich man who'd looted and plundered architectural wonders from around the globe. It was, she supposed, barely possible that this ceiling had been designed for the building, though she couldn't imagine a designer sufficiently confused to mate that ceiling and this lobby.

They rode the elevator to the Colwhistle office. Like its Portland counterpart, it featured a collection of brass plates by the suite door: attorneys, accountants, a chiropractor, an endodontist, and Will Colwhistle Financial Planning. Inside they found a small lobby with an African American receptionist, a pretty young woman with short, processed hair and neon red lipstick and nail polish. Lynne realized with a start that Hartford was the first place they'd been on this trip where she'd noticed more than a smattering of racial minorities. For the most part New England, like the Old England that had spawned it, remained mighty white.

Unlike Portland, this reception desk had nobody's name on it. Its occupant was tapping something diffidently into a computer when they walked into the lobby. Lynne and Jenna stood silently at the desk for a moment before she looked up. "Can I help you?"

"Will Colwhistle, please," Lynne said, her voice offhand and just a tad officious.

"I'm sorry, he's not here," the receptionist answered in a bored tone.

"How can that be? I was certain he was planning to meet us today," Lynne said.

"I don't think so." Still bored.

"And why would that be?" Still officious.

"Because I've never seen the man once." The receptionist leaned back in her chair.

"But this is his office. His name is on a plaque in the hall," Jenna put in. "Mail that we've sent to this address hasn't been returned."

Lynne listened with mixed affection and regret. What a facile liar she had raised!

"That's because it gets forwarded," the woman said. "I tell you, the man isn't here. He's never here."

"Forwarded to where?" Lynne asked.

"I'm afraid that's confidential."

"Well, does he get a lot of mail?" Jenna asked. "That needs to be forwarded?"

But the receptionist was shutting down, her window of indiscretion slamming shut. "If you leave a message, I'll send it along."

"That's all right," Lynne told her with a warm and friendly smile. "Tell him Mrs. Montgomery came by, and that I'll catch him in Montpelier."

✌

THE Mark Twain House was one of the ugliest buildings Jenna had ever seen.

When Twain coined the term "Gilded Age," he might well have been referring directly to the huge and garish structure he'd erected here. The exterior was burnt orange and black, a darker, smaller version of the Capitol monstrosity. It featured porches and balconies and chimneys and gables and turrets— pretty much every architectural excess and affectation the era had produced.

It had a Disney sort of feel to it, but this wasn't where the princess would find her true love. It was where the prince would be imprisoned and hung by his thumbs. It was pure Disney nightmare.

How could anyone reconcile the man who built this hideous place with the sometime Mississippi River steamboat captain, the young journalist who'd hung out in western mining towns, writing about jumping frogs and editing a Silver City newspaper? What on earth had he been thinking?

Once inside, it was obvious what he'd been thinking. He wanted the biggest, most original, most pretentious house that money could buy. Big as it was, that wasn't enough. He cheated; the stair railings at the building's core were lower than normal to make the house seem even taller. He had hired Louis Comfort Tiffany to decorate the place. If there had been an *Architectural Digest* during the Gilded Age, this house would have been a cover feature.

Everything was heavy and dark and grotesque, though not always authentic. The entry hall wasn't actually inlaid with mother-of-pearl, but was stenciled instead with silver paint. Wallpaper elsewhere that was supposed to look like leather was just heavy coats of paint. The overall effect was so bizarre and appalling that it hardly mattered what was real and what was faux. Faux probably didn't matter much, in any case, to a guy whose books were published under a pseudonym.

"The money for the house came from his wife Olivia, whose family was wealthy," the docent told them. "This meant that later when he went bankrupt after a couple of his schemes didn't work out, he could at least keep the house, because it was in her name."

"I'd think he'd have welcomed an excuse to get rid of it," Lynne murmured.

While Jenna wasn't entirely sure what she'd expected, this definitely wasn't it. Just last night she'd told her mother that she particularly wanted to see the Twain house because it was where he'd written *Huckleberry Finn* and *The Adventures of Tom Sawyer.* Obviously from memory or imagination, since nothing she'd seen here so far even hinted at humility, simplicity, or charm.

"He always said that the happiest years of his life were from 1874 to 1891 when he lived here," the docent went on. "As we move through the house, you'll see evidence of some of his fascination with technology. He went broke with a typesetting machine called the Compositor. Over in that corner is one of the first telephones, but it worked so badly he kept a written record of the sounds that came through—thunder, artillery, and so on. He had a stereopticon in one room and a typewriter in another. Samuel Clemens was the first author to submit a typed manuscript to a publisher."

And so it went, one gloomy room after another.

There wasn't a stick of furniture in the place that looked comfortable, and the only respite from dark, looming rooms and furnishings was an alcove filled with plants, the all-too-tiny conservatory. An atrocious fake Venetian bed that Clemens claimed to adore was grotesquely carved with angels that unscrewed on the corners. "He loved this bed," the docent said, "and he took it with him when he left here. He used the footboard as his headboard so he could see more of the carvings as he worked. There are a number of pictures of him writing in this bed. And eventually he died in it. He was born during an appearance of Halley's Comet, and he died seventy-four years later when the comet returned."

Jenna made short work of the gift shop, where she bought a t-shirt with a Twain quote: "If a man could be crossed with a cat it would improve man, but it would deteriorate the cat."

Outside Jenna turned to her mother. "Don't ask. I don't

know what I think about this, except that I wish I hadn't come. And as for the rest of this compound"—she waved an arm at the three other elderly buildings on this historical island, now surrounded by a decidedly less-well-maintained neighborhood—"I don't really care about seeing the Harriet Beecher Stowe House and I think it's too late anyway. So on to Amherst. But I better not find out that Miss Emily's house looks like Sleeping Beauty's castle."

"Didn't Miss Emily write 'Hope is the thing with feathers'?" Lynne asked.

Jenna nodded, affection clear in her smile. "Uh huh. Which is why that Woody Allen book was called *Without Feathers.* Is there any chance of finding someplace quiet and charming to stay tonight? I don't want cute, particularly. Just calm."

"Then calm it shall be," Lynne promised. "I was looking at a place up near Amherst. The units all have private baths and there's a continental breakfast, all set in a grove of maples. Shall I call to see if they've got a room?"

"Yes, please. Sounds perfect."

And it was.

Chapter 26

FOLLOWING *the women had turned out to be a royal pain, and he regretted not tagging the car when he had the chance, though he certainly had no reason at the time to think it belonged to anybody useful.*

First they went to downtown Hartford, where parking, ironically, was a bitch and a half. He managed to stay with them as they went into an office building, but they were out again so quickly that he couldn't imagine what they were up to.

Then they went to the parking lot at Nook Hill, where the Twain and Beecher Stowe houses were open to the public. They got out and the young blonde stretched languidly. She was a looker, tousled blonde hair, soft golden tan, long legs in a short denim skirt. Mother and daughter, he'd decided, though there hadn't been anything in the news to indicate the existence of the younger woman.

He watched them move toward the buildings. Tourists. And probably tourists who'd be there for a while.

It was too tricky trying to follow them directly. What he

needed was an advantage, and, like every good Boy Scout, he had come prepared. As he waited for them to disappear into the building complex, a Toyota pulled out of the parking spot right next to the driver's door.

Fate. Serendipity. Finally something was going his way. He didn't like to think much about the tasks that still awaited him.

He pulled the van into the snug parking space and slid over to the passenger window to do a little reconnaissance before getting out.

A box on the backseat was filled with neatly filed maps and brochures, along with various New England guidebooks: AAA, Smithsonian Historic, Fodor, Frommer, Michelin, and the Countryman Explorer Guides. These people were doing some serious sightseeing, which of course fit the description of the Montgomery woman who'd found the bodies. A travel agent.

He pulled on a pair of those handy latex gloves that all the pharmacies sold these days, then quietly opened the passenger door of the van and slipped out, leaving the door unlatched. First he dropped his keys and bent to pick them up, tucking the small tracking device into a protected spot beneath the chassis. Then, after casually glancing all around and noticing nobody who appeared to be paying any attention to him, he used the highly illegal slim jim to open the driver's door, then sat in the driver's seat and explored.

He was quickly rewarded by a legal pad on the floor of the driver's seat inside a neat folder labeled "Reservations." He memorized the key names and dates, sorry to see that most of them were so far afield. He'd have to really juggle his schedule to connect again.

Then he replaced the legal pad exactly as he'd found it, looked outside again to be sure the coast was clear, and exited the Chevy, locking the door behind him.

He got back into the van and went to take care of his other local business.

Chapter 27

AMHERST didn't disappoint.

Lynne was pleased to see that they were able to tour the Dickinson Homestead—Emily's room, anyway, the rest of the building being dedicated to unspecified educational pursuits—check out of their lodge, and get back on the road again by eleven the next morning. It was odd to think of a pretty young lady once known as the Belle of Amherst becoming so agoraphobic that she never went outside at all.

With only two days till their reservation at the Inn at Shelburne Farms, they'd decided to skip the Berkshires. True, photographs promised an area that was undeniably pretty, and yes, it had been home to a lot of literary figures. A landlocked Melville had written much of *Moby Dick* here and the Hawthornes had lived here intermittently. Edith Wharton, with the tremendous advantage of money not derived from writing, lifted the concept of writers' residences to a new and staggering height with The Mount, which Lynne privately thought might well be another version of the Twain House.

But mostly the Berkshires seemed to be a place writers drifted in and out of, partly, at least, because of its proximity to Manhattan.

The farther Lynne got geographically from the Maple Leaf Inn, the less likely her mother's venture—and Lynne's consequent tour—became. She was starting to take the Scarlett O'Hara approach to the whole thing. Tomorrow was another day. If the trip actually came together, she'd come back east and pick up the loose ends before it began. She'd need to see firsthand, in any case, that the Maple Leaf Inn was actually ready for guests.

She and Jenna headed north from Amherst, leaving the interstate to go west at Greenfield on the Mohawk Trail. Running some sixty-odd miles across the top of northwestern Massachusetts, this former Indian trail was still mostly isolated, with long expanses between indications of civilization.

For the most part, the houses along the sparsely populated highway were worn down and dilapidated, needing paint and somebody to gather up the junk cluttering their unkempt yards. This wouldn't seem remarkable, Lynne realized, if almost everything else they'd seen in New England weren't so spic and span. The single constant in these tired old residences was satellite dishes hanging off their unpainted exteriors.

Nature's display of color more than compensated for man's failures at maintenance, however. Gold foliage rimmed the roadside and small golden leaves floated out of the trees and across the highway. Coral sumac grew in drifts alongside the road. Across the hills and valleys, once-green vistas were brushed with the blazing crimson of maples and the gentle gold of ash and birches. Green fields were dotted with accents of dusky vermilion and crisp light yellow. Splashes of scarlet and saffron brightened the nearby hills.

The smoky scent of wood-burning stoves filled the air as they drove through tiny towns that time and everybody else had forgotten. They passed the statue of an Indian with MO-HAWK TRAIL spelled out in stone at Hail to Sunrise Park, then stopped down the road at a gift shop with a hand-lettered sign on the porch: GET YOUR TURNIP FESTIVAL TICKETS HERE.

"Dang, and we'll miss it," Jenna said, jotting it onto her list of oddball signs, below a recent entry for LIVE PARKING ONLY. How else would one park?

Jenna drove as they turned north and continued into Vermont on Highway 7. The roads with low numbers were usually some of the finest in New England because they tended to be the oldest. More and more splashes of red and gold appeared in the scenery as they passed by. And it was every bit as vivid as one could hope for.

This was why Lynne had come, why she'd agreed to her mother's plans for next year's tour, why she was able to cast off the worries and concerns back in South Hadford. There were plenty of magnificent natural wonders in the United States: artistically carved canyons, dazzling waterfalls, craggy beaches, fantastic caverns, mountain vistas, placid bayous.

These few weeks of colorful foliage in New England each year measured up next to any of them.

THEY paid homage to Robert Frost at his lottery-winning grave site at the First Congregational Church in Bennington, then slipped inside where an enthusiastic deacon was explaining the church's history to two busloads of visitors in Christian tour groups. The pulpit loomed high above the pew boxes, reached by stairways on both sides. The South Hadford church had replaced its colonial pew boxes with more modern rows, but here tradition ruled and the boxes remained, though decidedly non-authentic cushions had been added to sooth noncolonial derrieres.

They moved into downtown Bennington for a late lunch, and as they waited to be served, Lynne's phone rang, the soft, mellifluous tone she had reprogrammed back on Monday as she and Jenna fled the Maple Leaf Inn for the serenity of Strawbery Banke.

"Don't get it," Jenna said. "It's bound to be trouble. We're right in the middle of a nice meal in a nice town and there's nothing you can do about anything anyway."

The soft chime persisted.

"Attagirl," Jenna went on. "Now if you're really a tough cookie, you'll turn it off without even looking to see who's calling. And then call back later. Maybe."

As nearby diners began to look irritably in her direction, Lynne capitulated. "I can't help myself," she confessed, picking up the phone, recognizing Priscilla's number and saying, "Hello, Mom."

"Oh, thank heaven I got hold of you," Priscilla said, running her words together, her tone all breathless. "I just heard the saddest news. Louise Grant—you know, the wife of Mr. Grant who used to own this place—passed away yesterday."

Chapter 28

PRISCILLA was humming tunes from the *Camelot* sound-track and unpacking more of her dishes in the dining room, realizing how nice it had been to have the Wedgwood out for Lynne's getting-to-know-you party, when a knock came at the front door.

She peeked out the dining room curtains, saw Cindy Jackson, and went to let her young neighbor in. Cindy seemed distraught.

"What is it?" Priscilla asked, opening the door wider. "For goodness sake, come on in."

"It's Daddy," Cindy said, fighting for composure. "I was just at the hospital. He's still unconscious and now they're saying he's in a chronic vegetative state. Nobody knows when he'll wake up. *If* he'll wake up."

Priscilla had plenty of experience soothing the afflicted and bereaved. She moved into auto-comfort and circled an arm around the girl's shoulders. "Where's Bradley?"

"Here I am!" the youngster piped up, poking his head over the edge of the porch. "Gotcha!"

"Bradley, come on inside with us," Priscilla told him, not releasing Cindy. "Would you like to watch some television?"

Bradley hauled himself up onto the porch without bothering to go around to the steps. "Sure! Whatcha got?"

Even in her distress, Cindy seemed to register what she considered unacceptable behavior. She turned her head to give the boy a glare. "Bradley, watch your manners. Mrs. Jones will tell you what she has."

Priscilla had recently bought a video of *Pinocchio* with an eye toward . . . well, she wasn't really sure what she'd had an eye toward, but maybe she'd been unconsciously preparing for just this moment.

"Come along upstairs with me," she told him. "I've got a special Disney surprise for you. Cindy, why don't you go sit down in the kitchen and I'll be right back."

She hustled Bradley up to her room, scanned it hurriedly for anything that might get a young boy in trouble, discovered dozens of potential problems, then decided to trust his good behavior and settled him in front of the TV. Thank heavens he was past that awful stage where they put everything in their mouths, where they were smart enough to get the cleaning fluid bottle open but still dumb enough to drink the contents. Priscilla set an internal mental alarm for fifteen minutes to come back and check on him and returned downstairs.

Maybe it was time to get the TV set up in the parlor.

Cindy was sitting at the kitchen table when she returned. "The police keep bothering Mama, trying to find Daddy's business records. But Daddy isn't the kind of person who's ever kept business records, really. He'd work for people and put their payments in a little ledger and pay taxes, but it was all pretty informal. Now they're saying that he must have been involved in killing those people and hiding their bodies."

"Based on what?" Priscilla had actually been wondering about this possibility herself. Ever since Ralph's uncharacteristic fainting spell the first morning Lynne was in town, Priscilla had felt vaguely uneasy. The innocent didn't react that way, flu or no. And she realized now that Ralph probably hadn't realized the basement floor was being broken up until he actually arrived that morning. He'd been out of commission while the plumber and Jason made those arrangements.

Of course, if Ralph actually *had* been responsible for anything back all those years ago, he might not even be able to remember it. Could they put you in jail for doing something you didn't even remember? Well, obviously. They jailed drunk drivers all the time for accidents that occurred during alcoholic blackouts, and rightly so. She'd worried about that possibility constantly during the later years of her marriage to Tony Doolittle.

"I'm not sure," Cindy said. "I feel like such a baby. I just talked to Todd and he said he'd come home, but I don't want to bother him."

"He's your husband, Cindy. It shouldn't bother him to take care of you."

"I just feel like I should be doing something."

"You're watching out for your son," Priscilla told her gently, though in reality neither one of them was paying the slightest attention to Bradley. For all they knew, he was dangling out her bedroom window by one arm, having already drunk all her expensive perfume. "I'll run up and check on him in just a minute. Where's your mother?" She should have asked this first.

Cindy shrugged. "Out at the Washington Arms. I took her back before I came here. It's too stressful for her to just wait there at the hospital, watching Daddy."

"Tell you what," Priscilla said. "I'll call my sister and we can brainstorm a bit."

"She hates me," Cindy said. "She always seemed to have it in for Todd when he worked at Golden Mills."

Priscilla frowned. This was new information. "When was that?"

"Oh, back in the seventies, sometime."

"Well, I'm sure it was nothing personal and no reflection on his work," Priscilla assured her, though with Abby you

could never be certain. "Abby's just a little brusque sometimes."

Priscilla placed a hasty phone call to Abigail, who promised,
brusquely, to come right over.

BY the time Abby arrived, Cindy's hands were cupped
around a mug of Irish Breakfast tea and Bradley was still
watching *Pinocchio* upstairs. Priscilla had checked on him
twice and he seemed totally engrossed in the movie. The TV
was definitely coming downstairs. Her knees couldn't stand
too much of this up and down stairs business.

"I spoke by telephone with young William O'Keefe," Abigail announced when she came in. "He was reluctant to share
any information, so I then called Charlotte Roberts—you
know, Mr. Grant's secretary?"

Priscilla nodded. Cindy didn't move.

"Charlotte told me," Abigail went on, "that when the
boardinghouse was first opened in 1968, there were so many
physical problems with the place, particularly with the water
and septic systems, that after a year or two, Mr. Grant had to
completely close it down to do repairs."

"But does she know when that was?" Cindy asked.

Abigail nodded. "Charlotte was able to link it to outside
events. She's certain that he opened the place as a boardinghouse in 1968 because he was very involved in the Eugene
McCarthy presidential campaign at the same time, and between that and this property, she had to cover for him a lot at
the mill. And she was able to tie the work on the property to
late 1970 and early 1971 because again she was covering for
Mr. Grant." Her tone carried both surprise and disappoint-
ment, as if it had never occurred to her that one of the vice
presidents of the mill she considered her second home might
ever have been derelict in his duties.

"We introduced a new line of sweaters made of cotton, the
Hampshire Hills line, that same winter," Abigail went on.
"There were quite a few technical difficulties with that line,

though eventually it became very successful. But in the beginning, the equipment we were using wasn't entirely compatible with the fiber changes. I checked just now with somebody I know who's still working at Golden Mills. She told me the police have been there several times going through the mill records to work out the time frames for all these things. And she said one of them let slip that the records at Gradolf Hardware show Ralph making large purchases of cement that fall."

The doorbell rang and Priscilla sprang to answer it, in what she suddenly realized was an entirely preposterous hope that it might be Lynne and Jenna.

It wasn't. It was Todd Jackson instead. Todd was a lanky man, all knees and elbows, dressed in khakis and a short-sleeved white shirt. His rust-colored hair was thick and luxuriant, his blue eyes anxious and troubled. A redheaded Ichabod Crane.

"Is Cindy all right?" he asked, hurrying into the kitchen. Cindy struggled to her feet so she could collapse into his arms. Her distress was obvious.

"Let's get Bradley," he suggested, "and go to the park. We haven't been paying him much attention this past week, and I think he's scared."

"Who isn't?" Cindy said, but she nodded agreement and went upstairs to get her son.

After she was gone, Priscilla noticed Todd looking curiously around the kitchen.

"You've really fixed this place up well," he told her. "I like the way you've reworked the kitchen."

"That's mostly your father-in-law's handiwork," Priscilla said. "Did you see it before he began?"

Todd smiled. "A long time ago. I lived here in the mid-seventies."

"Really? Before Cindy mentioned it just now I had no idea." Priscilla hated being the last to know anything.

He nodded. "That's actually how I first met Cindy, though she was just a kid at the time. The Tracys were right across the street, in the house where we live now. I was working at the mill." He nodded at Abigail. "As you may recall."

Was there any male under sixty in this town that Abby hadn't terrorized in the course of employment?

"Todd was one of our best and brightest workers," Abigail continued. "I was sorry to lose him."

Todd shook his head and smiled for the first time. Abby might have just given him her equivalent of a gold medal endorsement, but he clearly still feared her.

Priscilla did some fast calculations. Cindy couldn't have been more than eight or nine at the time. "And you . . . stayed in touch with Cindy?"

He laughed. "Not at all. After a while I left and moved to Nashua. It was years later before I connected with Cindy again. We'd each been through a bad marriage by then and something just clicked. But I certainly never imagined that I'd be living in this cul-de-sac again. If it weren't for her parents' health problems, we'd still be in Nashua."

"This is a better place to raise a child," Priscilla told him. "What was it like? Living at the boardinghouse?"

Todd considered. "Well, it was comfortable but kind of formal, if you get what I'm saying. Each of us had a private room, which I imagine are the same bedrooms you still have upstairs. There was a kind of apartment in the back here where the managers would live." He gestured toward a back quadrant of the house, the library and the bedroom that was still full of boxes awaiting attention. When everything was done upstairs, Priscilla intended to move her own room down here, where she wouldn't be sleeping on the same hall as total strangers.

"There still is," Priscilla told him. "And how many of you were here at a time?"

Todd considered, quietly counting on his fingers. "Usually about six or eight, plus the managers. Most of us had single rooms but sometimes there were couples who'd be together."

"And the managers?" Abigail put in. "Were they couples as well?"

"Usually, though for a while there was a girl who did it all by herself, the cooking and everything. She had a baby and no daddy around, so it was a good spot for her. Cute little kid, too."

Priscilla assumed that when there was a couple, the woman would do the cooking and Todd confirmed this. "Except for this one couple, Betsy and Jack. Jack was an incredible cook. I sure hated to see them leave."

"Did Mr. Grant come around often?" Abigail asked.

Todd shook his head. "Hardly ever that I was aware of."

Cindy and Bradley appeared in the doorway. "Bradley wants to ask you something," Cindy said. She had *Pinocchio* in her hand.

Bradley's face was serious. "Can we borrow that movie? It's not done yet."

"Certainly," Priscilla told him. She looked up at Cindy and Todd. "Keep us informed."

"Of course," Todd told her, and the Jacksons left.

Abby left then, too, and Priscilla was alone once again. She tried to pick up where she'd left off unpacking the dishes, using deep breathing to relax. She only wished there were some way that relaxed state could continue, could flow into the mainstream of her life.

As long as she owned the Maple Leaf Inn, she was starting to realize, she could kiss relaxation good-bye.

Chapter 29

OF all the things he'd done this past week, this was the riskiest and most important. It was, he had convinced himself, all a matter of attitude.

He had the syringes from the daily insulin injections he'd given Raffles, his diabetic cat. Raffles had eventually succumbed, thoughtfully leaving behind his medical equipment. If Ralph had been diabetic, it would have been even easier. The insulin was still there in the refrigerator, maybe a little out-of-date, but drug manufacturers built in margins of error to those expiration dates, he was sure.

Not that it mattered.

Insulin was not the drug of choice.

He went to the library and reviewed the Physicians' Desk Reference in the reference room. His own blood pressure medication was an ACE inhibitor. He'd never really understood what that meant, but again, it didn't matter. He ground up half a dozen of them and steeped them in a small amount of vodka. Then, to be on the safe side, he added half a dozen more. There was no hurry. He could take as long as was necessary to dissolve them.

When they were ready, he filled two syringes. It never hurt to be overprepared.

Chapter 30

JENNA knew that back before they left California for New England—a time span that was starting to feel as far removed as the Hundred Years War—her mother had hoped to find a reasonably priced room at the Equinox in Manchester, Vermont.

The Equinox was, by all accounts, a remarkable resort, a place over two hundred years old where miscellaneous presidents and endless other important folks had stayed, in a town where the sidewalks were reputedly made of marble. It offered activities that ranged from golf to falconry. Alas, they had learned, two conferences had the place booked solid. All that was left were a couple of suites in the seven-to-nine-hundred-dollar range in the Charles Orvis Inn, which was apparently some kind of sub-hostelry. What could make them worth that kind of money Jenna couldn't begin to imagine.

But even those megabuck suites were gone by the time they reached Manchester, when Lynne insisted on stopping by to check on possible cancellations.

Jenna had been playing a little game with herself, thinking

about the things she could do with even the low-end one-night rental cost of one of those suites. A really great bicycle, though she didn't have room to store it. A fancy new TV—no, a whole home theater, complete with popcorn and a new microwave. Some racy lingerie from Victoria's Secret. A carload of Godiva chocolates. A six-pack of every beer they sold at Trader Joe's. A weekend in San Francisco. Even better, a long weekend of spa pampering.

She was relieved when they found a pleasant room in a charming motor lodge elsewhere in town, in a grove of sugar maples with foliage that was a rich blend of green and gold. The autumn air was crisp and dry, and they needed sweaters now to hold off the chill as they walked around town. Even the familiar displays of pumpkins and cornstalks and vivid chrysanthemums seemed fresher here, more vibrant.

In their perambulation, they admired individual leaves on trees and bushes that were changing color, stopping in awe several times at particularly striking exhibits of foliage. Then they draped the soft woolen shawls they'd bought in Portland around their California shoulders and splurged on an uptown dinner at the Colonnade restaurant at the Equinox.

"I want you to order whatever you'd like," Lynne instructed, as Jenna blanched at the prices. "Ignore the right hand side of the menu altogether. Every now and then it's nice to give in to self-indulgence."

Jenna, who already knew this, decided that the experiences she would count under that heading probably weren't things she wanted to share with her mother. "You got it, Mom. And you know, even with all that hassle back in South Hadford, this is a really cool trip. Thanks for bringing me along."

"The pleasure's all mine," Lynne told her. "Now let's look at the wine list."

EXPLAIN to me again, please," Lynne said at breakfast in the Marsh Tavern the next morning, "how it's possible for all this foliage to change color so quickly." The sugar maples outside their hotel room had lost all traces of green overnight and now glowed gold in the nippy morning air. "I always think about that scene in *Fantasia* where dragonfly nymphs paint the leaves, but somehow I suspect that's not scientifically accurate."

"*Fantasia* works for me," Jenna said. "Everything I know about foliage changes I learned from that handy little flyer for leaf peepers. It's all related to temperature and day length. When the weather gets colder and the days get shorter, the trees take that as a signal to go dormant. And that's where it gets a little screwy. Tree leaves are normally green because they contain chlorophyll. Trees use chlorophyll to make food so the trees can grow. When they stop producing chlorophyll, it breaks down. That's when we see the yellow and orange that are the actual colors of the leaves."

Lynne shook her head as she spread jam on a slice of toast. "Hard to believe that underneath that nice healthy green those leaves are actually gold and orange."

Jenna nodded. "The other colors—bronze and purple and red—are a little more complicated. Maples are the most dramatic. The maple leaves produce sugar during warm fall days, but the cool nights trap it somehow. The redder a leaf, the more sugar it contains. Oh, and sometimes the color has more to do with where the leaves are on the trees, though I couldn't tell you exactly why that is, not to save my life."

"Well, then, how do the leaves decide how long they're going to stay on the tree?"

"Haven't got a clue. But once they decide they're ready, all those leaves eventually fall onto the ground."

"And need to be raked up," Lynne continued, "which is one of my favorite memories of coming here as a kid. Of course, if you had a lot full of deciduous trees, you'd probably get tired of it pretty quickly. But you know, even though there aren't many things about fall that I miss in Southern California, I really do miss the smell of burning leaves. Though I don't think anybody anywhere lets you do that anymore, unless maybe you're in the Alaskan bush and then why bother? Sometimes I think we're really missing the boat in dealing with pollution. You can't tell me that burning leaves is less environmentally sound than SUV emission fumes."

"I wouldn't try to tell you that," Jenna said cheerfully. "I've learned never to argue with you unless I'm absolutely positive I'm right. And I've never smelled burning leaves, I don't think." At least not the kind of leaves she was willing to discuss with her mother.

"I guess it's all part of progress," Lynne said, "but sometimes it seems a little backward. When I was growing up, we usually lived in places that didn't have much winter, so I only got to experience raking and burning leaves a few times. I remember getting blisters from the rake, but it sure was fun jumping into huge piles of leaves and then setting them on fire." She laughed. "Listen to me. I've turned into an old geezer."

Jenna grinned. "Actually, you're more of a middle-aged geezerette. And a cute one at that."

Chapter 31

NICE and easy, that was the ticket. He'd bought the kind of nondescript uniform that orderlies and LVNs wore, had laundered it and one of those cloth hats several times so they wouldn't look brand-new. He bought rubber-soled shoes for silence and was surprised to discover that they also were remarkably comfortable. Couldn't keep this pair, of course, but it was something to think about later.

He had a battered clipboard, a stethoscope hanging out of his shirt pocket and a pocketful of latex gloves.

He'd worked on changing his facial structure with a fake moustache and pads in his cheeks, like Marlon Brando in The Godfather. He brushed a lot of talcum powder into his hair to make it seem lighter without the risky evidence of chemical hair coloring.

He was all set.

Security at the hospital was a joke. He already knew that from when he'd been here on other unpleasant business a few years back. Nothing had changed. Now, as then, nonchalance was the ticket.

He arrived just after the evening shift had come on duty at three o'clock. He'd heard on the radio that Ralph was now out of ICU and he'd gotten the room number out of a volunteer who answered the phone at hospital information. All of these were good signs. It was coming together. He could do it.

He came up the elevator alone, using a pen to hit the floor number, slipping on the rubber gloves as the elevator rose. He came out of the elevator and walked past a couple sitting in chairs there, wearing the exhausted expressions of people whose lives have come to revolve around the failing health of a loved one.

He passed Ralph's room slowly, saw him lying there. Alone. Deathly still in the bed nearest the door, the curtain between the beds drawn for the privacy of the roommate who had the window and could better appreciate the view.

He continued down the hall, stopped, looked around.

Nobody.

He moved back down the hall, slipped inside the room.

Closed the door.

Pulled the syringe from his pocket.

Held the IV line in his left hand, injected the needle into the port with his right. Pushed the plunger and emptied it into the IV line. Slipped the empty syringe back into his pocket and walked out the door.

Down the stairs, out through the emergency room.

Six minutes, total.

Chapter 32

JENNA had been looking forward for a long time to today's Vermont activities, the visits to places both physical and spiritual that seemed so central to the history and soul of the region.

Today was Essence of New England, a saunter through central Vermont with its maple and marble museums, its Green Mountains vistas and small town country charm. "Anything I can say about New Hampshire," Robert Frost had written, "will serve almost as well about Vermont." He certainly seemed to know what he was talking about, from all that she could see. The scenery was as gorgeous as what her mother had remembered in New Hampshire.

As they set out, with Jenna at the wheel again, puffs of cumulus cloud floated in a bright blue sky. Route 7 north had more foliage color than they'd seen anywhere so far.

"I wish I could figure out what those little pink bushes along the roadway are," Lynne fretted. "They look almost like azaleas, except it's the wrong region and climate and time of year."

"Why don't you just ask somebody?"

"Because I keep forgetting."

Besides the pink bushes and scarlet vines climbing telephone poles, many of the maples they saw carried a full spectrum of autumn color, blending green and gold and blazing crimson all on the same tree. They passed through small towns where fund-raising thermometers charted the progress of campaigns for United Way.

As they neared Rutland, marble shops began to appear amidst the changing foliage. In search of a fast bathroom, they wound through town, passing a stunning Rutland church constructed entirely of marble blocks in shades of white and cream. Marble was so taken for granted here that slabs of it were used to shore up the crumbling edge of a parking lot adjacent to Burger King. A guy waiting inside for his food wore an odd hat and baggy pants, looking like a Johnny Appleseed wannabe or a refugee from the Venice Boardwalk in LA.

This being Norman Rockwell country, they started at the Normal Rockwell Museum east of Rutland, then doubled back to continue north to the New England Maple Museum in Pittsford, leaving the Vermont Marble Museum in Proctor for last.

At the Maple Museum, they wandered through rooms filled with impressive murals of the Vermont seasons, along with equipment showing the history of maple sugaring. The exhibits began with the legend of how Indians had inadvertently discovered maple syrup by boiling "water" that came off the trees and discovering that it was sweet. It took a lot of boiling to reduce the sap to syrup, actually, some forty gallons of sap to produce a single gallon of syrup, which helped explain why the genuine article was so ridiculously expensive. Before the English taught the Indians to use iron cauldrons, sugaring had been an even more labor-intensive task, accomplished by dropping a succession of heated stones into hollowed-out trees filled with sap, to boil down the syrup.

Exhibits on the gathering of sap in winter had a decided Robert Frost feel to them as well—horses pulling wagons through stark winter woods with snow on the ground, the sugaring men clad in heavy plaid jackets and hats. Even such mechanization as was possible didn't make this sap gathering look much more modern.

"It seems like such an enormous amount of work," Lynne said, "though I guess there isn't all that much else to do in the dead of winter here."

"Particularly since the dead of winter seems to last about nine months," Jenna added. "I guess if you didn't know any other climate, it would seem perfectly normal to go trudging through the woods sticking spikes into trees in mid-winter."

"Late winter," Lynne corrected, as she cocked her head in puzzlement before a complicated and now-obsolete piece of sugaring equipment. "Some folks really like a winter climate, you know. They ski, they snowmobile, they skate."

"They freeze their butts off."

"That too. The one I always have trouble understanding is ice fishing. Why would anybody want to build a shack out on some frozen lake so you can sit by a little hole in the ice with a fishing rod?"

"I assume that's a rhetorical question," Jenna said. "Let's go find that tasting room, okay?"

The tasting rooms of Jenna's experience had all featured wine and she was amused to find the similarities here. There were little cups for sampling syrup of various grades, from Grade A, the lightest and most highly prized, through the heavy Grade C, used for cooking and not readily available outside New England.

It seemed terrifically decadent to swill pure maple syrup, but she gave it her best shot in the interest of research. They then sampled a bewildering assortment of other maple products: crystallized candy; hybrid spreads with fruit, mustard, and horseradish; zucchini chutney; and pumpkin, pear, and apple jams.

"You know what I feel like doing?" Lynne asked as they headed out to the car.

"Brushing your teeth?" Jenna asked.

"Great minds!" They laughed together and linked pinkies

as they had done so often when Jenna was growing up and they shared a thought.

It was a special blessing, Jenna knew, to have a mother with whom she was so simpatico.

REACHING the Vermont Marble Museum took a bit of extra navigation skill via a complicated set of detours on poorly marked back roads. They could tell they were nearly there when they began to come upon buildings constructed entirely of marble.

Proctor had been a company town in the purest sense of the word. Colonel Proctor had sent interpreters to Ellis Island to entice immigrants and meet his demand for skilled and un-skilled laborers. In the grand tradition of company towns, workers often ended up owing when they settled their ac-counts at the company store each pay period.

But they'd done some amazing work. The company had been the tombstone purveyor for US Government cemeteries since the Civil War, providing the same shape on all markers with a different configuration of information clear, through Vietnam. The area's marble had been used in the US Supreme Court, the Jefferson Memorial, and the Tomb of the Unknown Soldier.

The real showstopper, however, was the Hall of Marble, with dozens of varieties cut and polished to stand in display rows towering seven feet tall. Here were marble slabs from all around the world: Vermont Royal Red, ivory Roman Travertine, gray-striped Vermont Brocadillo, reddish brown Jasper with salami-like mottling, and burnt siena Ramello Roso from Italy.

Even the rest rooms had marble fixtures and walls.

LYNNE was leaning back in her seat, enjoying the experience of being chauffeured, thinking about Robert Frost and sugaring and fall vistas, when Jenna threw a zinger at her.

"How did you find out that your father had died?" Jenna asked, as they continued north toward Burlington and Shelburne Farms. She was at the wheel, eyes straight ahead on the highway.

Lynne abruptly brought herself to the here and now. It was a logical subject to raise, having recently visited a place that specialized in military tombstones, but there was just enough emphasis on "your" to make Lynne realize that this was a multi-part question, that Jenna was thinking of the death of her own father as well.

The parallels were strong. Both men had died in their prime, while their only daughters were away at college. Both had died without warning, had left young widows suddenly alone in worlds that had once revolved strongly around their husbands.

"Some people came up to campus from Monterey," Lynne said, suddenly feeling the fresh raw pain she had experienced that dreadful day when Greg the Invincible had crashed in the California desert. "A chaplain and one of Daddy's old friends who was teaching at the Navy language school down there. I guess that was probably the closest Naval installation to Santa Cruz, though I certainly wasn't thinking about that at the time. It was just after dinner and I was about to go to the library and work on a paper."

After all these years, she still remembered the topic, Cognitive Dissonance, though she had no idea what she was planning to say about it, or even what course it had been for. And she remembered the pain in the voice of Alan Reardon. *I've got bad news for you,* he'd said. But she knew that already, knew the moment that she saw him. *Your father's plane went down at China Lake this afternoon.* And after that she didn't remember much of anything.

"It was awful," she said now. "I kept thinking that there had to be a mistake, that Daddy couldn't possibly be dead. He'd always been so incredibly alive." She felt her eyes filling, wiped the back of her hand across them. "They waited while I packed some things and then Captain Reardon drove me home."

Home.

An alien concept to a military brat. Home had been a state of mind, for the most part, a succession of cookie-cutter residences in officers' housing around the globe, places where Priscilla's furnishings underwent minor changes over time, though certain elements were always the same. Daddy's dark brown Barcalounger. Lynne's own bedspread and curtains, a yellow floral print that matched the hooked throw rug she always kept beside her bed. The Chinese lacquer hutch where the liquor was kept. The bookcase that housed the *Encyclopedia Britannica.* Priscilla's collection of porcelain cups and saucers and the shadow-box shelving where they hung. Lynne suddenly realized that she hadn't seen those cups and saucers yet at the Maple Leaf Inn. They must have merged with the rest of the china and crystal that clogged the Inn's dining room. She wasn't sure whether this was good or not.

"You had a long drive," Jenna said. It wasn't a question.

"I guess. It was dark by then and I remember being glad nobody could see me cry. It seemed like the middle of the night by the time we got there, but all the lights were on and people were there with your grandmother."

Priscilla had been dressed in black when Lynne arrived, fluttering around while the other officers' wives tried to occupy her, to get her to stay still. Daddy's most recent portrait hung just inside the front door, draped with a black scarf. He looked incredibly handsome and irrefutably alive.

Standing in the doorway for a moment before Priscilla saw her, Lynne had seen for the first time just how vulnerable her mother could be. Then Priscilla turned and dissolved into her daughter's arms.

"I try not to think too much about it," Lynne said now. "At the time it had a sense of impossibility. I always worried when he was in Vietnam, and somehow I thought that once he was stateside again, nothing could happen." A cruel misconception. How could she have ever believed that there was anything safe about serving as a military pilot?

"I was cutting class," Jenna said, her eyes distant as she re-lived her own nightmare. This was why she'd brought the subject up, Lynne could tell. This trip had been triggering memories for all of them. "But I guess you know that, don't you? I had a test that afternoon and I was way behind in the reading. So I figured that I'd skip Psych and do my best to skim everything before the Shakespeare test." Her smile was wry. "Then you were there and I didn't have to take the test after all. I don't even remember if I had to make it up."

"I wanted to be there for you," Lynne told her, voice grow-ing husky. "I was in shock, of course. Even at the time I knew that. But I didn't want strangers to tell you, or even friends. I knew I had to do it myself."

She hadn't expected to find Jenna at the sorority house, had only vaguely known her daughter's schedule. The first few quarters she had memorized each term's lectures, labs, seminar times. But by Jenna's senior year, the details hadn't seemed as important.

Midmorning, the hundred-mile drive up to UCLA had moved swiftly, no traffic jams, no artificial obstacles to keep her from finding her daughter to tell her the awful, life-altering news. Monty's friend Lew had insisted on driving. Lew had been there at the beach when Monty carried his surfboard ashore, then suddenly collapsed and died. Lew had been at the hospital when Lynne arrived. During the drive up to UCLA: huddled in the passenger seat beside him, Lynne had made no attempt at conversation, had barely noticed the music Lew was playing. The Eagles. *Hotel California.* And Monty had just proven, beyond a doubt, that you could both check out and leave. Any time.

"I'm glad you did," Jenna said now, reaching out a hand that Lynne clasped tightly. "I guess it wouldn't have really mattered, but once I knew, I really needed you."

Jenna in jeans and a UCLA sweatshirt on that cold gray January morning. But barefoot when she came downstairs, California girl that she was. And in Jenna's widening eyes,

Lynne had seen the reflection of her own disbelief thirty years earlier.

When the cell phone rang, Lynne knew without looking that it was her mother.

"Ralph Tracy passed away in the night," Priscilla said. "Perhaps it was a blessing."

Chapter 33

HE couldn't find the sunglasses anywhere. They were brand-new, too. Designer frames, blended lenses, special case. Four hundred bucks it would cost to replace them, but the money didn't matter.

What mattered was where he had lost them.

He had last worn them on Monday morning, had tucked them in the side pocket of the khaki jacket he had worn to West Hartford. Somewhere that day it had clouded over and he'd removed the glasses, stuck them in the pocket.

And lost them.

They weren't in the basement apartment where he'd surprised Louise Grant. He'd noticed them missing as he prepared to leave the apartment, with everything properly positioned to suggest a heart attack. He'd even put the bottle of nitroglycerin in her hand to assuage the overly curious. He checked everywhere before he left, and they weren't there.

They weren't in the borrowed Bright Horizons van.

They weren't in his home or his office either, places he knew they couldn't be but felt obligated to check anyway.

They must have slipped out of his pocket when he sat behind the wheel of the rental car the Montgomery women were driving. He couldn't risk having them find the glasses. They'd open the case, and look at the glasses and then—this was the part that made him want to weep or scream or both—they'd notice his business card tucked into the lining. He'd lost his glasses before, you see, enough times that he now habitually kept identification with them. Several times he'd gotten them back because somebody'd found the card and rightly surmised that the owner would cough up a reward.

That wouldn't work this time. He had to get them back. Their itinerary had them leaving for California on Sunday. As they got ready to go, they'd clean out the car to repack everything.

They'd find the glasses.

They'd see the name.

They'd know.

He had to get to them first.

Chapter 34

LYNNE and Jenna dawdled through the rest of the day, meandering along twisting country roads, stopping to photograph covered bridges, taste-testing apple varieties that Lynne had never heard of before. They stopped at craft shops and woolen outlets, at scenic overlooks and art galleries, at charming antique stores and tacky souvenir shops. Most of them featured walls filled with maple syrup in every conceivable size of container, from utilitarian gallon cans to cute little maple leaf bottles that would maybe cover a short stack of pancakes.

After getting her mother's report on Ralph Tracy's death, Lynne turned off her phone. Anything that happened in South Hadford was going to happen whether she knew about it or not. She was a little surprised how liberating it was to totally on her own, with only her daughter and her own thoughts.

The scenery continued to be spectacular. All around them were pulsating displays of color, painted by a cosmic hand with coppery splashes running into burgundy-tinted browns, scarlet maples and lemony birches, amber shrubs and the occasional towering evergreen. These were the vistas for which the term "breathtaking" had been created.

Every direction they might turn held a postcard perfect view.

"What's cool about this scenery," Jenna said at one point, "is that when you normally look at a mountain forest, it's rich and deep and green, but you don't have a sense of individual trees. But once the leaves start changing, it becomes obvious that the view is made up of individual trees, hundreds and thousands of them. I love the way you can see the shape of a single tree against the others, even if it's twenty miles away. And I'm amazed at this, but even I can differentiate trees by their shapes and colors, just like the Leaf Peeper's Guide promised."

They began collecting some of the more spectacular leaves they encountered, pressing them between the pages of an old John Grisham novel they bought for fifty cents on a library sale shelf in one of the small towns they passed through.

Finally Lynne took a look at her watch and was surprised to find it much later than she'd realized. "If we're going to be able to see anything when we arrive at the Inn at Shelburne Farms, we really need to hustle."

"You know me," Jenna told her. "World class hustler."

The sun was just setting and they were fast losing their light when they arrived at the Shelburne Farms gate house. Sunset came early on these October evenings, and they were farther north than they'd been yet on this trip.

After checking in with a gatekeeper and getting directions to the Inn, they wound along a deserted forest road, illuminated only by their own headlights. Lynne had been vaguely aware that the grounds at Shelburne Farms, were substantial, but she hadn't realized just how extensive they were.

"Last night I dreamed I went to Manderly again," Jenna said, as the forest canopy closed over them. Lynne extended a pinky and Jenna linked it with her own once again. It felt warmly comforting to resurrect that childhood ritual, to remember the good luck that was supposed to come from shared thoughts.

Lynne sniffed, then laughed as the odors of manure from unseen dairy barns and wood smoke coming from what?—unseen cottages?—mingled in the evening air. "I think this is the smell of the nineteenth century," she said, just before they came upon the Inn.

The enormous mansion featured three stories of Queen Anne-styled red brick, with half-timbering, massive gables, steeply pitched roofs, and at least one circular porch.

"Good God," Jenna said. "It's the Mark Twain House, run amok."

Lynne nodded. "Or the house in Agatha Christie's *And Then There Were None*."

"Whatever. But we're definitely not in Kansas anymore, Toto."

THEY were greeted at the entry by a darkly handsome young bellman who carried their bags inside while they went in to register. A younger, more cheerful version of Mrs. Danvers welcomed them by name after they passed through the Main Hall, where a fire crackled as guests sat around, reading and being genteel. It was obvious from the get-go that gentility was going to be the hallmark of this experience. They checked in formally in an office lined with bookshelves, all full.

"If you find this interesting," the night clerk told them as Jenna craned her neck to read titles, "be sure to visit the library. The collection is superb."

Reaching their rooms was a complicated matter, involving several flights of stairs, long corridors, and the occasional blind turn. The corridors had deep red carpeting, with red and white floral wallpaper, white wainscoting and wood-work, sufficiently wide to accommodate some miscellaneous items of large, dark furniture and statuary.

As they followed the bellman, Jenna began to wonder if they should have been leaving a trail of bread crumbs by the time they finally reached their accommodations, two small private rooms off the third floor Play Room, now locked for the evening. Their lodgings had once housed governesses and tutors, back when this impossibly large place was a single-family dwelling. Other servants had apparently lived elsewhere on the grounds, but those tending the wealthy youngsters here needed more proximity. Though not, it seemed, their own bathrooms. Lynne and Jenna shared one with the third guest on their hall. All the guest rooms showed the occupant identities with hand-lettered name cards slipped into bronze holders on the doors. The card-holders also identified each room. Jenna was in the Gable Room, Lynne in the Cherry.

They hadn't made dinner reservations at the Inn because of uncertainty about their arrival time, so they decided to go into town. First, however, they noshed on the welcoming baskets of apples and crackers and Vermont cheddar from Shelburne Farms that they'd found in each room, with bouquets of fresh flowers.

Jenna dug out the Swiss Army Knife that her father had given her on her tenth birthday, to slice the apples and cheese. "This is probably silly," she said, "but whenever I use this I have this sense that Dad is with me, wherever I might be."

Lynne waved a hand. "What do you think he'd have to say about this place?"

Jenna laughed. "That anybody with this much money could live anywhere, so why on earth would they stay in the Arctic north?"

"I think you're probably right," Lynne said. "So. You want to go find some dinner?"

They headed downstairs via the service stairway at the rear, past an impressive deer head hanging between floors, and left by way of the Game Room to drive into town. They found a pizzeria that was loud and crowded and reminded Jenna of Westwood, filled with young people.

She felt a sudden stab of homesickness.

IN the morning Jenna woke early, put on running shorts, and headed down by way of the Play Room, now open to reveal two doll houses nearly large enough for a child to play inside, and a giant clipper ship in a glass case over five feet tall. Why it was necessary to close this up at night was a mystery, but not one she felt worth pursuing.

Downstairs she stopped off in the Library, which was stunning in its breadth and quality. About half the books were behind small metal guards with polite signs suggesting staff assistance to examine them. But even those books left accessible were often very rare and probably very valuable as well. Jenna frequented secondhand bookstores in Santa Monica, where "old" tended to mean mid-twentieth century. Here were thousands of volumes on every conceivable subject, including the eleventh edition of the *Encyclopedia Britannica,* the favorite of literati and librarians. She pondered a shelf of sixteen volumes by Mrs. Humphry Ward, wondering what she had written about and who she was and why her husband's name was listed rather than her own. A dozen or so leather bound volumes of James Fenimore Cooper would have fetched a fortune in Los Angeles, and shelf after shelf of books on exotic travel served as clear reminder that the wealthy have a perspective others can only imagine.

Outside, she found the building vaguely disquieting in its resemblance to the Mark Twain House, even larger and more ostentatious than it had seemed the night before. Beyond vast expanses of well-tended lawn, she could see the calm waters of Lake Champlain.

As she set off on one of the marked trails for a run through the woods, she had the outdoors to herself, sharing the woodland wonder with only its native creatures. Here some of the trees had already finished their fall display and stood bare of foliage, their leafy summer garb in drifts on the ground. Much of the path was covered with leaves and she began to relish the scent of them, the slight crunching sound that echoed with each footfall.

Squirrels chattered irritably as she passed, suggesting that she go elsewhere and take her fellow humans along with her.

She could definitely see their point. This was a natural wonderland, a community of animals who must surely resent the human presence. At one point she surprised two young deer who looked her way inquisitively, then fled back through the forest. Everywhere she went she saw birds of countless species, often in flock-like numbers. Surely it was time for them to be heading south.

On this briskly cool morning she'd debated wearing a sweatshirt, which hadn't really been necessary anywhere else she'd run on this trip. Halfway through the run she removed the sweatshirt and tied the arms around her waist. When she slowed to a walk, however, the crisp morning air was still plenty bracing.

Fall was coming to a close in northern Vermont, and winter was hard on its heels.

Chapter 35

ABIGAIL was sweeping her kitchen floor on Thursday morning when the phone rang. She had grown to dread the bad news that telephone calls lately represented and was tempted not to answer, but after three rings, an ingrained sense of duty forced her to pick up the receiver.

"Miss Chenonceau?" She didn't recognize the voice.

"Who is calling?"

"This is Todd Jackson, ma'am." Cindy Jackson's husband and Ralph Tracy's son-in-law. Who had never called her before.

"Yes, Todd. I'm so sorry about your father-in-law." Though when she thought about it, perhaps Ralph's death had saved his family continued problems and heartache. She could not imagine Ralph, whom she had always regarded as a plodding fellow who lacked imagination but did excellent handiwork, as being responsible for the deaths of the young people in Priscilla's basement. But his complicity to some degree seemed all but certain.

There was a moment of silence.

"Cindy and Doreen are taking it very hard," he said. "Would it be possible for me to come over? I need your advice on something."

Abigail sighed. Whatever he wanted, she was reasonably sure it wasn't simple. "Yes, of course."

He looked haggard when he arrived, gaunt and older than his years. What was he? Forty-five? Fifty? She ushered him into the parlor and sat expectantly. He didn't seem to be seeking solace over the death of his father-in-law, and surely Mountain Mortuary would be able to handle various details without her counsel.

"I'm sorry to trouble you," he began, "but—"

He didn't meet her eyes.

"Yes?"

"I just don't know what to do. You probably don't remember this and maybe you never even knew before the other day, but I lived at your sister's place for a couple of years in the seventies, back when it was a boardinghouse."

She hadn't thought about it for years, but once he'd mentioned the connection on Tuesday, it had come back to her. Todd had been one of the most steady and reliable members of the mill labor force, quickly working his way up to a position in the marketing department. It was Todd Jackson who hit on the idea of getting specific items from the Golden Mills line into upscale catalogues like Coldwater and Norm Thompson and National Wildlife, a venture that had proven spectacularly successful. The Christmas sweaters the company developed for those catalogues had become one of the biggest moneymaking schemes that Golden Mills had ever undertaken.

"What you don't know, what nobody knows, is how I came to live there." He hesitated, then finally met her gaze. His eyes were steady and troubled. "I was a military deserter, AWOL from the Marine Corps. I still am AWOL, though not under the name Todd Jackson."

Abigail had thought that after the past ten days nothing would ever be able to surprise her again, but this matter-of-fact statement left her stunned speechless.

"I had no idea," she said after a moment.

"Nobody did," he told her. "Almost nobody, anyhow. I was directed here by a group that was dedicated to helping deserters develop new identities so that we could stay in the United States."

"A group here in South Hadford?"

He shook his head. "I'd rather not say where the group was located. There are people who helped me that I don't want to compromise. I don't know where they are these days anyway. But part of the service these people provided was steering me toward Golden Mills and the boardinghouse. I was given a new identity and told that I could have lodgings and a job here so that I could build a new personal employment history." He smiled for the first time. "As you know, the plan worked."

Abigail's mind was reeling. He made it sound as if there had been an entire parade of deserters and draft dodgers passing through Golden Mills and Charles Grant's boardinghouse.

Had there been?

"Was Mr. Grant aware of what was happening?"

Todd nodded. "I didn't learn this until much later, but I was told he was. I don't know how often this happened or how many of us there might have been, but I stayed at the boardinghouse for almost two years before moving into my own place. I never talked about it, but there were a number of other guys there at the same time who struck me as likely to be in the same situation."

Other guys who had probably worked under Abigail at Golden Mills. She felt an unexpected sense of betrayal. Charles Grant's responsibilities had included personnel matters. People went through his office before interviewing with Abigail for specific production jobs. He had known they were military criminals and had referred them anyway.

"You didn't ask these other young men?"

He shook his head. "I couldn't tell for sure and I didn't want to risk making a mistake and having somebody turn me in. This was toward the end of the Vietnam War, but we still had people over there in Southeast Asia. If I'd turned myself in, or if somebody else had, they'd have put me in prison. Which was better than going to Vietnam, because you could be reasonably certain that you'd get out of it alive, but not something that a twenty-year-old kid wants to do with the next six years."

"This group got you identification papers?"

He nodded again. "Back then it was relatively easy to create a new identity. You'd check cemeteries for children who died young, before they were issued Social Security cards. Nowadays, you get a Social Security number at birth, but back then most people didn't bother till they were old enough to get jobs. Anyway, you'd write to the local jurisdiction saying you were So-and-So and needed a copy of your birth certificate. Once you had a birth certificate, you could get a Social Security number and build the new identity starting with that. I built my new identity by working at Golden Mills and living here in South Hadford."

Abigail was dumbfounded. He made it all sound so matter-of-fact. And she was still reeling at his direct implication of Charles Grant in this illegal—one might even argue treasonous—venture.

"It just happened that I really liked this area, and I was able to fit into the work I was doing well enough, so I decided to stay here. I got an apartment in town after a while and then moved to Nashua when I had a better job opportunity. I started taking night courses and got my degree in business. I never would have considered staying in South Hadford, or moving back, except that I met Cindy again and fell in love with her."

"And you think that this other deserter, Eldon Weibeck, was here to do the same thing?"

"As soon as I learned he was AWOL, I figured that was the only possibility."

"So why have you come to me? Why not the police?"

"Miss Chenonceau, I'm still technically a military deserter. That status didn't really matter to me until suspicion fell on

Ralph. Ever since his accident, I've been bothered by the fact that he went down to the stream."

Abigail frowned. "And why is that?"

Todd smiled. "Did you ever know my father-in-law to be a nature lover?"

"How would I know that?"

"Well, he wasn't. He might notice if it was snowing or raining, or maybe not. If you pointed directly at a flower or a landscape, he'd maybe grunt. Miss Chenonceau, he didn't care about nature before, and since his memory started to go he'd been very careful only to do things that were already familiar. I can't see him going all the way back behind the Washington Arms unless he had a reason. Like somebody took him down there."

How to put this gently? "Todd, one of the continued problems with Alzheimer's patients is that they wander off and get lost."

He shook his head. "Not Ralph. And don't you think it's a little odd that Ralph had that accident the same week that Mrs. Grant died?"

"An unfortunate coincidence."

"Maybe. But I'm not much of a believer in coincidence. I think that everything that's happened in the past two weeks is tied together somehow. And the common link is Charles Grant letting deserters build new identities in his boarding-house. I keep waiting to hear something from the police about this, but before his accident they kept focusing on Ralph. Now that he's dead, I'm afraid they'll just let everything stay as it is. That's not fair to Cindy and Doreen. And it's not fair to Ralph, either."

Abigail sighed. "Does Cindy know your military status?"

"Does that matter?"

For some reason, this angered her. "You've come here on your own initiative to give me information that makes me an accessory to a crime. I think that I'm entitled to the courtesy of a response."

"I'm sorry, ma'am. No, I never told Cindy or anybody else. From the very beginning I told people a simple story of my background that wasn't too far removed from the truth. The older I got, the easier it was."

"And your actual family, wherever they might be—do they know where you are?"

He shook his head. "I don't really have any family. That made it easier to become Todd Jackson. My parents died in an auto accident when I was twelve. After that I lived with an uncle who was—" He hesitated. "Let's just say he was difficult. I never figured he'd miss me much, in any case. He was a gung-ho ex-Marine and just about the only thing I ever did that pleased him was to enlist in the Corps. I checked on him a few years ago. He's dead now."

"So there's nobody from your . . . your other life that you stayed in touch with?"

"No, ma'am."

Abigail dropped her head into her hands for a moment. What did the modern military do about deserters? In earlier times, they'd been shot. But surely there was some more humane punishment today. There'd been some kind of amnesty back during the Carter Administration, she remembered, though she'd never paid much attention to the particulars, and in any case, Todd wasn't a draft dodger. He was a deserter.

Finally she looked up. "You must go to the authorities, Todd." She wondered fleetingly what his real name was. Had been.

He sighed. "I was hoping that you might be able to suggest to the police that the boardinghouse was sometimes used for deserters, without me having to be brought into it. Maybe say you remember something you once heard, or that Mr. Grant had told you."

As impositions went, this one was colossal. Abigail's mind was spinning. "What makes you think that I could tell the police anything that they'd believe, without some kind of specific information or corroboration?"

Now he actually smiled. "Around South Hadford, ma'am, your word is, if you'll pardon the expression, golden. You could point the police in that direction. And Mr. and Mrs. Grant are both dead now, so they can't be hurt."

He left one important detail unspoken. Abigail added it. "Do you think Ralph was responsible for hiding the bodies?"

Todd nodded. "I do, actually. I've given this a lot of thought. Ralph and Doreen bought the house where Cindy and I live several years before I first came to South Hadford. When they moved out to the Washington Arms and we came back here, we bought the place from them so they'd have a bit more capital. The Washington Arms isn't cheap. We paid the Tracys slightly less than market value, but when I got all the paperwork, two things jumped out at me. One, Ralph bought the place from Charles Grant in 1971, and two, he paid practically nothing for it."

"Thirty years ago," Abigail said, "real estate was considerably less expensive than it is today."

"I know that, but the house is fundamentally sound and the Tracys all have said that apart from a few cosmetic things like new paint, they didn't have to do any significant work on it when they moved in. Even though Ralph could easily have done any work on it himself."

"You're saying that the house was a payoff."

"I'm not saying anything. Except that the timing is interesting."

"It's beyond interesting," Abigail said, "but of course you know that. Todd, you have information that is extremely important. You must talk to the authorities and I can't do that for you. I have a suggestion that may work, however, at least momentarily."

Chapter 36

"THIS place is a mighty compelling argument against inherited wealth," said Jenna Montgomery, who herself had received an entirely unexpected fifty thousand dollars when her insurance salesman father died. Much of that money was still in mutual funds though lately she'd been making withdrawals at an alarming rate to help cover her living expenses.

Jenna was reeling from the combination of staying at the Inn at Shelburne Farms, which so far surpassed her expectations that she was barely able to process its excesses, and visiting the Shelburne Museum, which was the strangest conglomeration of stuff that she had ever encountered. Extraordinary stuff, to be sure, but stuff just the same, and surely unmatched anywhere on planet earth. Eat your hearts out, potentates and dictators.

Jenna and Lynne were eating an uninspired lunch after a morning spent barely skimming the surface of all that the Shelburne Museum had to offer. Of course, it wasn't a museum at all, really, but a collection of museums or, more correctly still, a collection of collections. The whole place had

sprung pretty much full blown from the mind and pocket-
book of Electra Havemeyer Webb, a sugar heiress who devoted most of her seventy-two years to collecting American
folk art and just about everything else she could get her
hands on. Whalebone pie crimpers, weather vanes, miniature
circus performers by the thousands, hatboxes, shotguns, tavern signs, cigar-store Indians—Electra collected them all.

They'd toured the steamship *Ticonderoga,* which had been
hauled overland from Lake Champlain nearly two miles on
specially constructed railroad tracks, to be dropped into a
crater dug for its permanent landlocked mooring. They'd
climbed to the top of the similarly relocated Colchester Reef
Lighthouse, also from Lake Champlain, that stood within
spitting distance of the steamship.

They'd lingered in the General Store, which housed the intact contents of a defunct turn-of-the-twentieth-century em-
porium in an old Burlington Post Office building. Jenna had
been particularly fascinated by the attached Apothecary
Shop, filled with patent medicines and remedies collected
from New England's pharmacies when the Pure Food and
Drug Act of 1906 changed the nature of pharmaceuticals forever. No more Dr. Williams's Pink Pills for Pale People. No
more Swamproot. No more laxatives with names like Kodol,
Sagwa, or Dr. Thomas's Eclectic Oil. No more blood wine or
marshmallow cream, which she was fairly certain had nothing to do with candy.

"It's not just the fact that she had too much money," Lynne
argued mildly.

"Well, maybe not. The woman was obviously a compul-
sive collector, and I guess you could even argue that she
saved a lot of these things from becoming landfill. But,
sheesh!"

"I agree that it's overwhelming. And if we weren't on a
relatively tight schedule, I'd be tempted to come back tomorrow."

"Mom!"

"Jenna, we haven't even looked in at least two-thirds of
the buildings here. It's all a matter of personal taste anyway.

The Quilt Museum is supposed to be one of the finest in the world."

"You could say the same thing about the duck decoy building, and so what?" Immediately before deciding to break for lunch they had stumbled into a house filled with nothing but a gazillion wildlife decoys.

"Different strokes," Lynne said mildly. "And face it, we may never be here again."

"You'll be here if you lead that tour."

"A mighty big *if* at this point. But you're right. I'd probably try to get everybody a couple nights at the Inn. Just so they could have the experience."

"Well, you'd better hope you have clients who really like dead animals."

Lynne laughed. "I'll willingly concede that the Beach Lodge gave me the heebie jeebies."

Patterned after an Adirondack hunting camp, the Beach Lodge at the Museum was crammed with major taxidermy projects. Three enormous bears, for instance, including one that Electra allegedly bagged herself, the fable further claiming that the intrepid heiress had felled the creature while her cowardly guides fled in terror. Somehow Jenna had trouble believing this tale.

It was beyond dispute, however, that Electra loved to hunt. The Beach Lodge included a moose rack more than seven feet across and a caribou with an odd third antler coming out of the middle of his forehead. That third horn was originally called the Snow Shovel because Electra (or somebody) thought that was its purpose. The building also held an assortment of spooky owls and menacing eagles, and even a couple of scruffy squirrels brought out recently by one of the heirs who found them moldering in an attic.

The collection of mounts wasn't limited to the Museum, either. The previous night after dinner, Jenna and Lynne had played pool in the Inn's Game Room, which they had entirely to themselves. A massive ram's head flanked by a couple of young deer mounts had been displayed over a fireplace large enough to comfortably roast an entire wild boar. Other walls held an eagle with wings raised, another ram, four older deer and a buffalo head the size of a washing machine.

"Onward," Lynne said, gathering up the refuse from her lunch. "I want to see the quilts, and the dollhouses, and maybe a couple hundred weather vanes. I haven't seen a world-class weather vane collection in *ever* so long. . . ."

Chapter 37

ABIGAIL hoped that her trust in both Todd Jackson and William O'Keefe was not misplaced.

Since there was no way of telling how strictly young William might interpret the law on military desertion—or even if he was aware of what that law might entail—Abigail had agreed to keep Todd's confidence overnight, to give him time to explain his background to his wife and mother-in-law. She wasn't really worried about Todd running off in the night. Maybe he'd done that once, and maybe he'd even believed he was doing the right thing back then. But he'd stayed put now for nearly thirty years.

Abigail liked to believe herself a good judge of character, and even with this shocking admission, she considered her assessment of Todd's fundamental integrity to be sound.

She hoped.

She had arranged for Detective O'Keefe to meet with her and Todd at nine A.M. at her home. William had grumbled a bit at what he seemed to consider an unreasonable request, but she had assured him that he would find the meeting worth his time. And Todd, once he had accepted the in-evitability of having to reveal his deception, seemed oddly relieved. He wanted to bring Cindy to the morning meeting, but Abigail had flatly forbidden it.

"We don't know how William will react," Abigail had told him as he was getting ready to leave yesterday. "If there's any kind of a scene, it isn't fair to subject Cindy to the un-pleasantness. She has enough to handle right now. The girl just lost her father."

Todd arrived first, at eight-thirty. He'd nicked himself shaving and had a tiny speck of tissue on his chin. He wore a sport coat and a tie and his hands were shaking.

"I'm nervous," he told Abigail as he sat at the kitchen table, watching her arrange a box of donut holes neatly on a Limoges plate. He took the coffee she offered but didn't taste it. "I've known Bill O'Keefe for years. His daughter and ours played soccer together until they both got too cool for it. I think I trust him. But Cindy's not sure at all. She's afraid she'll never see me again. I took her for a drive last night and told her everything." He shook his head regretfully. "She wasn't happy."

"Well, of course not. It's a tremendous shock to her. It was a tremendous shock to me, after all, and I haven't been mar-ried to you for twenty years."

His smile was wan. "After I told Cindy, we came back and told the kids that I might have to go away on business for a few days. That happens now and then, and Brittany's so freaked out by her grandfather dying that I barely think it registered with her. Bradley seemed all right with it. But he couldn't help but notice Cindy sobbing."

"He'll think she's crying because of his grandpa," Abigail told him. What a tremendous upheaval that young boy's life was undergoing, with the worst of it quite possibly still to come. And Brittany—well, Brittany's reputed self-absorption might serve her well through various future events.

"You're probably right," Todd said, stirring the coffee, even though he'd taken it black. "I just hope there's no media circus when Bill O'Keefe gets here."

"And how, precisely, do you believe that the media would be aware of any newsworthy event at my home?"

That brought a little chuckle. "Not from you, ma'am, that's for sure. But you can't trust a cop. They're trained to lie."

"They're trained to seek justice," Abigail told him, hoping it was true.

DETECTIVE William O'Keefe arrived at eight forty-five, and seemed startled to find Todd already there. Or maybe he was just startled to find anybody else there. Abigail had given him no specifics about what she wanted.

She poured him some coffee, freshened Todd's cup, dispensed donut holes, and then led the two men to her parlor.

"Todd has information that he and I believe will be very useful to your investigation," Abigail began.

William O'Keefe—it was almost impossible for her to think of him with the honorific "Detective" and nearly as difficult to think of him as "Bill"—straightened in his chair and turned his gaze directly to Todd.

"And that is?" the policeman asked.

Todd took a deep breath. "Long ago on a galaxy far away. . . ." He shook his head. "Sorry, Bill. This is difficult for me, and in a minute or two you'll understand why. So let's start with the part that'll be of the most interest to you." He took another deep breath. "I think I know what Eldon Weibeck was doing here when he got killed."

Detective O'Keefe looked at Todd with cop eyes. A moment ago they'd been a pair of soccer dads. Now the relationship had changed, perhaps forever.

"If you're planning to confess something, you need to know that you have the right to counsel, Todd. You have—"

Incredibly, Todd smiled. "Get the damn card out, Bill, and do it by the book. You already left out the part about how I have the right to remain silent. Miss Chenonceau here is our witness and I'd hate to put her in the position of having to say we didn't do things right."

Detective O'Keefe got out a notebook along with his Miranda card. After the formal warning, the two men faced each other squarely. Todd Jackson began his story and for the most part, William O'Keefe let him tell it without interruption.

When he'd finished, Todd leaned back in what seemed to be total exhaustion. Abigail could understand that. She felt utterly depleted herself, and all she'd done was set up a meeting and buy donut holes.

Detective O'Keefe smiled. "I think we may have a little leeway here. You planning to leave town, Todd?"

Todd shook his head. "Not until they cart me off to Camp Lejeune. I did a little research on the subject a while back. My situation is what the Marine Corps calls an Unauthorized Absence. Desertion, actually. It's not the same as being AWOL, because when you're AWOL, you maybe missed the plane or got drunk and forgot to get back or something. When you've deserted, it's for good. You plan to stay away indefinitely. And once you turn yourself in, which I guess is what I'm doing right now, they send some goons out to pick you up and take you to the brig."

"*The Last Detail,*" O'Keefe said abruptly. "Jack Nicholson on Shore Patrol, taking in Randy Quaid."

"Yeah," Todd told him. "Not one of my favorite movies."

"Could I have some more coffee?" O'Keefe asked, turning to Abigail.

She rose, surprised at the sudden stiffness in her joints. This was not the time to correct his grammar. Of course he *could* have some coffee, and he *might* have some as well. "Todd? More for you also?"

He nodded. "My last meal as a free man. Donut holes and coffee." There was almost a lilt in his voice, as if he had somehow liberated himself by squarely facing his past. Abigail, to her surprise, felt an almost maternal pride.

After their cups were replenished, Detective O'Keefe got serious. "Okay, Todd. Here's what we need to do. First off, call Cindy and let her know you're not in leg irons yet. You and I need to go talk to Niles Burton. Who've you told about this?"

Todd shrugged. "Miss Chenonceau. You. Cindy. I was going to tell Doreen, but Cindy asked me to wait."

"That could work to our definite advantage. You said you did some research on this desertion thing. I'll have to check on this, but it seems to me that if you've turned yourself in to the local authorities, namely me, and if the local authorities require your assistance on something else before we call in the Marines, you oughta be covered. If we can work this out, I'll be your character witness at the court-martial. Assuming there even is one. What happens once you're in Marine custody? Do you know?"

"They put me in the brig, for starters. Then it gets into a lot of mickey mouse stuff while they figure out what to do with me. Most likely by the time it all gets sorted out, I'd be able to get out without doing any additional time. Of course by then I probably won't have a job to come back to. Or a family."

"I wouldn't worry about the job. I hear you're pretty indispensable over there. And Cindy's a champ. She'll be here for you."

"I hope so."

"So they'll have you sitting around doing some kind of busy work for a while, let you run up some legal bills, then cut you loose?"

Todd smiled. "Actually, the legal bills are on the taxpayers. They'll give me defense counsel."

Abigail couldn't help but interrupt. "You mean the same organization that's prosecuting you is providing your defense? How can that possibly be?"

Todd's smile grew broader. "It doesn't have to make sense. It's the military. You know that old saying—military justice is to justice as military music is to music."

They all laughed then, and for the first time in nearly two weeks, Abigail had a feeling that at least one thing might work out.

Chapter 38

THESE past few days had been far too busy to even think about handling the Montgomery problem. But all was quieter now, and they seemed to be the only potential problem remaining, that mother and daughter. He could track them down, get the sunglasses out of the car before they cleaned it out and found them.

With a little luck. And so far, his luck had been holding.

Fortunately, he had their itinerary. And even more fortunately, he could call their location up any time, and they'd never know a thing.

Chapter 39

"I can see how it would be possible to spend a long, long time in Vermont," Jenna said as they packed the trunk on Friday morning after two nights at the Inn at Shelburne Farms. "Just about every place where we've stopped, I can imagine sticking around for a while. Though there doesn't seem to be much to do in the way of making a living here."

She was a fine one to talk about making a living, Jenna thought sarcastically. Five years out of college and she was working as a clerk in a bookstore. Friends who'd gotten law degrees or MBAs after graduation were making six-figure incomes and driving Lexuses and Mercedes. One of her sorority sisters was a multilingual business executive in Tokyo and another was rising with meteoric speed in a multinational company based in Brazil.

Nor were her classmates strictly limited to fields where they were making boatloads of money. A girl she knew was writing direct mail ad copy for the American Cancer Society and somebody else—a guy she'd admittedly known only slightly—was heading a South Central Los Angeles literacy organization.

In separate but related news, half a dozen of her good friends had gotten married and three of those already had children. While Jenna Montgomery did not hold a meaningful or remunerative position, could visualize no marriage prospects on the horizon, and remained ambivalent about motherhood. All the while working for scarcely more than minimum wage in one of the most expensive neighborhoods in the country. Hell, she could probably earn as much blending Frappuccinos at Starbucks.

"Keep in mind," her mother told her now, "that Vermont is one of the poorest states in the country. That it has a winter that lasts for eight or more months. That its population remains limited precisely because there isn't much industry or business here. That its income is largely from tourism, and that tourists, even my own lovely ones from Booked for Travel, are demanding and unpredictable."

"But you see what I mean, don't you? Every time we've stopped, I wanted to stay longer and see more. This racing around is exhausting. I don't see how you can stand it when you've got a dozen clients counting on you to do everything but apply their mascara."

Lynne laughed as she slammed the trunk. "That's a different type of travel, Jen. Even on the trips that cover a lot of territory, the options are limited. If this tour ever happens, we'll probably devote entire days to stops that you and I would wrap up in an hour and a half. Of course, part of the point of what we've been doing as we scout is to see how long a time *is* reasonable for these places and activities. I wouldn't have thought it would take so long to get to the Marble Museum, for instance, or to tour it adequately once we were there."

"Just so we have enough time at Ben & Jerry's," Jenna said with a grin as she took her place in the front seat and waited for her mother to start the car.

"Worry not, my child. That's something of a sacred pilgrimage for me."

Other pilgrims had beaten them to the holy font.

At Vermont's largest tourist attraction, attendants directed traffic in the parking lot as the biggest crowd they'd seen in New England milled around. Tours left every twenty minutes and a two-dollar admission fee earned you the right to wait in the gift shop—filled with bike jerseys, oven mitts, cookie cutters, and fifteen different styles of Ben & Jerry's t-shirts—till your tour started.

Overall, the tour turned out to be a pleasant and self-effacing look at a company that started out as a couple of guys making ice cream in a former gas station in Burlington. The commentary was simultaneously slick and folksy, explaining the mechanics of Ben & Jerry's ice cream production (they'd pioneered the addition of chunks) in segments orchestrated to the second by countdown clocks. Guides also reminded tourists that from the very beginning the company had believed in giving back to the community. From local softball team sponsorships to tie-dyed uniforms for the Lithuanian Olympic basketball team, Ben & Jerry's had also used that same conscience as a compelling sales tool.

AFTERWARD, up the road at the Cold Hollow Cider Mill, the folksiness seemed a bit more real and the process every bit as fascinating as they watched apples crushed between thick waffly plastic sheets, stacked like pancakes, and pressed till the cider seeped out the sides, to be caught and bottled. Not surprisingly, the whole place smelled like apples.

Chomping apples that they'd purchased out of enormous boxes outside the Cider Mill (three for fourteen cents, possibly the greatest bargain of the entire trip), Jenna and Lynne returned to the road. Jenna drove this next stretch on the interstate into Montpelier, through hillsides painted with breathtaking color. The spectacular display continued into Montpelier, with its glowing gold statehouse dome.

There was, of course, roadwork going on.

But it took no effort at all to find Will Colwhistle's final New England mail drop, not far from the Capitol. Here there was no real pretense at maintaining an office, just a storefront with private mailboxes and an indifferent clerk who knew nothing and revealed even less.

"What are we going to do?" Jenna asked as they got back into the car. "We've hit every address except Manchester and the guy's nowhere. It's like he doesn't really even exist."

"We know he exists," Lynne said, settling back in the passenger seat. "But I can't figure out what he wants from your grandmother."

"Word has to be getting back that we've been stalking him," Jenna said, negotiating some complicated turns on the way out to town in search of Barre and the Rock of Ages granite quarry.

ROCK of Ages, like so many of the native businesses they had visited, wasn't all that easy to find. Traveling along back roads, Lynne began to wonder if they'd ever reach it, if perhaps they were lost once again.

When at last they arrived, they had just missed one of the guided bus tours of the active quarry. Jenna and Lynne, with a single meeting of the eyes, decided they didn't care and went outside to the original quarry, opened in 1885 and now abandoned. A short walk past piles of what the granite industry called "grout"—miscellaneous discarded rock—they came upon the quarry, some three hundred fifty feet deep and nearly filled with water. Small trees with leaves of amber and gold clung to its rocky edges.

It was a rather ho-hum experience, actually, and Lynne decided that if she returned with a group, they would definitely take the guided tour. In the gift shop she was pleased to see that, unlike the Marble Museum, most items were made in the USA. She bought a small slab of polished red granite for a paperweight and, over Jenna's mild grumbling, got directions to the manufacturing center down the road.

It was well worth the stop. From second-story observation windows, they watched a vast workspace buzzing with activity. Huge slabs of granite were being polished to the familiar gloss

with water and a buffer. Other workers engraved individual
stones by adhering rubber stencils to the polished granite, cutting out the required letters or designs, then blasting away the
exposed areas with a pellet abrasive. Additional work—carved
roses, religious statuary—came at the very end of the process.
Here it was quite possible to ruin an entire piece, as illustrated
by a saintly figure with a prefrontal lobotomy.

"A keeper," Lynne said as they left. "And I almost forgot it
was all about dead people and cemeteries."

But going through the town of Barre, they were reminded
one last time of the function of the business. Hope Cemetery
was filled with row upon row of substantial granite headstones in perfect alignment. Barre took care of its own.

FARTHER along Highway 2, the Cabot Creamery offered a
multitude of dairy products from Vermont cows, those famous
black-and-whites that seemed more prevalent in Vermont advertising than in Vermont pastures. They had no cheese curds
and the Visitor's Center staff claimed not to be familiar with
them, which took Lynne rather by surprise. Since the Sonoma
Sojourn when Ryan Atherton had introduced her to curds, the
very youngest incarnation of cheese, she'd assumed they were
a staple sale item for all cheesemakers. She and Jenna made do,
however, glutting on samples, buying creamy white cheddar
chunks for the road, and moving on.

Just outside the Visitor's Center, Lynne found more of the
pink-leaved bushes she'd been wondering about for days.
They had labels on them, Northland and Jersey. But Northland and Jersey what? Still befuddled as she headed out of
town, she noticed a garden nursery, made a fast turn into the
parking lot, and asked. A helpful young woman identified the
exotic bushes for her.

They were blueberries.

LYNNE and Jenna both stopped paying attention to exactly where they were as they came into New Hampshire from Vermont, crossing the Connecticut River that gives the two states their twisting shared boundary. And so they got a bit lost trying to find The White Birches, a bed-and-breakfast near Franconia.

Being lost turned out to be a wonderful gift from nature. At the wheel, Lynne slowed to fully savor the sense of autumnal solitude on a deserted two-lane road winding somewhere through the White Mountains forest.

"This is still Frost country, isn't it?" Lynne asked.

"You betcha," Jenna answered. "I think we've definitely stumbled onto the 'road less traveled by.' And you know what? It's pretty amazing."

The road itself was barely two lanes, with occasional trails heading off its sides toward unmarked and unknown destinations. Drifts of fallen leaves swept across the road in shades of copper and brown and orange, losing some of their color once they left the trees.

"We could be alone in the world," Lynne mused.

"Lucky us," Jenna answered.

Eventually they encountered a crossroad with a number Jenna could find on the map, and they resumed the drive to The White Birches. When they found it, not far outside a small town, across from an elderly cemetery and otherwise alone in the woods, Lynne was thrilled. She'd gambled on this place. Most of the other places they'd stayed at or examined had been recommended by friends, or fellow travel agents, or her New Hampshire relatives. But The White Birches was relatively new, and after reading a couple of guidebook descriptions, she'd decided to take it on faith.

The grove of trees which had given the place its name was splendid, their white bark peeling gently as the leaves above clung to the branches in golden glory. The white frame building featured a wide front porch with a collection of pumpkins and gourds piled casually around tubs of mums. A couple in their sixties or early seventies held hands as they slowly moved back and forth in a glider on one side of the porch.

For just a moment, Lynne felt the flash of bitter loss that sometimes hit her offguard when she saw an older couple so devoted to each other, the shared elderhood she had envisioned for herself and Monty. But she merely smiled and nodded greeting to them as she and Jenna went inside.

They jingled a bell on the desk that said REGISTRATION in the front entryway and perused the selections in a basket of apples labeled HELP YOURSELF. A white-haired woman in a handknit sweater came round the corner with a smile on her sweetly weathered face. She looked like an advertisement for the book *When I Am Old, I Shall Wear Purple*, and indeed the sweater was primarily eggplant.

"How wonderful to have you here!" she announced. "You must be the Montgomerys."

"We are indeed," Lynne assured her.

"Let me just show you your room and then we can get Ted to bring up your bags," she offered. "I'm Lois DeVry."

"We can get the bags ourselves," Lynne assured her, "if you'll just show us where we're headed."

The room was large enough to hold two double beds, a pair of dressers and matching armchairs flanking a small fireplace with a painted fireplace fan in place. "The central heat is on," Lois DeVry assured them, "and I'm afraid this fireplace is mostly just for show, but if you want to join us downstairs, I was just about to light a fire in the living room."

She told them of a restaurant within walking distance that had excellent chicken and dumplings, informed them breakfast would be in the dining room to the south of the entryway from seven to nine-thirty, then graciously excused herself.

Lynne turned to Jenna when she was gone. "You realize, I assume, that this is what your grandmother believes she's going to be doing."

Jenna grinned. "If she can pull it off, it'll be a helluva gig."

They brought in their bags, then wandered outside into the rapidly chilling late afternoon. The sun seemed to be setting significantly earlier each day. Here some of the leaves had already fallen, revealing the graceful patterns of the dark trunks and branches of mountain and white ash.

"At this point," Lynne said, "I think the foliage is a crapshoot. One solid rain can knock most of this right off the trees, and that will be that."

"I'm content," Jenna told her. "If every leaf in New England fell off right now, I'd still feel I've had the trip of a lifetime."

"I'm inclined to agree, except that I'd really hate to miss those red maples down in South Hadford when they're at their peak."

Jenna laughed. "I wouldn't worry. Grandma won't *let* them fall. If they try to drop off too soon, she'll be out there with a stepladder, an extension cord, and a glue gun."

ON the way to dinner they stopped in the old cemetery, surprised to find it shabbily maintained. "Guess there's nobody new moving in here," Jenna said. "You know, when we first started driving around New England, all those cemeteries seemed kind of creepy to me. Now they just seem normal, and natural. Even when they're deserted, like this one."

"Back when most of these folks were buried," Lynne answered, noting a family resting together since the early nineteenth century, "there weren't any perpetual care agreements." She stopped to look at a marker for Solomon Merriweather, who'd shuffled off the mortal coil at the age of seventy-three in 1842. As she passed by and glanced back, she found writing on the rear of the tombstone as well: "Killed by Charles Sawyer."

So much for idyllic White Mountain little towns. The crime blotter was written on the tombstone for all eternity.

Chapter 40

JENNA awoke with a sense of sadness on Saturday morning.

Tonight they'd be back at the Maple Leaf Inn and tomorrow afternoon they'd fly home to California. It had been a fantastic trip, bodies in the basement or no, but she hated to leave with so much unresolved. Grandma's inn-keeping venture seemed more uncertain than ever, particularly if a place like the one where they were currently staying was her goal. This place was too big and far too much work for one woman in her eighties to even consider.

She had never met old Ralph Tracy, but nothing anyone had said made her believe he could have killed anybody. His survivors would carry the stigma of accusation, in a part of the country where history was a way of life and memory ran long.

They had checked in with Priscilla, who confided in hushed tones that Todd Jackson was a Vietnam deserter, now claiming that Ralph had been murdered because he knew too much. The whole problem with Ralph, as Jenna understood it, was that he remembered too little. And she didn't know what to make of the revelation of Todd Jackson's faked identity, except that it seemed ridiculous to cart him off to some military prison for acting to save his own life.

Not that deserting was a surefire lifesaver, at least not for Eldon Weibeck. And what of Sydney Shackleford, heiress to a slave trade fortune, self-styled sixties radical? Who'd have reason to kill her? Jenna and Lynne had decided there was no reason to even try to gain admission to the Mont Blanc compound, across that well-fortified covered bridge. The Shacklefords were not receiving, and they were of a social class accustomed to doing as they pleased.

They did, however, plan to drop by unannounced this afternoon at White Mountain Candles, the company that had grown up around the commune where Sydney lived in 1970, thumbing her nose at her rich and conservative family who lived so nearby at the Mont Blanc compound. Lynne had left several messages on a machine that announced the place was temporarily closed, thank you very much. Odds were good that nobody would be there at all.

And then, in barely forty-eight hours, it would be Monday in West LA. Jenna would be plopped right back into her unfulfilling job in the doomed occupation of bookselling, never certain from one month to the next when she'd have to dip into her inheritance for her share of the rent on a ridiculously cramped apartment.

In her heart of hearts, she had hoped that something would happen on this trip to point her in some new direction in life. All she'd really learned in that regard was that traveling was fun, keeping irregular hours was appealing, inn keeping was hardcore labor and, being well-read didn't much matter to anyone outside of academia.

Good life lessons, she supposed, but ones that left as many questions unanswered as they resolved.

Chapter 41

LYNNE was relieved to find the sky clear and the foliage conditions pretty much unchanged as they set off through the White Mountains after a simple but perfectly prepared breakfast at The White Birches. Maybe they'd get to see those red maples in South Hadford in full splendor after all.

As they headed down I-93 going south through the heart of New Hampshire, she marveled at the splendor of the scenery. It didn't even really matter that the craggy façade of the Old Man of the Mountain had crumbled into oblivion, revealing a bit of rebar that had apparently been used for some geological cosmetic surgery. The geezer wasn't necessary here. Every view was fantastic.

The parking lot at the Flume, a deep gorge with a briskly flowing brook, was filled with cars. She regretted not having made this trip earlier, on a weekday. Still, you had to do *something* on the weekends, and the Flume Walk was one of the must-do experiences of the White Mountains.

They bought tickets in a Visitor Center that featured an enormous stuffed moose at its center. The object was to scare people into respecting the animals that were so often heralded by MOOSE CROSSING signs, and as far as Lynne was concerned, it was a highly effective warning.

They headed off on foot toward the Flume Walk, eschewing the bus that was available for the less scenic lower part of the trail. Even the lower trail was crowded, and by the time they joined the bus travelers, the path was jammed. It reminded Lynne of the men heading for the Alaskan gold rush fields on the Chilkoot Pass, trudging up the grueling mountainside in single file.

The wooden walkway alongside the rocky, rushing waters of Flume Brook led through a narrow gorge much like the River Walk in Zion National Park, where the canyon walls stood so close together you could almost touch them on both sides. Lynne and Jenna kept moving briskly, past tourists shooting pictures, families with babies in backpack carriers, and more young children than they'd seen anywhere on the trip so far.

At the top of the Flume, the trail moved off into the woods, and this part was considerably less crowded, as a large percentage of their fellow Flume-walkers turned back the way they had come. As Lynne and Jenna hiked through the woods, they often had the moist and mossy trail largely to themselves. Discarded leaves lay in drifts at the feet of the trees they had once nourished, while lush green moss climbed the trunks of those same trees.

There were lots of stately green conifers in this forest, watching in bemusement as the fickle deciduous trees that surrounded them shed their food source. Mossy rocks loomed large where they'd been abandoned millennia before by the receding glacier.

The only thing that would have made the trail more perfect would have been a covered bridge. Sure enough, when they rounded a curve on the trail, there one was. Even better, it was a pedestrian bridge. They discovered as they came to cross it that it had been constructed with wooden pegs rather than nails. They stopped and had another tourist take their picture there, one last time.

And then, shortly thereafter, they were back at the base of the trail.

Chapter 42

HE picked them up at the Flume, a far larger parking lot than he would have preferred, but one where his presence would not be noticed or remarked upon by anybody. There were huge crowds, and he had chosen a small SUV for today, a car that would blend in all too effortlessly.

He cruised the parking lot until he came upon their rental car parked near the entry with a continual parade of people passing by. Once he'd found it, he again cruised until he had a spot of his own where he could wait till they reappeared. He would follow them and wait to see where they were going. There had been question marks next to the activities planned for today on the list he'd read when he broke into the car in the parking lot at the Twain House in Hartford.

Flume?

Mont Blanc?

White Mountain Candles?

He called it right that they'd go to the Flume, but after that, he wasn't sure of their route—if, indeed, they were sticking to the schedule that he'd seen. However, there were really only two ways to get from the Flume to Mont Blanc and the candle place. Either they'd go south on I-93 and pick up Highway 112, the Kancamagus Highway, or they'd go north on I-93, then cut over on Highway 3 to Highway 302 through Crawford Notch.

He'd probably have to improvise a bit, but improv could sometimes be the best solution to problems not yielding to traditional methods.

He settled back to wait.

Chapter 43

LYNNE had been looking forward to driving the Kancamagus Highway ever since her mother had first proposed that she visit New England in October. Arguably the best known scenic route for foliage in all of New England, the road was crowded with leaf peepers out to catch one last vestige of autumn glory. This was the last weekend anyone could reasonably expect to find colorful displays in the White Mountains and most of northern New Hampshire. Any day now a cold wind or rain would blow the rest of the leaves off these northern trees and the mountains would hunker down to await winter snows.

Named for an Indian chief of the Penacook Confederacy who tried unsuccessfully to keep the peace between English settlers and Native Americans, the Kancamagus was two lanes wide and barely thirty-five miles long. They picked up the highway in Lincoln and headed east, past hillsides with ski runs sculpted out of the colorful hillside foliage, nature's version of a clipped French poodle. Here there were frequent signs warning:

BRAKE FOR MOOSE
IT COULD SAVE YOUR LIFE
HUNDREDS OF COLLISIONS

Starting on the western end through the White Mountain National Forest, they found trees planted right down to the roadway, the landscape beyond having an almost paint-by-numbers feel. This tree bronze, this one crimson, that one over there a brassy gold. At one of the frequent turnouts they stopped and admired great clusters of red berries on an unknown shrub, watching a thoughtless tourist pull down a branch and pick a spray. A girl emerged from the privy and announced, to nobody in particular, "Whatever you do, don't look down."

The eastern end of the highway, along the Swift River, had more conifers, with spectacular views looking back toward the west. Misty clouds hovered over the treetops, and just when Lynne thought it couldn't get any better, she saw a small bear emerge from the woods ahead and scoot across the road.

At the highway's end in Conway, they stopped at a souvenir store and bought a Moxie, the soft drink they'd been wondering about throughout the trip. The drink had a faint taste of root beer, and they agreed it hadn't been worth the wait.

Then they set out in search of White Mountain Candles.

Jenna cast her glance sideways at her mother. "Do you really think we'll be able to learn anything that the police haven't?"

Lynne shrugged. "Nope. But I want to see it. This whole business seems to have started out there. And I'm fascinated that what started out as a hippie commune managed to morph into a major league business."

THE major league business, tucked away from civilization, was reached via a winding road lined with scarlet maples, a side trip that would have been worthwhile just for the foliage. A discreet sign as they left the main highway pointed them toward White Mountain Candles and the tiny town of Longmeadow. It was the only sign they saw before reaching the town, which seemed unspoiled by traffic or tourism or even much in the way of services for its local residents.

They stopped at a small grocery combined with a post office. The few small businesses were closed for the weekend and even the gas station/propane distributorship across the road seemed deserted. The grocery was quiet, with a single clerk, a woman whose steel-colored hair was pulled back in a ponytail at the nape of her neck. She wore faded jeans and a plaid flannel shirt. At a table near the post office part of the building, another similarly dressed, middle-aged woman with a mop of dark curls sat sipping coffee and reading a magazine.

In many ways the establishment reminded Lynne of the General Store on the grounds of Shelburne Museum. Its stock was more modern, but the small-town combination of services seemed almost timeless.

Lynne and Jenna got cans of cold soda from a cooler. "We're looking for White Mountain Candles," Lynne said as the ponytailed woman met them at the checkout counter.

"No reporters allowed there," the woman told them in a decidedly unfriendly tone. "Best you just turn around and go back."

"We're not reporters," Lynne said sweetly. "And I was under the impression that they offered factory tours. There was a sign off the highway directing us down here. This *is* Longmeadow, isn't it?"

"It is. But they're not open for thrill seekers either. No tours just now. Wrong season."

Lynne laughed. "I make my living in the travel industry, and I know there's never a wrong season for tours. Particularly not in New Hampshire during peak. I understand why they might want to discourage visitors just now, but I assure you that we're not being simply nosy."

The woman stared at her. "That'll be three dollars for the drinks."

The sign at the cooler had said they were seventy-five cents apiece. Bad news had delivered inflation to this little corner of New Hampshire.

Lynne laid three dollar bills on the counter. "I'm Lynne Montgomery, and this is my daughter Jenna. My mother owns the building in South Hadford where they found the remains of Sydney Shackleford. As a matter of fact, I'm the one who found her. Jenna and I were passing through this part of the country anyway, and we wanted to stop and pay our respects. I won't pretend we aren't curious, of course. But more than that, my mother's never going to be able to open her bed-and-breakfast while this is hanging over her. And frankly, we're all just baffled by how on earth Sydney found her way to southern New Hampshire. I was hoping maybe somebody here might know."

The woman with the magazine had been listening. Now she stood and came over to the counter.

"I'm Nancy Taylor," she told them. "I work at White Mountain Candles."

She did more than work there, Lynne realized. There had been a sidebar on White Mountain Candles in one of the newspapers, with mention of CEO Nancy Taylor, who had been with the operation from the very beginning. Nancy Taylor had described Sydney Shackleford's actions as "headstrong but heartfelt." Meeting her here was a real stroke of luck.

Lynne again introduced herself and Jenna, feeling an instant liking for the woman.

Nancy's handshake was cool and firm. "So you're the travel agent from California, right?" At Lynne's surprised nod, Nancy smiled. "When somebody you've been wondering about for a third of a century finally turns up, and it looks like she's been dead all that time, you pay attention to the details. Though the story where I read about you didn't explain why you were here, or how you happened to find Sydney."

She gestured at the table where she'd been sitting. "Come sit down for a minute."

As they joined her at the table, Lynne offered an abbreviated version of events. "Jenna and I have been traveling around to set up a tour for next year when my mom's bed-and-breakfast opens up," she concluded. "Though I have to say I'm not so sure that's going to happen, what with all that's been going on."

"Your mother must be pretty energetic," Nancy told her. "Mine's down in Florida playing Bingo. So let me guess. You wanted to see White Mountain Candles to include it on your tour."

Lynne shrugged. "It's a possibility. But I have to admit I probably wouldn't have stopped if it weren't for . . . all this. We saw Eldon Weibeck's mother down in New Bedford last weekend. It didn't sound as if Sydney and Eldon had very much in common, so that made me more curious about you all at the commune."

"I'm about the only one left from the original group that was here. A couple of the others are still silent partners, but . . . I hope you aren't planning to drop in at Mont Blanc."

"It had crossed my mind," Lynne admitted.

"Well, you might as well uncross it. I can't imagine that they'd let you in, and the whole place is about as impenetrable as those European castles set on mountaintops."

"You've been there?"

Nancy nodded. "Back when we were still in school. It was pretty awesome, actually, but I think Sydney was embarrassed by it. They had a whole sports complex there, with an indoor swimming pool and handball court and a bowling alley. Now they've probably got it all tricked out with exercise equipment and rock climbing walls."

"Well, I guess that scratches Mont Blanc. And I think we're running out of possibilities. Jenna and I are supposed to go back to California tomorrow. I hate to leave my mother hanging like this. Jenna has to get back to work, but maybe I'll stick around a little longer."

"I've closed things down for a while at the candle factory,"

Nancy said. "I was over there this morning until a while ago when I came in for some coffee and company. I'm glad I happened to be here when you showed up."

"So are we," Lynne said.

"We had too many reporters through here over this last week, pretending to take the tour and asking lots of rude questions. I took down the signs for now, and Martha here has been helping deflect sightseers. But you're right about peak. Normally I'd be out there waving the tourists right in. It's costing us money to be closed."

Lynne clucked sympathetically.

Nancy sighed. "And then on top of everything, we've had cops." She made it sound like an affliction, like scurvy or lice or scarlet fever. "We don't usually get a lot of cops up here. They came back yesterday afternoon with a search warrant and stayed for hours. It was the third time they've been here."

This had to be in reaction to Todd Jackson's revelation about how he'd come to South Hadford. Priscilla had called all agog with the news yesterday afternoon, leaving a message while they were at the Quilt Museum at the Shelburne Museum.

"Were they looking for records of military deserters and draft dodgers?"

Nancy stiffened. "So you know about that? It isn't in the news yet. I was online about an hour ago and I didn't see anything."

Lynne hesitated. "Only what I heard from my mother, and she's not always the most accurate reporter." No need to explain that after Priscilla's call, she'd phoned Abigail to get the real lowdown, and that initially Aunt Abby had pretended not to know what Lynne was talking about. If she ever needed a truly important secret kept, Lynne realized, Abigail Chenonceau was just the ticket. "But it explains a lot if that building in South Hadford was somehow part of a smuggling operation."

"Not smuggling," Nancy said. "At least that's not what the police told me." She wasn't admitting any knowledge, and who could blame her? "They said that deserters and draft dodgers had lived there to create new identities."

"And they came here looking for what? *Records?*"

Nancy nodded. "I know. It's ridiculous. There wouldn't be any records, of course. Even if that was something we'd been doing—and it wasn't—it isn't the kind of thing that you'd put in some kind of ledger book. Or file folders. They even downloaded everything off the computers, as if there'd been PCs back then."

"I'm so sorry," Lynne said. "Here you're finding out that your friend has been dead all these years, and then you have all these hassles on top of it. It's been pretty awful down at my mother's place, but we aren't . . . well, emotionally involved."

Nancy Taylor looked off into space for a moment. "Emotionally involved," she said slowly. "I guess you could say that, yeah. I met Sydney when we were both freshmen at Radcliffe. I was on scholarship and Sydney—well, Sydney wasn't."

"So you knew her a long time."

"Not long enough. She was a friend. And I always thought something bad must have happened to her. She wouldn't just disappear. I always thought it was related somehow to the family hassles that the Shacklefords were having about what to do with Mont Blanc and some of the family property on Nantucket. Sydney and some of her cousins wanted to sell that property and do something socially relevant with the proceeds."

Like the heirs at Shelburne Farms, Lynne realized suddenly, who had sold off part of the acreage and created a foundation to manage the rest. "And did that happen? I don't know much about the Shacklefords except what I read in the papers."

"Nope. As I understand it, the whole issue just died off without Sydney around to spearhead it. Sydney always had this absolute conviction that she could do whatever she wanted. I guess that comes from growing up with money."

"Did her money help you all make ends meet at the commune?"

Nancy nodded. "It did. But by the time she disappeared, we were actually doing pretty well with the candle business. Not running it in any kind of businesslike manner, of course. And there were some lean times after Sydney disappeared. But we managed."

"When exactly did she disappear?"

"I told the cops that. It was a couple weeks before Christmas. She went home for Thanksgiving, or over to Mont Blanc anyway, and then she came here and helped us with the candles for last-minute Christmas orders. These days we have all the Christmas stock finished by August, usually, but back when we were just getting started, we didn't know to do that sort of thing."

"Was Eldon Weibeck with her after Thanksgiving?"

"She had a guy with her," Nancy said after a moment's hesitation. "I'm not telling you anything the police don't seem to know, so don't think I've got some big revelations or anything. I didn't know who the guy was. She called him Weezer and he called her Minerva. I don't know why. He helped with the candles for the Christmas orders and then the two of them took off and that was that. We never saw or heard from her again."

Lynne frowned. "Did she leave stuff at the commune?"

Nancy laughed. "Oh my, yes. Expensive stuff, too. Her KLH stereo and her Nikon 35mm camera with all its lenses. Plus a lot of clothing and books and stuff. When it seemed like she wasn't coming back and we needed her room for somebody else, I was the one who packed all her stuff up. I found about six hundred dollars in cash in the toe of a boot."

"What did you do with it all?"

"Well, we used the stereo and camera, and after a year or so, we put the money toward the rent. Times were pretty lean then. After a while, girls just started wearing the clothes."

"What about her car?"

"As far as I know, it never turned up. She had an MG convertible, which is a ridiculous car to have in this climate, but she really liked it. She was driving it when they came and went in December. Her registration renewal came here the following fall, but by then it seemed pretty clear she wasn't coming back."

Lynne considered carefully. "Did she ever have other strangers with her? Guys?"

Nancy laughed. "All the time. It used to bug her that guys might be attracted to her because of her money, but not enough that she wouldn't fool around with them. She was very much into losing her inhibitions."

"Incredible," Lynne said. "Thanks so much. I'm glad we happened onto you."

"As long as you're out here, would you like to come see the candle factory?" Nancy offered.

"We'd love it," Lynne told her.

Chapter 44

HE rather enjoyed crossing the state on the Kancamagus Highway, allowing himself the pleasure of fall vistas along with the business of the Montgomery women. He gave them plenty of space, not wanting to attract attention on what was, after all, a back road. Indeed, at one point he came upon their car parked at a scenic turnout and passed them by. He stopped at the next turnout after that and waited.

He followed them the rest of the way on the scenic road, then continued with them as they drove northeast, away from Mont Blanc.

White Mountain Candles, then. A business he knew was closed. This was starting to feel like his lucky day.

Chapter 45

WHITE Mountain Candles looked like the cover of a New England Autumn coffee table book. A large wooden building built of logs was surrounded by a grove of birch trees with peeling white trunks and vibrant yellow foliage, nestled into a hollow ablaze in scarlet and bronze. A smaller log cabin sat farther back in the clearing.

"This is the factory," Nancy told them as they got out of their cars in a modest, empty parking lot strewn with drifts of gold and crimson leaves. "Most of it is shut down right now, except for what I've been fiddling with this morning. C'mon and I'll give you a fast tour."

"I don't want to impose," Lynne said, though of course she did.

Nancy laughed. "After having the police pawing through every order we've gotten in the last thirty-five years, my notion of imposition has changed. Stay here and I'll go around back to open the place up. You might as well get the full impact of our charm." She disappeared behind the building.

A few minutes later, they could see lights going on inside

through a glass front door. Then Nancy was swinging the door open wide to let them in.

The first thing Lynne noticed when she went inside was the overwhelming sweet aroma of dozens of candle scents, all competing for olfactory supremacy. Maybe it was seasonal or maybe it was an overactive imagination, but after a moment she thought that pine and cinnamon generally predominated, overpowering the more subtle aromas.

The second thing she noticed was a large gift shop on the left, its exterior walls faced with peeling birch logs to create an entirely charming rusticity. The store lights were off but a window display featured several very large white candles embedded with scarlet maple leaves.

The third thing she noticed was that, apart from the gift shop, everything was spanking clean and well-lit and very modern in design. Two staircases at opposite ends of the lobby led up to the observation gallery. At the top of the stairs, she could see a wall of windows, undoubtedly overlooking the production area. This was a classic self-guided tour setup, with arrows directing people to go up on the left and exit on the right, directly in front of the appealing gift shop entrance.

Nancy led them onto the production floor through an unobtrusive door under the far stairway. The production floor gleamed in front of them, all stainless steel machinery and assembly lines. In here the scent was even stronger.

Jenna sneezed.

Nancy laughed. "You get immune to it after a while," she said. "In the beginning when we did it all in the kitchen, I used to really love the point where we'd add scents, always way more than the suggested amount. Somewhere along the line, it all turned into business, including the scents."

"It's a nice business," Lynne said. "And I did look at your website the other night, I confess. I was impressed. You could have been all cutesy, the way a lot of these places are. But even with the historical overview, you came out seeming . . . well, dignified, I guess is what I mean."

"We're all a little allergic to cutesy," Nancy said. "Dignified is what we aim at, though 'commercially successful' is what we always secretly hope for."

"Looks like you make both those goals," Lynne said, looking around. "I played around with candle making a long time ago, but I never got much past crayons and paraffin, poured into quart milk boxes. I had one nice mold, but I could never get the wick to work right. I'd end up with a shrunken part down the middle."

"A common problem in the home market," Nancy said. "We sell candle making kits, too, and we've tried to fix that. You're welcome to one of the kits if you want to take another crack at candle making."

"I'm going to run out to the ladies' room," Jenna told them, heading back out toward the lobby. Lynne had seen signs for rest rooms located near the gift shop.

Lynne smiled. "Forgive me, but it sounds a little too much like a Girl Scout craft project." She nodded toward Jenna, just leaving the room. "And you may have noticed that my Girl Scout is grown up now. So tell me, how do you make candles with stuff in them? The pine needles and maple leaves and such?"

"The candles with inserts like pine needles and berries and summer flowers—those are done in two stages. We build the exterior in molds that are only about an inch thick, and then when those are hardened, we add the wicks and centers. We use two different kinds of wax so that the center will melt down first and you can refill it with votives then."

"Very cool," Lynne told her, and she meant it. "That other building out back. It looked older than this one."

Nancy nodded, "It's the original building where all this began. It's bigger than it looks, but still not all that large. We used to have ten or twelve people living there most of the time and it never seemed crowded. Of course, we were younger and a lot more tolerant. Not to mention stoned most of the time. The parking lot is where we had the vegetable garden. We had an awesome root cellar, and we were able to grow just about everything we ate."

"Who lives there now?"

"Nobody. It's set up as offices. We do a lot of shipping and also a lot of special orders for catalogues, and all that's handled out of that building. It could never make the fire code anyway. This building was built to some very rigid specifications. Wax candles are, after all, designed to burn, and the object is to have that happen somewhere else."

"So nobody actually lives on the grounds anymore?"

"Nope. We've all grown up and moved out. Like I told you, I'm the only original left on the premises. Here, Lynne. Let me show you what I was doing when I went into town earlier."

Nancy led Lynne to a workstation away from the machinery and flicked on some electric burners under a glass cook-top. "This is kind of an experimentation station," she explained. "Sometimes we'll have demos going on here during busy periods. The customers like it." She stirred each of several small pots of different colored waxes and one larger one holding perhaps a gallon of red. "The smaller pots hardened a bit while I was in town, but I can show you with this red."

She pulled out a granite slab from a freezer and ladled some red wax onto the smooth surface. Then she used a tool that resembled a rubber kitchen scraper to spread it evenly. "I've been fiddling around with silhouettes again. I used to like these back in the early days. Back then we'd cut them into finished candles by hand, but obviously we need something more mechanized here."

The wax was cooling quickly. She made a few slashes with a sharp little knife, then carefully removed a small maple leaf design. "Wrap this around a white candle, and it will glow really nicely in your mom's B&B dining room."

Lynne shuddered. "You had to remind me."

Now that the two of them were alone, Lynne thought carefully about what she wanted to say next. In a very brief period she had grown extremely fond of Nancy Taylor and she didn't want to lose that sense of camaraderie. But there were things she really needed to know.

"Let me ask you a hypothetical question," she began.

"Sounds dangerous," Nancy told her. She didn't seem to be kidding.

"Suppose that somebody who'd been living here back in the late sixties had a friend in the military who was AWOL, and that friend didn't plan to go back. Because, say, there was a war going on in Vietnam."

"Yes?"

"If that person didn't want to leave the country, say, and wanted to establish that new identity with a job and a residence somewhere, where do you suppose that person might have gone?"

Nancy offered a half smile. "California, most likely. We all talked about going to California back then, remember?"

Lynne smiled back. "Actually, I was lucky enough to already be in California. I was a Navy brat and that's where my father happened to be stationed when I was in high school. So I went to UC Santa Cruz and never left the state. Until I started working for a travel agency, that is."

"I thought you owned the agency," Nancy said with a little frown.

"I do now. I bought it after my husband died."

Nancy looked appalled and embarrassed. "I'm so sorry," she said. "How horrible! I didn't know."

Lynne had liked her before, and she liked her even more for this genuine expression of sympathy and dismay. "Of course you didn't. But back to my hypothetical. If this hypothetical military deserter didn't want to go to California, at least not yet, where do you suppose he might have gone?"

Nancy sighed. "I heard rumors at the time," she said carefully, "that if somebody without much in the way of work history wanted to get a job and a place to live with no questions asked, there was a knitting mill in New Hampshire where that person had a good chance of getting hired."

"Did that rumor say where the place was?"

She shook her head. "I never knew. I think Sydney did. She's the one who was involved with Mobe at Harvard. I was more of a flower child, not so political. The kind of girl who'd get into making candles."

"Is it possible that Sydney brought guys here back then, fellows who wanted to lay low for a while?"

"I wish I knew I could trust you," Nancy Taylor said.

"All I want to do is get this cleared up so my mother can get on with her project and I can go home. Sydney's dead, Nancy. She can't be hurt by anything that comes out now. In a way, it makes her kind of a heroine, I think, for acting on her convictions."

"Easy enough for you to say. You don't have a business being threatened by the police."

"The police can't do anything to your business. If they're putting pressure on you, it's so they can lean on somebody else. The house where Sydney's body was found in the basement belonged to . . ."

"I know who it belonged to. I read the newspapers. The name Charles Grant didn't mean anything to me. It still doesn't. But it's possible, just barely possible, that back then I might have heard about an older man who'd become actively anti-war after his son came back from Vietnam with his head all screwed up."

A male voice came from behind them. "I believe that's my cue."

Chapter 46

BOTH women jumped at the intruder's voice. Lynne turned toward it, a feeling of dread pouring over her.

A man stood in the middle of the room about ten feet away from them. She had never seen him before, but the gun he was holding looked like a hundred deadly weapons Lynne had watched in movies. It was huge and it was shiny and it was pointed right at them.

The man was unremarkable in appearance. You might see him managing a coffee shop or selling washer-dryers at Sears or toiling over a drafting table in some engineering department, and ten seconds later you'd forget him. He could have been anywhere between forty and sixty-five. His hair was thin and graying, his complexion sallow, and his body decidedly unfit.

Not that any of that mattered. The gun, as Lynne's cop son David always pointed out, is a great equalizer.

Nancy spoke first. "Who are you? Am I supposed to know you?"

He shook his head. "Not at all."

Lynne frowned. "Then does that mean that *I'm* supposed to know you?"

He shrugged. "You can play dumb if you want."

This was horrifying. She wasn't playing dumb at all. She really *was* dumb. And where in God's name was Jenna? She'd be done in the rest room by now. Lynne sent a lightning prayer out that Jenna would be smart enough to stay out of sight. Lynne had already lost Monty. She couldn't bear it if anything happened to Jenna too.

"Where's the girl?" he asked.

Damn. How to warn her?

"She went to the bathroom."

"Call her. Now." He waved the gun and Lynne stepped over to the lobby door.

She stuck her head out and called. "Jennifer Lee! Come here please. Jennifer Lee!"

Then she heard Jenna's voice. "Be right with you, Mumsy."

"How did you know where to find me?" Lynne asked, moving away from the door and back into the room, playing for time. If he talked a bit, maybe she could figure out who the devil he was, and why he was holding a gun on her.

"I've known exactly where you were ever since midday Monday," he said, "when you visited my mother."

His mother!

Midday on Monday, Lynne and Jenna had visited Louise Grant in West Hartford, had asked about her husband Charles and his boardinghouse property. Had looked at family photographs showing two daughters and a son, been told that the son was a businessman in Boston.

But not all the time, it seemed.

"You're Charles Grant's son," Lynne said, as odd bits and pieces of information fell into place. "Johnny. The one who went to Vietnam and spent a long time in the hospital when he came back. Of course!" She frowned. "But your father was a Vietnam dove. His secretary said he put money into the McCarthy campaign."

"It's just John now. And he wasn't a dove when I was

being drafted," Johnny Grant said. "He was a goddamned flag-waving hawk and he intimidated me into enlisting in the Marines instead of going with the Army as a draftee. It wasn't till he saw what happened to me that he changed his tune. Came and saw me in the hospital in San Diego and cried like a baby. Where's that girl? Get her ass in here!"

"Jennifer Lee! I need you now."

Jenna appeared in the doorway. "Sorry, Mumsy." Her eyes widened at the sight of the gun, but she didn't seem entirely surprised. "Wha—"

He waved the gun. "Over there. With your mother. Now."

Jenna said nothing as she moved toward Lynne. Either she'd figured out some kind of plan or she was scared witless. Lynne wasn't sure which possibility horrified her more.

"You were injured in battle?"

"I was . . . no. I wasn't injured, not any way you could see." He nodded at Nancy. "You had it right when you were talking before I came in. It was my head that was all screwed up. Post-traumatic stress disorder they call it nowadays, but back then it didn't have any fancy names. Nobody could figure what the problem was, and they just kept telling me to suck it up, but I couldn't. They kept moving me from one place to another, my family, once I was out of the Marines. The Marines were happy to let me go, too. I didn't reflect too well on their Semper Fi bullshit."

"So you were at the boardinghouse when Sydney Shackleford and Eldon Weibeck came there," Lynne suggested. Finally things were starting to fit, to make sense.

"They weren't supposed to come," he said. "They weren't supposed to be there. It was closed, being fixed up. The plumbing was all screwed up and my dad had to shut down the house. The old man had been putting deserters through there as a kind of penance for me being fucked up, but he had to close it for repairs. But that kid went AWOL and the girl brought him anyway, even though they weren't supposed to come."

"How did you happen to be there?"

He laughed bitterly. "I'd run away from the place where

they had me then, this kind of fancy funny farm in Massachusetts. Lots of long discussions about my childhood, not that it made a frigging bit of difference. I wasn't having nightmares about growing up in a small town in New Hampshire. I was having nightmares about cutting the heads off Viet Cong. All I wanted was to be alone. After I got away, I hitched up to South Hadford and I figured I could crash at the boardinghouse, 'cause I knew it was having work done. Everything would have been all right if they hadn't come."

"What happened?" Lynne was almost afraid to hear the answer. But as long as he was talking he wasn't doing anything else, like shooting them.

"They sneaked up on me," he said. "Woke me up and it was like some kind of a flashback and I was in the Nam again. All those fighting skills came back and I broke the sonofabitch's neck, just like that. Then the bitch started screaming and I just had to make her shut up."

Blunt trauma, the medical examiner had said. Skull fracture for Sydney, broken neck for Eldon.

"And your father covered up for you."

Johnny Grant nodded. "He bribed the handyman. Told me he could make it like nothing ever happened. Nobody'd miss them cause nobody knew they were there. I was back in the funny farm by then, locked down but good."

"So Ralph Tracy cemented the bodies into the basement floor."

"Who knows? I never asked. I just knew they went away. And after a while, and a couple more funny farms, they decided I had some kind of chemical imbalance and started pumping pills into me." He offered a lopsided grin. "Which has made me a productive member of society."

All while he talked and raged, Nancy had been inching back toward the bucket of hot wax and Lynne had slid along at the same rate. Now from Lynne's right, a splash of hot red wax flew toward Johnny Grant. It caught him in the chest and face and left arm but not, unfortunately, on the hand that was holding the gun.

He gave an awful shriek and fired once blindly. Wax was

dripping off his face and arms. Then he grabbed Jenna by the hair and pulled her toward him, still waving the gun.

But Jenna was as tall as he was, and she was left-handed, and suddenly she had the sharp blade of her Swiss Army knife in her left hand. She slashed backward and he shrieked as a streak of blood appeared on his right thigh. When he jerked in pain, he loosened his grip on her hair. She twisted, used her left arm to knock the gun out of his hand and stepped back just as Nancy smashed the empty wax bucket onto his head.

He crumpled to the floor, blood pouring from the slashed leg, wax hardening into an oddly grotesque mask on his face and right arm. He kept screaming.

"I don't suppose anybody has any handcuffs," Jenna said.

Nancy was digging in a cabinet in the back of the production floor. She came back with a length of metal chain. "This'll have to do for now," she said, "but we'd better get a tourniquet on that leg. Looks like you got an artery, Jenna. Nice aim."

Jenna was already pulling her belt from the loops on her jeans. When she hesitated—Jenna had always been squeamish, which made her performance just now all the more remarkable—Lynne took the belt from her and wrapped it securely around his thigh. The flow of blood dwindled to a trickle. Meanwhile Nancy trussed him with the chains. He was beginning to look absurdly well restrained, like somebody in a Houdini escapathon.

"We need to call for help," Lynne said, looking around. Her adrenaline was still coursing madly.

"All taken care of," Jenna said. "I was afraid I wouldn't be able to get cell phone reception here, but I managed to get through to 911 before I came out onto the floor. I was upstairs looking through the window when he came in, see. So you didn't even really need the name code. But I'm glad to see it still works, Mumsy."

Lynne hugged her daughter fiercely. "Me too, Jennifer Lee."

It was a silly name code they'd used for twenty years now,

Jennifer Lee and Mumsy, a shorthand to tell the other that it was time to leave, or something was wrong and required private attention or—though it had never come to this before today—that a man with a gun was holding one of them hostage.

Chapter 47

LYNNE was intrigued to discover that when the State Police told an airline that you were needed on official police business and had to change a reservation, the airline changed that reservation without complaint or surcharge. She hoped not to need this information again.

It was only forty-eight hours, in any case, from Sunday to Tuesday, their new departure date. And they probably wouldn't even have needed that long, except for that old New England emphasis on thoroughness.

Detective Niles Burton drove up from Concord and arrived at White Mountain Candles in the late afternoon on Saturday. Some time later, he got down on the ground with a flashlight and located the tracking device that Johnny Grant had put on Lynne's rental car on Monday, probably while they were inside talking to his mother in her basement flat in West Hartford. While the crime scene technicians checked the rental Chevy for Johnny Grant's prints, they discovered a glasses case that had fallen beneath the driver's seat. It contained a nice new pair of prescription sunglasses and a business card for John Grant, President of Grant Garages Inc. in Boston.

Grant had been currently driving an SUV belonging to somebody who garaged it in one of the half-dozen parking garages that he owned in the Boston area.

Grant himself had been taken to the nearest hospital, where he was under police guard as doctors treated him for wax burns and a deep, nasty slash on his leg.

As things began to sort themselves out, Detective Burton borrowed Nancy Taylor's office in the White Mountain Candles administration building. She had it furnished in sleek modern ash, with splashes of color from bold modern paintings. Lynne found herself wondering what the history of this room might be. Had Sydney Shackleford slept in this room, with or without Eldon Weibeck? Had other deserters waited here in the anonymity of a sixties commune for a go-ahead to move up to Canada or down to the boardinghouse in South Hadford?

"John Grant seems to have made a habit of 'borrowing' cars from clients he knew wouldn't be using them. Once he had that tracking device on your car," Detective Burton said, "he could come and go as he needed to, and track you down with very little trouble. He couldn't afford to follow you, because his absence for a prolonged period would be noticed. So he probably just made day trips out of Boston. And of course he had to be in South Hadford for his mother's funeral on Thursday."

"Did he kill his mother, too?"

"We'll find out when the exhumation order's signed," Burton told her. "Because she was elderly and died at home, the folks in West Hartford had no reason to suspect anything. Her doctor there signed the death certificate. We'll be looking for anyone who might have seen him in her neighborhood that day."

"And Ralph?"

"Now that we know what to look for, we'll check again out at the Washington Arms where he fell originally. He hasn't been buried yet, so we'll also be able to get an autopsy on him done in the next day or so."

"Poor old Ralph," Jenna said.

Detective Burton shook his head. "Poor old Ralph almost certainly was the one who put in the concrete floor at your grandmother's place, and whoever put that floor in cemented those bodies in it as well. The payoff seems to have been the house the Tracys bought for a song from Charles Grant after Ralph was finished with the basement floor." He leaned back. "And now, I think we've done all we need to here. Can you come up to Concord on Monday to sign statements and help us tidy up whatever loose ends remain?"

"Do you need my mother as well?"

"Yes, please."

JENNA was mostly silent on the drive back to South Hadford Sunday morning, and Lynne thought she seemed troubled by her role in regaining control at the candle factory. It had been well after dark on Saturday by the time everything got squared away at White Mountain Candles. By then Lynne felt as if she'd known Nancy Taylor for years, and when Nancy offered her spare bedroom to Lynne and Jenna, they accepted instantly.

As a little treat to themselves this morning, they decided to begin the journey back to the Maple Leaf Inn by heading west on the Kancamagus Highway, a road Lynne hadn't expected to drive again for at least another year. She found she liked going east-to-west even better and made a mental note for her tour-planning file.

Lynne was driving and Jenna had her seat angled back and her long legs splayed. Jenna hadn't slept well last night, had been up several times. But Lynne knew better than to push. Jenna would talk in her own sweet time. That time came as they cruised south on I-93, surely one of the most spectacular interstate routes in the country.

"I never told you this because I figured it would alarm

you," Jenna said slowly, and Lynne felt herself becoming alarmed reflexively.

"What, honey?"

"Well, I don't know if I can get this to make sense. I took a couple of self-defense courses up in LA after I graduated, thinking it would probably be a smart idea—you know, young single woman living in a nasty city full of criminals and perverts, all that."

Lynne, who knew exactly what her daughter was talking about, also knew to keep her mouth shut.

"It was always really abstract," Jenna went on. "I mean, the moves were very specific and they'd always talk about it in a way that made it sound like you were in danger, but the fact of the matter was that you were being attacked by the partner you were working with, not some crumbum with a gun or a knife. I always wondered if I'd be able to do anything when it was really necessary. And now that I know I can, I don't . . . I don't know. I just don't seem as satisfied by it as they always said you'd be. I mean, I hurt that guy. He could have bled to death."

"He didn't."

"Because you and Nancy were there to take charge of things. Once I stabbed him, I was pretty much worthless."

"Jenna, that was your part of the operation." She put her voice into the *Mission Impossible* tone that she'd used just a few days ago. "Your mission, Jenna Montgomery, was to neutralize the subject so that your agents in charge could carry on." She switched her voice back to normal. "Sweetie, you were amazing. You had the presence of mind to call for help first, you came out prepared with a weapon, you took your time until it was just the right moment, and we all came out of it alive. Which was not Johnny Grant's intention, I can assure you. I can't begin to tell you how happy I am that your father gave you that Swiss Army knife and that you had the guts to use it."

The police had found full gasoline cans in the back of the SUV Johnny Grant was driving, and while he wasn't saying anything at all on advice of what looked to become a flotilla of attorneys, his intentions seemed clear.

"If you say so, Mom."

"I say so."

"Mother knows best," Jenna said, and Lynne extended her pinky.

THEY were home in plenty of time for Priscilla's Sunday evening dinner, chicken fricassee. Priscilla was claiming it was a family standard, but it didn't seem familiar to Lynne who was, if she recalled correctly, Priscilla's only child. Maybe it had been a standard of Tony Doolittle's family, or Harvey Jones's.

Priscilla had invited Abigail, who arrived with a pound cake and a box of frozen strawberries. Lynne put a couple of bottles of Chardonnay into the freezer once she learned the menu, and the wine flowed freely as they sat on the front porch of the Maple Leaf Inn with a platter of baby quiches left in the freezer after the tea party.

The two red maples had shed about half of their foliage now, and a thick carpet of ruby-colored leaves lay on the lawn. The late afternoon wind blew cool, and all three generations of Lynne's family wore their soft woolen shawls from Maine. Lynne was starting to feel guilty about not having also brought one for Abigail, until Aunt Abby noted brusquely that you could accomplish the same thing at a fraction of the cost with a couple of yards of wool from the fabric store.

Lynne had been carefully avoiding mention of the future of the Maple Leaf Inn. She had failed at all attempts to dampen her mother's ardor and at this point, she figured it wasn't worth the energy to argue. She was bitterly disappointed at not having been able to corner the elusive Will Colwhistle, and had no idea what to do next about that extremely loose end on this trip.

Priscilla surprised her.

As they sat on the porch Priscilla said, "I almost forgot to tell you."

Instinctively Lynne braced for the worst. Priscilla wasn't one to forget good news. At the same time, she caught a tell-tale scent of something burning in the kitchen. She could put off her mother's announcement by mentioning the burnt smell, but if she could smell it out here, the fricassee was probably already ruined. She held her tongue.

"I had a registered letter on Saturday from Mr. Colwhistle. He explained that he's developed some health problems and has been forced to cut back on his client list. He's sold my mortgage to the First Bank of New Hampshire."

Lynne felt herself exhale. A real bank. All that skulking about, what Jenna had so aptly labeled stalking—it seemed to have paid off. Jenna caught her eye and grinned.

Lynne raised her glass. "To new beginnings for the Maple Leaf Inn."

"In more ways than one," Priscilla said, raising her own glass. "I spoke to a lovely Realtor here in town while you girls were on the road. I've decided that running a bed-and-breakfast is more work than I'm willing to do in my old age. The place goes on the market next week, and the Realtor feels quite confident that the notoriety will help sell it quickly."

The hand that Abigail had raised with her wineglass seemed to tremble a bit. "And what will you do after you sell this place, Priscilla?"

Priscilla smiled. "I've decided I'm too far away from my girls. I'm moving to California."